Praise for *The C*

"Vivid depiction of New Orleans' m
as Andrew Jackson gathers Creoles, ~~p~~
to oppose a massive British assault. ~~\~~ ......, ...a being
played out against the full Jambalaya of America's most intrigu-
ing city—settings range from Creole mansions and Ursuline
convents to Quadroon Balls and Congo Square. It's amazing to me
how much social and historical information has been deftly folded
into this compelling narrative. I couldn't put it down!"

—DR. BRUCE ELLIOTT, professor of history
at Stanford, UC Berkeley, and Sonoma State

"Three strong female protagonists give fresh perspectives on a culture unique to New Orleans during the imminent British assault.
Love, loss, and class anxieties mingle with war and triumphant
resilience. A vibrant and engaging story!"

—TOM MITCHELL, PhD, author of the Winning Spirit series

"A dramatic story full of rich historical details. A free woman of
color who acts as the local healer/midwife, a young white prostitute
who yearns for a better life, and a Creole plantation mistress desperate to provide a son for her husband—these and other colorful
characters navigate the tumultuous events surrounding the Battle of
New Orleans. Race and class barriers fall in this tale of patriotism
and war, love and loss."

—BARBARA RIDLEY, author of *When It's Over*

"As Sue Finan develops her characters, the reader is drawn in by the
historic detail of New Orleans in the early 1800s. This is the setting
for a story of strong women, from different walks of life, using their
strengths to help Andrew Jackson win the Battle of New Orleans.
A great read."

—GABRIEL A. FRAIRE, Healdsburg, Ca.
Literary Laureate Emeritus

"Contrary to what many history books would have us believe, wars have never been fought by men alone. Set in the vibrant city of New Orleans during the War of 1812, Sue Ingalls Finan's historical novel *The Cards Don't Lie* braids the experiences of individuals from a wide range of cultures, classes, races, and genders to create a fuller picture of that conflict, and especially of the crucial roles that women played in it. Finan's extensive research helps to bring both the setting and its characters to life for modern readers."

—JEAN HEGLAND, author of *Into the Forest*,
Windfalls, and *Still Time*

"The best historical fiction enriches our understanding when the historical evidence is scarce—but can also give voice to those who are usually overlooked, such as women and people of color. Sue Finan's *The Cards Don't Lie* admirably accomplishes both of these objectives. An enjoyable journey through an underappreciated era in American history— the War of 1812 and, more specifically, the events surrounding the dramatic Battle of New Orleans—the author employs an innovative narrative structure, using cryptic yet revealing tarot cards, that propels the story forward at a dramatic pace."

—CHRISTOPHER D. O'SULLIVAN, Professor of history
and international studies at University of San Francisco
author of *Harry Hopkins: FDR's Envoy to Churchill
and Stalin, Colin Powell: A Political Biography,
FDR and The End of Empire: The Origins of American Power
in the Middle East*, and *Sumner Welles: Postwar Planning
and the Quest for a New World Order, 1937-1943*

The
CARDS
DON'T
LIE

The CARDS DON'T LIE

A NOVEL

Sue Ingalls Finan

She Writes Press, a BookSparks imprint
A Division of SparkPointStudio, LLC.

Published 2018

Printed in the United States of America

ISBN: 978-1-63152-451-6 pbk
ISBN: 978-1-63152-452-3 ebk
Library of Congress Control Number: 2018941947

For information, address:
She Writes Press
1569 Solano Ave #546
Berkeley, CA 94707

She Writes Press is a division of SparkPoint Studio, LLC.

This is a work of fiction. Names, characters, places, and incidents either are the product of the author's imagination or are used fictitiously. Any resemblance to actual persons, living or dead, is entirely coincidental.

To Jim:
I did not know this writing was in my cards
Until you inspired me

With love

~

September 1780

"The most important battle of your life will take place where the trees have beards. Some men wear the skins of animals, and an outlaw will ensure your victory. And I see three plucky and extraordinary women. Quite mysterious," says the gypsy, as she splays the cards out on the table. "Just who are you, boy?"

"My name is Andy. Andy Jackson."

Tarot: THE HIGH PRIESTESS

Revelation: Hidden influences will be at work.

~

August 1812

Her arms outspread, her eyes fixed on the ceiling, the priestess began speaking. Yet it was not her normal voice; this utterance was a much lower-pitched and distinctive sound. It was the *loa* who was giving emphatic instructions, and the client listened carefully.

"You will protect yourself by burying a small bag of ginger and mandrake roots in your backyard. Once you have buried them, you will sprinkle rainwater over them. Burn a white candle of peace and gratitude each night for nine nights."

The energy then seemed to diminish, and moments later it was gone. The priestess, as if emerging from a trance, focused her eyes on the client and smiled. Now speaking in her customary way, she said, "Go in peace and abide in plenty."

"Thank you, Catherine," replied the patron.

Tarot: THE NINE OF SWORDS

Revelation: Desolation; failure; misery; suffering.

⌒

Sheila gently wiped her exhausted daughter's forehead with a damp cloth. "You're doing well, Marguerite. It'll be just a little bit longer, and then you and Jacques will be parents!"

The elderly doctor, summoned to the large manor house the day before, nodded his head. Holding his forceps like a conductor's baton, he was prepared to aid the wife of the plantation owner in the final stage of delivery.

"Would you like some more water, dear?" asked Sheila.

Instead of answering her mother's question, Marguerite's face turned crimson as she grasped the bedsheets. Her body grew rigid as she screamed, "It's ripping my insides out! I can't take this much longer!"

"Yes, you can, Marguerite," replied Sheila. "Remember how we talked about it? I think labor pains are similar to the most severe stomach cramps ever. And that's what you're experiencing. Why, your friend Claudia said it was as if you had to pass a cannonball inside you!" She laughed at the memory.

Marguerite, though, did not laugh. She roared again in pain.

Sheila responded, "My goodness! You sound like a bellowing bull, my darling! Now, you need to be brave."

Patting her daughter's hand, she continued, "Think of

Jacques—how pleased he'll be to be a papa! And I guarantee once the baby is here, your pain will be practically forgotten."

Marguerite shrieked again. "It's like a red-hot poker! Get it out of me!"

Sheila looked at the doctor questioningly.

"The tissues at the opening of her birth canal are rupturing," he whispered.

"I heard that," Marguerite cried. "I'm going to die!"

"Nonsense! Happens all the time! Bear down now, Madame de Trahan," the doctor said cheerfully.

She gripped the sheets again and pushed down with all of her strength. Her baby crowned.

"Ahhh! Just one more big push, now, Madame de Trahan," encouraged the doctor, as he encircled the baby's head with his instrument.

Marguerite took a deep breath, held it while tightening her body, and then bore down again, shoving the child out into the doctor's reach. She groaned, then grunted and sank back on her pillow.

"Congratulations, my darling! It's all over, and now you're a mother!" exclaimed Sheila, as she bent over to kiss Marguerite's forehead.

Straightening up to address the doctor, she asked, "And do I have a grandson?"

Silence.

Made apprehensive by the doctor's silence, Sheila moved to his side.

The doctor held the lifeless infant, the umbilical cord wrapped three times around his tiny neck, shook his head sadly, and whispered, "I'm afraid the boy did not make it, Sheila."

Marguerite's eyes grew wide as she saw the regret on her mother's face and the motionless, diminutive body the doctor was holding and screamed once more.

"Noooooooo!"

Tarot: THE EIGHT OF CUPS

_Revelation: The decline of an undertaking,
often accompanied by despondency._

~

It was another of the Capitol's hot, humid days in late summer. Dressed in his customary black suit, President James Madison was in his office in the new mansion, preparing for a meeting with his cabinet. His face was wizened with worry; this "second war of independence" against England was quickly aging him. He wiped his sweaty forehead with his handkerchief once again.

There was a hammering knock at the door, and Edward Coles, Madison's personal secretary, charged in.

"Edward! You look distressed!"

"Bad news, Mr. President. Another of our merchant ships was seized on its way to France. All of its cargo was taken."

"Damn those British!" Madison flung down his quill and stood up.

"Any casualties?" he asked the taller man.

"Not this time, sir. But they did take some of the crew."

"First, Jefferson's embargo didn't work, and now we're stuck in this war," said the president, as he sat down.

"Yes, sir. Up and down the seaboard, the people are suffering massive hardships, and they are furious. No one prospers when commodities are rotting on the docks, waiting to be loaded on the few ships willing to risk sailing."

"More hypocrites, Edward. The merchants up and down the northeast coastline, the richest men in the nation, crying over the embargo against England while refusing to give a ha'penny for support of our navy."

His secretary agreed. "Even though you limited the trade sanctions of the Embargo Act to only England, the merchants blame you for the depression, their idle ships, and the unemployed seamen cluttering the ports."

"Well, at least the English can't seize the ships or impress the sailors while they are tied to the docks. They can call it the Dambargo all they want, but they are making plenty of money on the damn smuggling up the coast to Canada."

He paused, thinking of the pro-war arguments of war hawks Henry Clay and John Calhoun. But without unified popular support from the country, the war effort was enfeebled. Besides the East Coast's lack of assistance, many troops in the militias refused to fight outside their own states. Plus, the Commander-in-Chief suspected that a number of his generals were incompetent.

"Anything else, Edward?" he asked, rubbing his eyes. "I'm feeling the onset of another headache."

"Unfortunately, yes, sir. Our defense of the northern territories is not going well."

"Is this another Fort Michilimackinac, where we gave up—raised the white flag without firing a shot?" asked Madison.

"Worse, sir," answered Edward. "The Potawatomi Indians have massacred the entire Fort Dearborn garrison and the civilians under their protection."

"Another disaster, and another of our isolated frontier forts gone, thanks to the damn English supplying guns and powder to the Indians. Yet my miserly opponents in Congress are against increasing the army by more than a few thousand men, at the same time insisting the way to win this war is to conquer all of Canada—*all of Canada*. Do they have any idea the size of the army needed to take and hold all of Canada?"

Edward shook his head. "They're not accountable. You are the Commander-in-Chief, sir."

The President pinched his nose and massaged his sinuses. The headache was getting worse. He sat down again while his secretary waited.

"Any good news?"

"No. Brigadier General William Hull, at Fort Detroit, supposedly in order to avoid a massacre, surrendered his troops."

"Supposedly?" repeated the President, raising an eyebrow.

"Sources say that we actually outnumbered the British, sir. Some say that it was a cowardly act on Hull's part."

"The entire garrison?"

"General Hull had over two thousand troops, sir; plus we lost twenty-five hundred muskets and thirty cannon."

"Devastating, Edward. And Forts Niagara and Erie have been fiascos also. It's been only two months, and already we have no army left in the West."

Edward nodded in agreement. Mr. Madison's War was not going well.

Tarot: THE KNIGHT OF PENTACLES

Revelation: The coming of an ordinary matter.

⁓

There was a knock at the door.

"Madame Caresse, Madame Caresse, *s'il vous plaît?*" It was a child's voice, at first hesitant with her request.

After a short pause, the knocking became a rapid pounding. And, no longer hesitant, the child was screaming. "Madame Caresse, it's urgent! You must come right away!"

Mumbling, "I hear you, I hear you!" under her breath, Hortense shuffled her large-boned frame toward the front of her mistress's cottage. Yawning, she opened the door; it was five o'clock in the morning, and she had awakened only fifteen minutes ago.

"*Entre, mon petit chou,*" she said, looking down at the neighbor girl, Antoinette. "My, my! For being only seven years old, you make an awfully big noise! So I guess *ta mère* is having her baby now?"

"*Oui,*" replied Antoinette, wringing her hands, "and Maman is moaning an awful lot!"

The maid nodded. "You sit down here in the *salle* by that fire Scamp just lit, and I'll get Madame Catherine."

"No need, Hortense," said Catherine Caresse, coming into the parlor, her petite figure already clothed in a practical shift. Catherine's hazel eyes sparkled as she greeted her young neighbor. "*Salut*, Antoinette! I had a feeling your *maman* would be delivering soon; we had a full moon last night!"

"*Oui*, she started having the pains yesterday before dinner-time, Madame Caresse, but she wanted to wait until they got really close before calling for you."

"Your *maman*, she did not eat dinner, did she?"

"No, she was not hungry," replied Antoinette.

"*Très bien*. Hortense, is the *café* ready?"

"*Oui*, madame. I put the water on to boil as soon as the fire was ready and the lanterns lit."

"Excellent! A cup before we go, then."

"But, madame, you must come now; my *maman*, her pains are close!" pleaded the girl, continuing to twist her hands.

"Now, Antoinette, to leave the house without sitting for coffee is bad luck, and this is a day when we must have the best of good fortune. Come, sit! Hortense, do we have any sweets for the *café*?"

"*Oui*, Madame," replied Hortense, as she filled four cups with steaming coffee. "There are a few molasses biscuits in the tin on the buffet. I'll put them on a plate."

"Excellent," said Catherine. "Scamp! Come on out and join us!"

A young boy of color, about three years older than Antoinette, slipped out from the back gallery. "Hello, Antoinette! Nice to see you. Awfully early, but nice!" he said with a shy smile.

"Hi, Scamp" was her bashful reply.

Hortense sat down after bringing the biscuits to the table. Scamp immediately helped himself to two of them. The two women sipped their coffee as Antoinette squirmed in her chair.

"Antoinette, do you have hot water available?"

"*Oui*, madame. And we have lots of clean cloths for Maman and *le bébé*."

Catherine took a final sip of her drink. "As always, excellent *café*, Hortense! And the cookies are still fresh and delicious!"

"Thank you, madame."

"I think it is time to get the street lantern, since it is still dark." Smiling at Antoinette, she said, "It seems that our little cabbage here has no appetite for coffee or sweets."

Jumping up from her chair, Antoinette cried, "So, we can go now?"

"*Oui*, we'll be on our way. Hortense, is my valise ready?"

"Yes—as always, here by the door," answered the dark-skinned maid, as she walked toward the entryway.

"Good! I believe Antoinette can help me with that."

Handing Antoinette the medicine bag, Hortense gazed into the child's eyes. "You are to carry this for Madame Catherine. Now, be careful, *chou*! There are medicine bottles and poultices inside. Can you do that?"

Antoinette slowly nodded.

"Scamp will carry the lantern. And don't worry, Antoinette; Madame Catherine is the best midwife in La Nouvelle-Orléans. *Ta mère* is going to be fine!"

Antoinette looked solemnly at her and said, "*Oui*, Madame Hortense!"

"Thank you, Hortense," said Catherine. "I believe we're prepared. I put some candy and toys on the altar for Papa Legba, and I have his talisman in my pocket for Jeanette to hold."

Catherine took her shawl off the peg by the doorway and wrapped it around her shoulders. After tucking her light brown, curly hair under her *tignon*, she held the door open for her young neighbor. "So, Antoinette"—she smiled—"do you think you will soon have a brother or a sister?"

Tarot: THE HIGH PRIESTESS

*Revelation: Entry into a different world of confusion
and bewilderment will lead to a different destiny.*

———

Young Peter Sidney slowly regained painful consciousness. He stifled a moan and tried to hoist his six-foot frame from the floor into a cross-legged, seated position. Once he had achieved that goal, he noticed a puddle of smeared, viscous fluid directly under his right knee. However, the throbbing in his head took precedence. Peter felt the back of his cranium. He kneaded a massive, aching knob, its swelling bulge tender to his touch. Nausea, then, and he vomited. More sticky fluid. Some of it in his lap.

He felt an odd rocking motion but was not sure if it was he or his surroundings that were moving.

"Well, blow me down; you're finally awake, then, Landsman!" The hearty voice came from about three feet away, and it sounded vaguely familiar.

"Come on, now—up you go. We have to get you presentable. Follow me."

Peter tried to stand up and get his balance in order to walk behind the voice's shadowy shape. The man leading him had a sturdy lantern, but it did not shed much light. Peter's head was dizzy, and his legs were wobbly. He had to plod in a stooped position to avoid hitting the ceiling.

After his eyes adjusted to the darkness, he glanced to his left and right and realized that he was in the hold of a ship. Sea chests, sails, and supplies were packed into the hull's overcrowded storage space. Continuing to keep his head low, he inadvertently kicked over some kind of container that sloshed water on him.

"Careful of the buckets, Landsman. They're mighty handy when they're full and we're fighting a fire. Of course, we need them when we're taking on water, too."

They stopped by a trunk, and Peter noticed that the man had some sort of uniform on.

"This is the slops chest," the older man announced.

Taking out a key, he opened the chest and selected some of its contents. Handing them to Peter, he said, "Put these on. You'll find our clothes more suitable than the civilian garb you're wearing. You'll be paying me for these garments from your future wages. I am Nathan Scott, the purser."

Still groggy, Peter sluggishly stripped off his soiled clothing and donned the leggings, shirt, coat, and trousers.

"I heard one of your friends at the pub say that you were the best carpenter in town. For your sake, I hope that's true. We need a few more buckets with covers made for the men who become ill."

His eyebrows raised, Peter looked at the smaller man. The purser realized Peter did not comprehend.

"You know, because the sick can't make it to the head. Here's your first rule to remember: always use the head. It's a seat with an opening at the bow. Any unclean behavior on your part will get you severe punishment. Do you understand?"

The purser did not wait for an answer. "You are now in His Majesty's Navy, and you will, of course, serve the king or be flogged."

Nathan Scott smiled somewhat at his last announcement, his gums displaying several brown teeth remaining in his mouth. Reaching into his pocket, he pulled out a little pouch. He took out a small sheet of tobacco and bit off a chunk. He chewed on it a bit. Then, with his tongue, he adroitly moved the wad over to rest between his left cheek and gum. Looking back at Peter, he held out the block and said, "Care for a plug of tobacco, Landsman?"

Peter didn't answer.

"No?" The purser chewed some more, then spat on the floor. "You'll be getting a tobacco ration yourself soon; just remember that no open flames are allowed onboard. Obvious reasoning, you know. So you're best off if you chew the stuff."

Apparently, more of the tobacco plug had dissolved in his mouth, and the purser spat again. "Mmm. And did I mention that you also get a portion of rum every day? Now, I know you like your ale, but I suspect you'll enjoy the rum, too. Just make sure to add some lime juice to it. Some of our new 'recruits' didn't pay attention to my advice. First they lost their teeth; then their bones and brains deteriorated. Scurvy, you know. Nasty disease." And, again, Nathan Scott expectorated.

How does the purser know that I like my ale? Peter abruptly recalled where and when he had first heard this man's voice.

The night before, to mark his sixteenth birthday, he had been having a few ales with friends at the Spotted Dog Pub in Penshurst Village. A group of men entered the tavern and insisted upon "helping" him celebrate by plying him with more alcohol. The Good Fellow of the Hour, they called him, engaging him in conversation and lavishing attention upon him. He'd gone outside to relieve himself, and that was the last he could recollect.

The "generous" men, including Nathan Scott, Peter now

realized, were a press gang, looking for able-bodied crew for their warship—the so-called recruits.

He gingerly felt the lump on his head again. They must have smacked him with something solid and dragged him off to the ship.

Still feeling stupefied and now somewhat in shock, Peter followed the purser to the upper deck. While gratefully gulping great lungsful of fresh air, he observed the seamen, intent upon their work, adjusting ropes, inspecting sails, and scouring the deck.

Then he heard spine-chilling howls of pain. They were coming from a man laid out on a mess table and held down by three other sailors. A tub was located nearby.

"Bite down on the musket ball, Charlie!" yelled one of the husky mates holding him down. "It will keep you from biting through your tongue!"

The screaming man was having his left leg amputated.

"Ah, a shame, you know. Charlie had a bad fall from the crow's nest."

Peter gave Nathan Scott a blank look.

"Up there!" The purser pointed to a basket lashed to the tallest mast. "Compound fracture. Everyone hoped for the best, and the doc tried to remove the loose bone splinters, but the leg just wouldn't heal. Putrefied."

A screw tourniquet had been applied a few inches above Charlie's knee. While assistants held the outside of the leg in a steady, straight line, the surgeon, looking like a butcher in his long white apron, stood on the inside of the limb, sawing about four inches below the kneecap. The surgeon worked decisively and quickly, slashing through skin, fat, and tendons. Charlie's agonizing wails continued.

Peter watched, horrified, as the surgeon cut the inside half, making sure to remove all the muscles to the bone. He applied a strip of leather to keep the area clear, before slicing and severing the lower limb. The assistant who had been holding the lower leg turned and tossed the detachment into the tub.

Charlie was now barely whimpering. With a crooked needle, the surgeon tied up the arteries and then removed the tourniquet.

Charlie had lost consciousness.

Peter smelled steaming tar and continued to watch in dismay as the surgeon used boiling pitch to stop the bleeding and seal off the wound.

"Poor Charlie," said Nathan Scott, shaking his head. "I hope he makes it. He's a good sailor."

Tarot: THE FOUR OF SWORDS

Revelation: Stillness needed to assemble one's thoughts and organize one's life.

⁓

M arguerite's baby was about to be added to Jacques's family vault in St. Louis Cemetery. His tiny cypress casket was positioned next to the whitewashed-brick crypt.

Marguerite was sitting on top of one of the taller tombs nearby and looking down. A small number of friends had come to lend support to the family. She saw them all below, including her self. A servant held a parasol over her head, shielding her from the sun.

Bizarre, she thought. _Why, there's Mother down there, and Père Antoine, too. And there's me! Yet here I am, up here. But there's that person—she looks like me and acts like me—down there, with them._

She waved to the people; called to them, _Yoo-hoo; look up here! I'm up here!_

No response.

They don't seem to see me up here. How odd. But I'm sure they would like to be up here with me, to see what it's like!

Marguerite looked around with awe at her surroundings.

What a fantastic view! I can see the river from here, even though it's eight blocks away! And I can see the carriages parked behind that wall on Basin Street!

She looked downward again. _And all these vaults—so many_

tombs are shaped like small houses. Yes, yes, she chided herself. *If the caskets were buried below the ground, the water, when it rises, would make them float to the surface.*

She gave a little shrug. *Not nice to see Aunt Jacqueline floating off! Plus, this way, with the little houses, we can have multiple burials in one home! Very clever; like a little city, really, with flowers and pretty iron fences and people coming to visit—like those down there!*

Marguerite watched as the small group gathered around the de Trahans' fashionable monument, one of the tallest aboveground tombs.

It's lovely—for a sepulcher, she thought. *Elegantly sculpted images of the poppies of sleep bordering the door. Our de Trahan name carved into stone. A graceful serpent underneath swallowing its tail, the symbol for eternity. Actually, that's awfully gruesome. But that's what it's all about, isn't it?*

And there's my baby down there, in that casket. So small. So cold. So dead.

She stared at the tomb's hollow opening. *They're going to bury him—insert him through that opening, into that cavity. His grandparents are already in there. And he'll be swallowed up. Just like them. Forever.*

My beautiful baby boy. And I can't stop them. If I could, I would make them stop.

So, is this what grief is? Being helpless?

She began to analyze the proceedings. *Look at me. I look so very sad,* she observed. *Everyone does. All that black,* she thought. *Black shapes embracing one another, exchanging a few words, nodding. Everyone behaving just so in Death's company.*

She felt a chilling presence touch her neck and then crawl down her flesh.

Ahhhhh, Death, and here you are. I know it's you. Are you watching them, too? There's the doctor, and three couples from our neighboring plantations. Those two older women? They're my mother's friends from church. You already know who their husbands are . . . were—you snatched them several years ago.

Hmm. Père Antoine is starting to pray. But you and I both know that prayers don't do any good. Silly Père Antoine.

She continued addressing her cold, clammy, clinging specter. *Deciding who will be next to capture their last breath?*

You can take me. Doesn't matter. I don't care. You'll get no struggle. I'm already released. You can't do any worse. I surrender. Go ahead!

She looked again at the group below. *My self: I wonder, do you see me here? The others can't—or won't. I'm obviously already departed, perished, finished. Ha! I'm just not dead yet.*

She gazed down at the little assembly again. *Death, stare at them with me. Who is next to be cast into a chamber in your little community?*

She saw her self step next to her mother, who was fingering a rosary. She saw Sheila reach for her hand and squeeze it. She noticed her self brush a fly away.

Ugh. Flies. I'll bet they're your pets, Death. They're despicable. Their dull buzz. That tedious, irksome drone.

Which is getting louder . . .

Owwww! What's happening? The buzzing noise—it's getting worse, pushing down on my brain. Pounding. Stop it!

She saw her self below clenching the crown of her head with both hands. She was pressing her fingers through her black lace veil into her scalp, her palms compressing her temple, squishing her forehead.

This clamor—it's getting heavier, the pressure. And it's building, swelling out, bulging in my skull.

"I'm not going away, Marguerite."

The voice was coarsely unpleasant; sounding mocking, snide.

Who are you? What do you want?

"*I am your friend, Marguerite,*" the repugnant voice assured her. "*I want you to know the truth.*"

The truth? The truth about what?

"*Your life is useless, Marguerite. What kind of a woman are you? Not much of a wife, that's for sure. No heir for Jacques. He's depending on you. But you've let him down.*"

But I've tried! I've tried so hard!

"*You've tried; you've tried so hard,*" he simpered, mocking her tone.

And then he roared, "*You are a failure! Your husband deserves a wife who will give him children.*"

Now cajoling, wheedling: "*But since I'm your friend, I have a plan for you.*"

What are you talking about?

"*Why don't you think about ending your life now? Then you can be with your baby. Down there. I can show you.*"

No! Get out of here, you nasty ogre!

A different voice, lighter, even lyrical: "*Marguerite, don't listen to him! You're grieving; you're in a dark place. But you must be strong; you must pull through!*"

"*Huh!*" The harsh voice again. "*You are weak! Look at those women down there. Three of them are your age. They have children who survived infancy. They're here to gloat. They're not your friends. Ask yourself: Why them and not you? You should be envious.*"

Marguerite could see her self below, shaking her head. *Yes! I'm bitter! And angry, too. Why didn't my baby live?*

She squeezed her eyes shut.

"*Because you are useless, Marguerite. And did that silly saint of fertility you prayed to help at all? Did he intervene on your baby's behalf? He played a cruel joke on you, Marguerite. You should punish him!*"

Opening her eyes again, she pursed her lips and clenched her fists. *You're right! How dare he! I will demand that Père Antoine put St. Anthony's statue upside down in a corner of the church!*

"*That's the spirit! Now you're on the right track!*"

And I said the rosary every day and made generous donations to the church's poor box. What good did it do me? So unfair!

"*Now, slow down here, Marguerite!*" It was that second voice again. Gentle. Tender.

But Marguerite was livid.

What! Marguerite demanded. That first voice was right. She wanted to rage, destroy.

And the throbbing pressure in her head was becoming more severe.

"*You know many women lose their babies—some in childbirth—and how many others die before their fifth birthday?*" the second voice said soothingly. "*Those women down there are your friends. They were your classmates at the Ursuline Convent School. You have known them for a long time. And they have lost children, too. They know your sorrow. They are here to comfort you, just as you were there for them. Remember!*"

Yes, but . . .

"*This sadness will never go away, but it will become less painful. And eventually you will want to ask for St. Anthony of Padua's help again. You must have faith! You must think about the future! St. Anthony will help you conceive once more and ensure safe childbirth. Don't listen to the evil one.*"

"*Nonsense! There is no future. Silly St. Anthony is never going to listen to you. You will never have another child. Because you are worthless, Marguerite.*"

"*Don't listen to the Devil, Marguerite! Trust me!*"

"*Bah! You know I'm right! None of those people down there cares about you. And look at all that praying you did.* God *doesn't even care about you! Forget about that silly saint; forget about those people down there. Just end it now!"*

Marguerite took a deep breath.

"Destruction. Easy to do."

"No, Marguerite, no!"

From her high perch, Marguerite looked down again upon the assembly. She saw her self grip the tip of an iron railing tightly. A jagged thorn from a climbing rosebush pierced her glove. She watched as a small red drop appeared.

Blood.

The voices were still. The heavy pounding throughout her head was subsiding. Also, she was becoming fully aware of her body's senses down below, especially the stabbing pain in her finger. Yet here she was, still above the crowd. Feeling quite unsteady. In both places. Panic.

I'm frightened. What's happening to me?

She saw her self inspect the blood from her finger and then turn to grip the iron fence again with both hands. Her awareness of her body below was growing more tangible.

More blood. And not from her finger. She knew she was still weak from childbirth, and now she perceived heavy bloody discharges accompanying her every move.

The fear became dismay. *Damn! What if my rags are saturated? What if there's blood on the ground below my skirt? Good thing I'm wearing black. But what if it shows? How appalling!*

Although she knew that Père Antoine was conducting a very short ceremony, she was suddenly aware that her body couldn't remain standing there. She saw her legs wobble. How humiliating if she were to faint. And with blood running down her legs. She tried to hold on to the railings to balance. *I must brace myself; I can't let myself go.*

Death's voice came back and laughed. *"Of course you can,*

Marguerite! Do it! Hit the ground. Serves you right! Do it, Marguerite!"

"No! Stop it!" she yelled back at him. "I'm in control! Now leave me!"

Sheila looked at her daughter in surprise. "Are you all right, dear?" she whispered.

Marguerite's eyes opened wide as she realized that she was grounded. And there seemed to be only one of her. Just to be sure, though, she raised her head and looked up at the taller tomb nearby. No one was sitting there, looking back at her.

Still weak, she tried to take a deep breath.

And gagged.

Despite the fragrance of the roses and flowers planted by the families who owned each tomb, she was becoming nauseated. The smell of the decomposing corpses in the burial chambers was overwhelming. She choked down the bile.

I must remain strong.

Sheila grabbed Marguerite's arm and helped her stagger to the cemetery wall. She leaned upon it, still unsteady.

"You will survive, Marguerite; you will survive." The message was softly reassuring.

And then absent. The voices, the pounding, and the aching in her head ceased. Marguerite looked up again at the top of the pediment tomb. Empty.

She closed her eyes once more.

Yet the mourners continued praying, the sun continued shining, and the flies continued buzzing.

Until Sheila lightly tapped her shoulder. The ceremony was complete, the small casket was no longer in sight, the mourners were slowly withdrawing.

Marguerite leaned heavily upon her mother and tottered over to the black-draped coach. The coachmen assisted her in mounting the steps. She sank into the seat and then laid her head in her mother's lap.

On the return trip to their home, neither woman said a word; the only sounds came from the hoofbeats. Sheila gently massaged her daughter's head. Marguerite wondered if she knew about the voices. Perhaps her mother was trying to eliminate them forever?

The two black Morgan horses pulling the carriage trotted through the avenue of trees leading up to the house and came to a halt in front of the home's entrance. The young footman riding on the back platform jumped off and opened the carriage door. With Sheila's help, Marguerite stepped down precariously and looked out to the meticulously landscaped green. The sturdy oaks and cedars bordered the grounds all the way to the Mississippi River, the nearby water lily pond glittered delicately in the sunlight, and the ornamental benches where she frequently fed the birds had been polished. All was as it should be. Except . . . Jacques was not there.

Marguerite pondered her husband's whereabouts. She had not seen Jacques since her labor had begun. As per tradition, he had gone to a nearby plantation to await the baby's arrival. A manservant had been sent to the neighbor's place bearing the sad news, but the domestic had returned only with a note: "Marguerite, I'm sorry."

And that was it. She had not seen or heard from him since. Where was he? Was he suffering from their baby's loss, too? She certainly hoped so. She hoped he was miserable. How dare he not be here to comfort her!

"Do you need some time alone, dear?" They had reached the porch, when Sheila interrupted her daughter's thoughts.

Alone? She felt totally isolated! Nevertheless, Marguerite quietly responded, "I just need to tidy up, Mother." She told her maid to get a bowl of water, along with some more clean rags.

Now cognizant of Marguerite's sticky problem, Sheila put her hands on her hips and scowled. "*Mon Dieu!* I knew this would happen! Didn't I tell you not to go to the burial, Marguerite?"

Obviously agitated, Sheila spoke even more loudly, and her tone went up along with her indignation. "In your condition! Everyone would have understood that you were indisposed. But no—you had to go! And now see what you've done; I certainly hope you haven't ruined that dress."

Appalled, Marguerite stared at Sheila for a moment and then screamed, "*Ferme ta bouche*, Mother!"

Instead, Sheila's mouth dropped open.

Marguerite turned away and, not wanting to argue further, slowly inched her way toward her bedroom.

Even as her maid gently removed the blood from her legs and assisted her in wrapping strips of cloth around her groin, Marguerite could still feel herself shaking with rage and frustration. Now exasperated at her mother and furious with her husband, she felt her brooding thoughts gnawing aggressively at her.

An hour later, although she had changed her dress, Marguerite still did not feel "refreshed." She made her way into the quiet drawing room. She thought of her infant inside the soundless and still casket. Collapsing on the low sofa, she reflected that her fragile baby's body, too, was cushioned in its coffin. One. Dead. And Jacques. Departed. Had she lost both her baby and now her husband, too? She felt herself becoming more and more depleted; her heart pitched around inside her emptiness.

She glimpsed herself in one of the gilded mirrors on the wall. Her usually creamy skin now looked pasty. Her face was gaunt, hollow, unoccupied, her ash-blond curls also drooping. A true reflection of her wretched self.

Sheila, still raw from her daughter's rebuke, came in but said nothing. She motioned to a servant to bring a glass of orange-blossom water for Marguerite to sip.

"Why?" Marguerite finally broke the silence. "Mother, I'm miserable. And it's not only because of my baby. Where is Jacques? Why isn't he here, with me? I don't understand!"

"Now, dear," Sheila said soothingly, as she tried to think of an explanation for her son-in-law's absence, "men are different. I'm sure Jacques is distraught and can barely handle the death of the baby himself. He'll come to you when he feels he has the strength to support you."

"But we should be consoling each other. I need him!"

"I believe he is avoiding you because he probably feels powerless to change anything. His hopes and dreams for the future were dashed, too."

"But—"

"He needs time to deal with losing the baby in his own way. You know Jacques is a very private person, and has always had difficulty expressing his feelings, Marguerite. But that doesn't mean he doesn't have them. The child was his heir. I'm certain he is deeply grieving the loss of his son."

Sheila thought a moment and then added, "In fact, darling, I did overhear one of the servants saying that Jacques has been working long hours, refusing to leave his office. That's typical of some men, you know—immersing themselves in work in order to shut out their troubles. I'm sure that's it. In fact, I gather that the only person allowed to enter the building is his manservant, Tobias. Knowing how delicate you are, Jacques must be protecting you from his suffering. I'm certain that he does not want to inflict even more pain on you."

Marguerite, her eyes wide, looked at her mother in astonishment. "Oh! I didn't know! I've been so selfish, thinking of my own needs. My poor husband. I must go to him!" she said, about to push her way up from the deep cushions of the sofa.

"No, no! Don't be too hasty, dear; let him cope in his own way. Plus, you are obviously in no condition to see him now," said Sheila. "You must use this time to heal yourself. Your bleeding has not stopped yet; I suspect you need more sleep. Are your breasts still painful?"

"They're still a bit tender, but my milk is drying up."

"Good. Now, let's get you back to bed for more rest. My precious daughter, you are young, you are beautiful, and you can and will become pregnant again. We'll put all this unpleasantness behind us. And next year, I'm confident that you'll be presenting a precious little baby de Trahan to Jacques."

Tarot: THE THREE OF CUPS

Revelation: A happy matter: the birth of a child.

~

As soon as Catherine entered Jeanette's cottage, she knew which room held Antoinette's mother. The grunting phase had begun. The pushing would start soon.

Smiling when she encountered her laboring neighbor on her bed, Catherine said, "Hello, Jeanette. I see it's time. Let me make you more comfortable."

"Ah, Catherine. I'm so happy to see you! The pains! I don't know how much longer I can do this. I'm so tired. And I need to go to the toilet!"

"Not really, Jeanette; Antoinette told me that you haven't eaten in a while. You're feeling pressure on your rectum from the baby descending, and that's good news! Let's get these linens changed, now!"

With Scamp's help, Catherine removed the covering blanket and replaced the wet padding as Jeanette raised her hips.

After Jeanette settled again onto her back, Catherine said, "All right, now, put your legs on these pillows so that they're above your hips. . . . *Bien!* Now, bend your knees a little."

With sure and gentle hands, Catherine massaged the pregnant woman's distended stomach with a salve of lard infused with a liquor of sumac leaves, sage, and swamp-lily root.

"Mmm. That feels so good!"

Catherine smiled. "I made lots of this liniment for you to use after the baby is born. It will reduce stretch marks."

"I'm looking forward to that already," said Jeanette.

The midwife got some of her necessities from the medicine case and placed them on the nightstand: a piece of valerian root, catnip leaves, olive oil, powdered snakeroot, and shavings of willow bark. She arranged her other essentials: scissors, a jar of rainwater, and a silver two-bit piece with a hole drilled in the middle.

After taking a bottle of red wine out of her bag, she said, "Scamp, will you put this on the dresser? And, Antoinette, please lean this picture of St. Anthony of Padua against it. *Merci.*"

Then Catherine placed the charm of Papa Legba in Jeanette's hand.

"Here, squeeze Papa Legba and entreat St. Anthony for a safe childbirth," she said.

"Ohhhhh," the drained woman groaned. "I've been praying a long time now. I just wish it were over."

"You're going to be fine, Jeanette," said Catherine. "You've done this before. You are strong, healthy, and at full term. Scamp and I are here to help you. And so is Antoinette."

The young girl, eyes wide and extremely pale, was speechless.

"Antoinette, get a cup of hot water for your *maman.* Scamp, you go with Antoinette into the kitchen and keep the water boiling." Turning to Jeanette, Catherine showed her the piece of valerian root. "This will take care of your nerves," she said. "We'll add this to your tea. And the willow bark in the tea will take away some of the pain."

"Oh!" For the first time, Jeanette smiled. "Please make it a big cup—because right now I have lots of pain."

As if to prove her point, she grabbed Catherine's hand and screamed.

"Bear down, now, and push!" counseled Catherine, massaging the vaginal opening with the olive oil.

Another scream.

Antoinette returned with the cup of hot water. Catherine placed a pinch of willow bark into a tea infuser and steeped it in the water. Removing the infuser from the cup, she held it so Jeanette could sip.

"Ahhh. It's warm. And . . ." Another scream.

"Push, Jeanette. Good, good."

Jeanette's nut-brown face reddened as she pushed down yet another time and let out an ear-piercing yell. Catherine put the cup of tea on the nightstand and moved toward the foot of the bed to monitor the baby's progress. She smiled at the young mother.

"Reach down, Jeanette, with your hand. That's right! Can you feel the head? Good! Another big push, now . . ."

Jeanette grimaced, clasped both hands on top of her stomach, gave a loud groan, and shoved down with all her might. The baby slipped into Catherine's hands, giving a lusty cry.

"*Bien, bien*, Jeanette! Congratulations! You have a son," said Catherine, as she held up the baby for the mother to see.

"Eww," said Antoinette. "It's messy!"

"'It,'" said Catherine, raising an eyebrow warningly at Antoinette, "is your beautiful baby brother. And you'll see something else somewhat bloody come out soon, Antoinette. That's called the placenta, which nourished your baby brother before he was born. All normal, and yet marvelous! Now, I want you to get fresh sheets and blankets for your mother while I take care of your new brother."

Catherine snipped off the umbilical cord with her scissors. To prevent the child from becoming a bed-wetter, she made sure that the stub was turned to the infant's left side. Then she gently washed the baby. After swaddling the newborn in a soft cotton cloth, she put a wool cap on his head and presented him to his mother.

"He's beautiful, Jeanette! And hungry!"

The new mother received her son, then sighed happily as he nuzzled and sucked at her breast.

Antoinette returned with the fresh bedding, which Catherine maneuvered under and around the tranquil mother and suckling child.

"What can I do now?" asked Antoinette, eager to appease and please Catherine.

"Take these wet and soiled bedclothes to the courtyard to be laundered. Scamp will show you what to do. I need to give your *maman* a sponge bath, and then she should have some soup."

"I'll get the bathwater, too," said Antoinette, as she sped off to the kitchen.

"How are you feeling, Jeanette?" asked Catherine.

"Wonderful, mostly. Isn't he exquisite? Look at all this hair! And his eyes—they're almost a violet color! He looks very much like Antoinette when she was born."

"And they both have your beautiful complexion, too. What will you name him?"

"Pierre, after his father. Oh, I can't wait to show him to his daddy!"

"I have forgotten, Jeanette—does Pierre have any other sons?"

"No, just daughters. So my baby will be special. And Pierre has promised that he will send my son to France to be educated."

"*Oui?* Our *petit* Pierre already has a grand future! Ah, here's Antoinette!"

The young girl had returned with a large pail of hot water and poured it into the basin. "I'll get the soup now," she said. "It's your favorite, Maman: crab-and-shrimp gumbo!" She hurried back outside to the kitchen.

Opening her medicine bag, Catherine got out her marble mortar and pestle. She took out a small sack of rosemary sprigs, parsley leaves, and rose petals.

"I expected you to deliver sometime soon," Catherine said, smiling, "so I prepared these last night."

Looking into the medicine bag again, she pulled out another small container of olive oil. Emptying the sack of flowers and herbs into her mortar, she crushed them with the pestle and then added a little bit of the oil. She poured in a cup of water from the pail, let the mixture steep for a few minutes, and slowly stirred the scented brew into the bathwater.

Catherine threaded a piece of cord through the hole in the silver two-bit piece. She took the now-sleeping baby from Jeanette, placed him in a beautifully carved walnut cradle, and then tied the cord around the baby's left ankle to bring him good luck. Helping the new mother sit up more comfortably, Catherine tenderly bathed her neighbor's body.

"You'll have other assistance besides Antoinette?" she asked.

"Yes, my sister Augusta will be coming to help. I'll send Antoinette to fetch her. But right now, after I have some gumbo, I think I'll just want to take a nice nap."

"I'm not surprised. But you did have a relatively uncomplicated delivery, Jeanette. I remember Antoinette taking a couple of days to appear. And I had to use forceps to help her out."

"Yes, you're right, Catherine. Little Pierre's birth was much easier."

Catherine continued, "We will stay until Augusta comes. I have not seen her since she had that horrible toothache. How is she doing?"

"She is well; that prickly ash bark you gave her worked wonders. She's grateful that you saved her tooth."

Catherine remembered also having prepared a tailor-made

charm bag of allspice, moss, and cedar. "I suspect my special gris-gris helped, too," she said.

"We are very fortunate to have you, Catherine. You are a great healer. I'll never forget how you cured my brother's alcoholism with eels. Thank you for all you do."

"I am blessed and grateful to possess these gifts of healing, Jeanette. I enjoy being able to give assistance in one way or another."

Jeanette inhaled deeply. "The water's fragrance is delightful. I suspect this particular bath is significant, too?"

Catherine smiled. "I knew it would please you. It's specifically for mothers who have just given birth. These special ingredients will help open the door for new opportunities, Jeanette—for you and little Pierre!"

"Maman! Here's the gumbo!" cried Antoinette, bursting into the room, spilling a bit of the tureen's soup. Scamp followed the girl, carrying bowls and spoons.

"And Tante Augusta is here, too!" Antoinette announced.

"Perfect timing," said Catherine, as she started to gather her supplies.

"Well, well, well!" laughed Augusta, as she came into the room. "I was hoping you wouldn't start without me, but it looks like I missed all the fun!"

After kissing her sister hello, Augusta looked down at Pierre. "Another gorgeous baby, Jeanette!"

Then she turned and gave Catherine a hug. "So good to see you, Catherine! And you've performed your amazing marvels again. Are there any instructions for taking care of Jeanette and my new nephew?"

Catherine gave Augusta a small bag of the powdered snakeroot. "Just a couple of suggestions, Augusta. If Jeanette has cramps, make a tea using a tablespoon of this. You can make a cup of tea for yourself, too; it's excellent for anyone's good health."

Handing Augusta an even smaller bag of the catnip leaves, she said, "Now, with this, use only a pinch, with six tablespoons of warm water. Then dip your finger in it and put it into the baby's mouth. It will prevent him from getting hives."

"That gumbo smells wonderful. Can you stay, Catherine, and share some with us?"

"I'd love to, Augusta, thank you, but I need to go home and take care of some business. I'll be back in a couple of days to see how you're all doing. Perhaps then. Ready, Scamp?"

Catherine finished her packing and put the picture of St. Anthony, along with her scissors, into her bag.

"Don't forget the bottle of red wine," said Jeanette.

"Oh, that's for you and Augusta." Catherine smiled. "I've been told that it's the best medicine of all!"

Tarot: THE TEN OF WANDS

Revelation: Bearing an oppressive burden.

⁓

The purser hailed one of the sailors, who was down on his knees, rigorously washing the deck boards. "Benjamin! Meet the Landsman. You are to show him the ropes." The purser turned to leave, then added, "And keep him busy!"

Looking up, the young, muscular seaman nodded to Peter to get down and join him. Peter knelt down dutifully and, upon closer inspection, saw that Benjamin had been scrubbing at various drips of tar that had splattered from strands of rope in the rigging. The sailor was using a hog-bristle deck bumper, but he handed Peter a large, abrasive sandstone.

"Use this holystone, Landsman," he said. "See how it resembles a bible?" Benjamin chuckled at his joke. Peter, however, was not in the mood for humor.

Noting Peter's lack of amusement, Benjamin continued, "We are to remove all the pitch marks until the planks are spotlessly pure and white."

Peter grasped the stone and began to scrub. The smell of vinegar in the cleaning solution was not unpleasant, especially compared with the stench of some of the unwashed sailors.

"Hist! Aren't you the one they kidnapped recently?" his new tutor asked. "What's your name?"

"I'm Peter Sidney, from Penshurst. I thought the press gangs only took seamen; I know nothing about sailing. They must have made a mistake."

Scouring more slowly now, Benjamin replied, "No mistake, Peter. King George III is desperate. In the war against America, the Royal Navy doesn't have enough enlisted men. And many of those who do volunteer desert whenever possible. The pay is late, the food is terrible, the discipline onboard is brutal, and the combats are bloodbaths."

"Well, then, why did you join?"

Benjamin gave him a glum look. "I was pressed, too. From an American ship! We're what they call the King's bargains; they don't have to lay out much money for us. Do you have any other questions?"

"Just one: tell me what I need to know to survive."

Tarot: THE WHEEL OF FORTUNE

Revelation: Good fortune; victory;
a surprising turn of luck.

~

E dward Coles knocked rapidly and then entered the President's office without waiting for permission. Although he was out of breath, he had a huge smile on his face.

"Do come in, Edward!" said President Madison, raising his eyebrows. Noting Edward's eagerness, he added, "I suspect this is important?"

"Sorry, sir; yes, sir. It's very good news indeed, Mr. President!"

Madison nodded wearily and put down his papers. "I would love to hear some good news, Edward. Do sit down."

"Thank you, sir," said Edward. Unlike the President, though, the secretary did not relax; he sat on the edge of his seat.

The President took a sip of his tea and leaned back in his chair. Nodding to his secretary, he said, "This war, it's aged me. And after last week's difficulties—the East Coast merchants blaming me for the depression, plus the frontier West losing their forts—yes, by all means, what do you have to report?"

"It happened just off the coast of Nova Scotia, Mr. President! The HMS _Guerriere_ was attacking the USS _Constitution_!"

"The _Guerriere_! It is one of the most galling of the British ships for stopping and searching our vessels! And . . . ?"

"And our men gave them quite the battle, sir! We won! It was all over in just thirty minutes!"

"Excellent! Who's the captain of the *Constitution*, Edward?"

"It's Isaac Hull, William Hull's nephew."

"Is that right? Glad to see that he's not as spineless as his uncle, the general who surrendered all of his troops at Fort Detroit!"

"Yes, sir. Isaac Hull and his crew rescued ten impressed Americans; plus, we now have over two hundred British prisoners. And the *Guerriere* has been demolished, sir!"

"And the frigate *Constitution*: What kind of shape is she in?"

"Only modest damage, sir. Evidently, the British cannonballs actually bounced off her oak hull. Some have been calling her Old Ironsides because she withstood the attack so well."

"Finally, a victory! That is excellent news, Edward! I'd say the Royal Navy is not so invincible after all!"

The President thought a minute and then leaned forward in his chair. "When the *Constitution* returns to port in Boston, she and her sailors should be honored with a parade. It will be good for morale."

"It's already being planned, sir."

"Good. Hmm. And will you tell Mrs. Madison to be sure our dinner tonight is extra special? We're hosting a couple of the congressmen and their wives. We can make it a small celebration. I hope this news will inspire more confidence and enthusiasm in Washington as well."

"I'm certain that Dolley will be happy to make your dinner into more of a festive occasion, sir," said Edward, with a twinkle in his eye.

The President laughed. "You know your cousin well, Edward!"

After the secretary left his office, Mr. Madison placed his hands behind his head and leaned back again in his chair. "Finally, a victory!" he repeated, smiling.

Finally.

Tarot: THE FIVE OF WANDS

Revelation: A time of struggle; the battle of life.

~~~

Peter quickly memorized Benjamin's advice; he did not want to test the reasoning.

"When it's your turn to sleep, swing your hammock from the ringbolts between your assigned rails. And make sure you're in the right location. Also, don't ever take someone else's belongings, or some dark night you could get tossed over the rail.

"And take off those shoes, or you'll slide off the deck on your own. If Captain's in a hurry, he won't stop to rescue an ordinary seaman or even a dozen of us."

Peter quickly removed his shoes.

"See? It's easier to grip the deck with bare feet. And when we're in a battle, sand is spread on the deck to keep you from skidding in the blood."

"How considerate," said Peter. He looked around at the weather-stained seamen. "Why would these men sign up for such a hazardous life?"

"They're not all volunteers. Quite a few of them have been impressed," said Benjamin. "Others, I've heard from the sea gossips, have been sent from the British jails. Not sure which ones, though."

They all looked gruff and grizzled, and Peter wondered

which were which. And those who had been imprisoned—what were their crimes? And he was going to be in battle with them?

Benjamin interrupted his musings. "Here—I have an extra bandanna for you to use." He handed Peter a large, colorfully patterned neckerchief. "The cloth protects your jacket from the grease and tar in your hair."

Seeing Peter's quizzical expression, Benjamin added, "You can put tar in your hair to keep the lice under control."

Peter nodded; he was already having a problem with the varmints.

"And in battle," Benjamin continued, "you wrap the bandanna around your head to cushion your eardrums against the pounding of the guns. Greenhorns like you who don't cover their ears when the cannons fire get bleeding ears and go deaf."

Then Benjamin smiled. "Ah! There's the bell for our dinner. We get three squares a day, on that wooden plate you got. Watch out for weevils, though—they're often in the hard biscuits. The good news is that the meat hasn't gotten rancid; we haven't been out to sea long enough for that to occur."

"Aren't there animals onboard?" Peter asked. "I'm sure I heard sheep bleating, and I think those are chickens squawking right now."

"Oh, we ordinary seamen don't get to eat any of the pigs, poultry, or goats in the manger; they're only for the officers. On the other hand, they do attract rats."

"And that's a positive because . . . ?"

"If you're able to catch one, they're pretty good roasted. There's your fresh meat! Otherwise, we have to wait until we're in port."

Benjamin laughed at Peter's expression. Then he sniffed the air and groaned. "We're having cabbage tonight, probably with salt beef. They call it sauerkraut because it's thoroughly soaked in brine. But at least we'll have the rum to wash it down. By the way, don't pretend to be sick; your rum rations will be stopped."

Peter's look was again doleful.

"Don't worry," said Benjamin. "You'll make sense of it. Just be sure to learn the knots I showed you and which one a job demands—there's the bowline, sailor's knot, and clove hitch."

Peter's look was now doubtful.

"You'll be working the lines and trimming the sails in no time."

"Right," said Peter, yet not with conviction.

"Of paramount importance, Peter, is to learn to read the skies, the weather, the winds, and, most crucial, the mood of the commander! Understand?"

"Aye, aye."

Two sailors walked by, bearing a long, lumpy sack. "Uh-oh," said Benjamin. "There goes Charlie. I heard he wasn't going to make it; I guess gangrene got him after all."

Peter looked up from scrubbing the deck in time to see the sailors hoist the bundle over the side of the ship, swing it back and forth several times, and release it into the ocean. Peter raised his eyebrows at Benjamin.

"When you die onboard, the sailmaker sews you up into your hammock for burial at sea. We call it the canvas coffin. There's a cannonball included to make sure you go directly down into the deep. Your garments, of course, are added to the slops chest."

Peter shuddered.

Knowing what he was thinking, Benjamin continued, "Your garb belonged to a Frenchman."

"What did he die from?"

"Being hanged. He was a prisoner of war." Then Benjamin gave Peter a lopsided grin. "The clothes look much better on you, though!"

Tarot: THE FIVE OF CUPS

Revelation: Sadness; regret over loss.

⁓

Marguerite was having her breakfast in bed, when she heard a knock.

"Come in, Mother!" she called out, as her maid started to open the door.

"Hello, Marguerite."

It was Jacques.

Marguerite almost dropped her cup of cocoa. It had been three weeks since the funeral.

Her husband held a bouquet of flowers and gave her a small, almost shy smile. "I hope you are getting better," he said.

"Jacques! Oh, Jacques!" she cried, holding out her arms. "My darling. I have missed you terribly!"

"I'm sorry, Marguerite." He remained standing by her bed, still holding the flowers.

Marguerite dropped her arms. Her outstretched fingers curled into her palms, forming fists, and her face screwed up as she glared at the man motionless before her. Anger surged through her. "Why weren't you here with me? I needed you! You have no idea how much I have suffered!"

Jacques looked sheepishly down at the floor. "Yes, well . . . it was difficult for me, too, Marguerite. And I thought it best not to make you even more miserable. I needed to respond to the death in my own way." He looked at her again. "I'm truly sorry."

Marguerite's face muscles slackened, and she sagged into the sheets. "Oh, Jacques, please forgive me for my outburst. I wasn't thinking of your anguish. That was selfish of me. Mother told me you were inconsolable."

"Yes, of course; we've all had a difficult time. But it's behind us now."

Marguerite quickly sat up straighter and put on a perky smile. She began speaking very quickly. "But we can try again, my darling. We must try again. Soon! I have regained much of my strength. Every day I can stomach a little more food, and I take a small stroll in the garden with Mother. She assures me that I am getting better all the time. Look," she said, pinching her face, "I have color in my cheeks! We'll have another baby, Jacques—a strong baby, a son. I just know it. . . ."

Marguerite realized she was babbling. Jacques just stood there, his green eyes watching her. He seemed to be in a daze.

"Jacques? Are you all right?"

"Hmm?" He nodded his head. "Oh, yes, I'm fine, Marguerite." He placed the flowers on her bed. "I am happy to know that you are getting well. I must get back to work now."

He blew her a kiss and left.

Tarot: THE MOON

Revelation: A time of confusion, oscillation, and uncertainty.

~

Peter had learned quickly from Benjamin's tutoring these past three weeks. He became accustomed to the ship's creaking, groaning, and occasional churning through the ocean. A couple of times, on days when the sky was blue and the wind brisk, the sails seeming to suck in their cheeks, he felt the synergy of the ship's strength and the seamen's competence. That was when he almost experienced contentment.

Almost.

But there had been other days when dark squalls stormed across the decks and the horizon pitched. The taut sails, the rigid ropes, and the tense sailors integrated as one force while the ship plunged through the swirling sea. During those times, Peter consciously blocked out his panic, but the terror could not be forgotten.

And, as Benjamin had said, conditions were horrible. Peter got only four hours of sleep before his next watch. He hadn't bathed yet and slept in his clothes, and because the head could not be used in bad weather, he had to join his mates in relieving himself in the buckets lined up in the bilge: the dark, damp, fetid lower deck. Benjamin had joked that they would have better conditions in jail.

The entire crew had daily gunnery drills, as well as sailing the ship. Peter learned to set the rigging and the sails, and if he was not doing carpentry work, he was expected to continue the duties of cleaning, painting, and polishing.

There was also leisure time. Benjamin had introduced him to the art of scrimshaw. He himself was carving a ship on a whale's tooth, but ivory was hard to come by, so Peter was learning on a small chunk of wood. He was scratching his version of a gull on it.

Evidently, it was not a very good rendition. "Is that a cross you're making?" Benjamin had asked recently.

"A cross?"

"It looks like a cross with eyes, but I didn't know you were religious!"

"I'm not. And it's a flying seagull. See? Here's the beak, and these are the wings. . . ."

Benjamin nodded, then added cheerily, "Aha! I see it. A flying seagull. Good job!"

Now, in the carpenter's shop (where he was less likely to be disturbed), with his needle, Peter was trying to improve his detailing of the gull. As he added scores to the bird's wings, he heard the master-at-arms yell out, "All hands, witness punishment!"

Peter had been told about these happenings, but this was the first captain's mast that he would observe. He quickly put the wooden piece in his pants pocket and hastened to join Benjamin and the rest of his shipmates at the gangway.

He was too late to hear the charges, but he did recognize the terror-stricken man brought up for discipline. It was Harry, a young sailor, who had been impressed from a merchant ship. He was blubbering, "I'm innocent! I didn't do anything! It's all a mistake!"

Two men stripped Harry's shirt off and lashed him by his wrists to an upright ship's grating. The boatswain's mate swaggered forward with a coarse red woolen bag. He removed a cat-o'-nine-tails from the bag and examined each of the waxed, braided cords.

"The cat's out of the bag now!" Benjamin whispered to Peter. The mate looked up and scowled as he scanned the crew.

Harry was still mewling. "It's not me. I didn't do it. Please!"

With a smirk, the boatswain's mate shook his head and took aim, ready to strike. He violently whipped the knotted ropes in an intense blow to Harry's pale, bare back. The small knots tore the skin.

Peter gasped when he saw the hideous red welts left by the first strike, and then winced with each of the following eleven brutal slashes that bit into the flesh.

Harry's back was raw meat. He was no longer able to stand on his own; he was hanging by his wrists. But the brutality was over. He was cut down from the grating and taken below to the sick berth. The surgeon was waiting to rub salt into the wounds to prevent infection. Meanwhile, the boatswain's mate, still with a smug smile on his face, unhurriedly removed the congealed flesh and blood from his whip.

Eight bells rang. It was noon—time for dinner. As the crew went mutely to their mess tables, Peter stayed close to Benjamin and sat next to him.

"Why?" he asked quietly.

"Harry was lucky," Benjamin replied, in a hurried whisper that grew husky. "He was accused of going to another man's hammock. He could have been hanged. But he got off easy; they just charged him with indecent behavior."

Benjamin noticed that Peter wasn't eating. "Hallo, what's the matter? You're not hungry? It's salt pork and pease porridge today, and the cheese isn't rancid yet."

"My insides feel like they're spinning around. You can have my portion," mumbled Peter. "But I'll be drinking my full ration of rum grog."

"Be careful, my friend," warned Benjamin, smacking his lips after swallowing some gulps from his mug. "On an empty stomach, you could become 'groggy,' and then you could have a meeting with the cat yourself!"

Peter looked back at Benjamin and shook his head. Reluctantly, he broke a biscuit and, using a piece to scoop up a lump of the porridge, shoved it into his mouth and began chewing.

Tarot: THE TEN OF SWORDS

Revelation: Sudden misfortune;
difficulties to absorb.

~

June 1813

The USS *Chesapeake* left Boston Harbor early in the afternoon of June 1. She sailed out to meet the HMS *Shannon*, which had been blockading the port for the past fifty-six days.

The frigates were a close match in size and force; however, the British vessel was low on provisions, and the Americans had a larger crew. Just before four bells of the fifth watch, as the two vessels drew closer, the Americans let out a confident cheer.

It was a bit too premature, though, as within the first five minutes of engagement they each suffered serious damage from the other's cannon fire. The *Chesapeake* was also losing its leadership. Three officers died at the helm.

The British frigate *Shannon* was now within boarding distance and threw grappling hooks onto the *Chesapeake*. The dismayed American crew quickly rallied and counterattacked.

"Don't give up the ship!" yelled Captain John Lawrence, himself mortally wounded.

Fifteen minutes of horrific hand-to-hand fighting followed, resulting in the *Chesapeake*'s loss of 150 dead and wounded.

And Edward had to report to President Madison that the Americans gave up the ship.

Tarot: THE NINE OF PENTACLES

*Revelation: May experience enthusiasm and
interest in a new field of work.*

～

A fact Peter soon realized: pay for both the recruited and the impressed sailors ran months, even years, in arrears.

Another reality: One out of every four sailors deserted His Majesty's Navy.

So: Peter Sidney, impressed at Penshurst Village, deserted. Like the hundreds before him, he jumped overboard and swam away.

The flat and low coral island was beautiful. Peter began walking along the sandy white beach while the surf gently lapped at the shore. He noted turtles and a couple of very long lizards sunning themselves among the lavender-colored succulents. Farther inland, he found salt ponds studded with mangroves, and wading flamingos, herons, and terns. Cattle, donkeys, and inquisitive goats helped themselves to water in the chalky puddles or sought shade under the white-flowered trees. It was an ideal place, thought Peter, where ships might stop to take on supplies. At least, that was what he was hoping. In the meantime, though he knew it was a silly comparison, he felt as if he were the hero of his favorite book, *Robinson Crusoe*.

It was his third day on the island when he saw the pirates. He crouched behind one of the trees, hugging its root system, as

47

if to blend in. He felt something pecking at the back of his shirt. It tickled. Not wanting to move, Peter tried to ignore it. Then he brushed his hand behind his back, hoping it would stop.

It didn't. Finally spinning around, Peter found himself looking into the eyes of a goat.

Peter tried to swat at it. "Scoot! Scoot! Go away!" he hissed.

It looked at him, seemingly unperturbed, and then it bleated.

"Shove off, now, I say!"

No effect. Another bleat.

"Ahoy, mates! Look what we have here!"

Peter looked up from his crouch to see a giant of a man, brightly dressed, arms akimbo, glaring down at him menacingly. Three men were with him; one had a pistol drawn. Peter quickly got up, eyes wide, raising his arms in surrender.

The pirates surrounded him, scrutinizing him closely.

"I suspect it's one of them English king's sailors. Wonder where his ship is," observed the man with the pistol.

"Just looks like a bilge rat to me!" another responded.

Peter remembered the slop buckets in the bilge on the Royal Navy's ship. It was considered the filthiest dead space for obvious reasons. Bilge rat: not a nice comparison; not a good start.

"Well, mates," said the giant, folding his arms across his immense chest, "what shall we do with him?"

"Wait!" sputtered Peter.

"Yesssssss?"

"I'm Peter Sidney from Penshurst Village in Kent, England. I escaped from the British Navy. Perhaps I can be of service to you. I am a carpenter!"

The large man looked at Peter, and a rumble started in his stomach and grew into another booming exclamation.

"A carpenter, you say! Well, today's your lucky day, Peter Sidney. *Our* carpenter, Jack, has a bursted belly from lifting one of his own barrels. Didn't realize how heavy it was, I guess. What do you say, mates?"

"Aye!" They all nodded.

And Peter was led off to yet another ship.

Tarot: THE SIX OF WANDS

Revelation: Good news and conquest.

~

September 1813

"Come in, Edward."

"Mr. President. It's a message from Commodore Oliver Perry."

"Good news from Lake Erie?"

"Yes, sir. The commodore's words: 'We have met the enemy, and he is ours.' The British Lake Erie squadron has surrendered."

"This is a first, Edward. Never before has an entire British naval squadron surrendered. Outstanding!"

"Yes, sir. We have taken more prisoners than Commodore Perry had men onboard."

"And the captured vessels?"

"Two ships, two brigs, one schooner, and one sloop. All brought back to Presque Isle."

"Excellent! Not only will that secure the northern borders of Ohio, Pennsylvania, and western New York, but it will make it much more difficult for the English to supply Detroit."

"This may be the turning point in the battle for the West, sir."

"Indeed, Edward. Commodore Perry should receive some sort of medal for his heroic achievement!"

Tarot: THE SIX OF SWORDS

Revelation: Passage away from difficulties.

⁓

It was Peter's fourth, uneventful day as a pirate aboard the *Dorada*, and he was inspecting the inside of the hull for any minor battle damages. He was also brooding about his fate again, when he heard Bartholomew playing a lively jig on an accordion.

As Peter watched several men laughing and dancing, his mood lifted. One of the fellows beckoned to him to join them. His spirit soared even more when they began singing a familiar tune with ribald lyrics. As each sailor added a verse, Peter's frame of mind became more buoyant.

When his turn came, he enthusiastically delivered, "And now for number eight, and she says, 'You're my best mate!'"

His new peers joined in, bellowing happily, "Roll me over in the clover; do it again!"

A few tunes later, Bartholomew took a break and Peter went over to talk to the musician. "Great entertainment, Bart! Wonder if you know a little ditty from my homeland; don't know the words, but I could whistle a few bars. . . ." Peter began to pucker up.

Bartholomew reached out to grab his shoulder. "No you don't, Peter. Whistling onboard will curse us with a terrible storm!"

"Really?"

Bartholomew's nod was stern. "Aye!"

"Good to know."

"Try humming the tune, though; I can play by ear. Always looking for new music. That's my job. Keep the boys from getting bored; don't want them getting drunk. So if my music keeps them moving, makes them merry, then this ship is run efficiently."

"You're a valuable member of the crew!"

"Thanks, but certainly not as crucial as you, Peter! We're lucky to have found you, since Jack is still recuperating from his hernia. All of us depend on your keeping the ship's leaky seams in check!"

"Keeps me busy—lots of wood around and beneath us!"

"And you may even be asked to fill in as a surgeon if we go into battle!"

"What? I can't possibly; why, I wouldn't know what to do. . . ."

"Think about it: you have similar tools and cutting experience. If we have many wounded, who else? That happened a couple of times when I was sailing on merchant ships out of Boston."

"Boston? You're an American?"

"Aye, but when President Jefferson started the embargo, I was unemployed. That's why I signed on a coastal trader headed for New Orleans. Now, *that's* a dancing town! Those Creoles can always find a reason for a party or a ball: weddings, baptisms, holy days—even after a funeral! I'm not a churchgoer, but I sure like how religion's practiced in New Orleans, compared with Boston. I'll never go back there! But I missed the sea and signed on with Captain Lafitte."

Changing the subject, Bartholomew said, "You seem to be adapting well, Peter; you apparently approve of our privateering."

"Privateering? So, *that's* what you call it!" Peter laughed.

"Of course! We're merchants operating private armed vessels. We've been given a letter of marque. It's a document that authorizes us to capture the ships of that country's enemies. Therefore, the crews of such ships are also called privateers—not pirates."

"What country hired the *Dorado*?"

"The Republic of Cartagena."

"Never heard of it."

"It's on the northwest coast of South America. Declared itself independent of Spain in 1811."

"But what about the loot you take from other foreign ships?"

"Yes, well . . . that all ends up in New Orleans, too, and the proceeds are divided among the crew. You'll see! But whatever you call it, you're feeling more comfortable within our operation?"

"Definitely! Much better than I did in the English navy. Although," he added, "some things are the same."

"Like what?"

"Well, the crucial jobs of the gunners, sailing masters, boatswains, carpenters, and surgeons are also held by the most skilled. And some of your rules are the same as those of King George's vessels."

"Such as?"

"Drunkenness and gambling for money are both forbidden, fire safety is imperative, and weapons have to be well maintained and fit for service at all times."

"Same rules on the merchant ships, and of course they make sense! And there are differences?"

"Absolutely. The captain of the *Dorada* was elected by the crew members, as well as the rest of the officers. And although breaking the rules leads to punishment, the crew decides the severity."

"Aye. Each of us has an equal voice in the affairs of the ship, as well as an equal share in the captured loot. That's different, and better than the merchant ships, too."

"Also, there's more free time. Unless I'm busy cleaning and repairing my weapons, doing my carpenter's mending, or needed for normal ship maintenance—"

"And don't forget raiding!"

"Right. Raiding . . . Hmmm."

"Don't worry about it, Peter. But you were saying?"

"There's more free time. I can play cards, checkers, or back-gammon, dance, sleep, or talk, whenever I want."

Yes, Peter thought, *the pirates' code of conduct is simple and fair, and I have willingly sworn my allegiance.*

Of course, if I hadn't, I would be marooned on a deserted island with only one bottle of water, a pistol, powder, and shot.

Still, Peter missed his home in Penshurst. He felt like an outsider. The other crew members were cautious around him; many of them were French or Spanish and did not like the English. *I wonder if they think King George impressed me to decrease the number of inmates in English jails.*

Plus, although the crew had gathered provisions on "his" island, he surmised that eventually the food aboard the *Dorada* was bound to be like that of the Royal navy. *I'll wager this food, too, will be meager, pickled, and infested.*

Last but not least, he worried about the ship. *It could sink!*

Bartholomew broke into his thoughts.

"You're frowning now, Peter. What's the matter?"

"Huh? Oh. Sorry, Bart. To be honest, I don't really feel like I belong yet, but I hope to. There's a sense of trust, respect, and, of course, freedom onboard here. It's a fellowship like my pals in Penshurst have."

"Give it time, Peter. They'll get used to you."

"Good." He smiled. "So, besides sinking—"

"Won't happen!"

"Or being killed in battle, what's the worst that could happen?"

"You could be captured by a ship of another country's navy and impressed or even hung."

Seeing Peter frown again, Bart patted him on the back. "Don't worry. Our leader, Jean Lafitte, is smart and shrewd. We'll be home in a couple more days, and you'll meet him."

"Home?" asked Peter.

"Yes! Before you joined us, we picked up some slaves and goods from a Spanish ship. They'll be auctioned off to plantation owners when we get to Barataria, which is our home."

"Where is it?"

"Barataria Bay is south of the city of New Orleans, in the new state of Louisiana in the United States."

"And the American government allows this auction?"

"Absolutely not!" Bartholomew laughed. "Governor Claiborne despises Jean Lafitte. The auctions are held secretly, but they're well attended. The Louisiana Creoles love our goods. They can't import them legally, because of the war and embargo, so business is good."

"Besides the auctions, what else is there to do?"

"The city of New Orleans has plenty of pleasures for a fellow like you, Peter! Do you like Opera? Theater? Cockfighting? Billiards? The racetrack? But first you'll need to take care of the *Dorada*. She has to be careened."

"Careened?"

"Don't worry—we'll all be helping you. Several times a year, during low tide, the ship is turned on her side and secured. Then, under the carpenter's supervision, we carefully scrape all the seaweed and barnacles off the bottom of her hull. Come high tide, she flows back into the water."

"And is able to sail faster without all the critters and muck hanging on?"

"Right. As privateers, we spend a great deal of time cleaning and repairing—not only the ship, but also our weapons. Which reminds me: you'll need to get yourself a boarding ax to slash through rope netting, and several pistols. Some of the seamen carry six at a time in a sash slung over their shoulder—keeps their hands free for fighting, you know. And maybe a musket, which you can always use as a club. Your choice."

"Oh. Yes. About the raiding; I, um, don't really know much about weaponry. . . ."

"You will. And actually, although we're well armed and always ready to attack, we also have four to five times more men than you'll find on a merchant ship. We only want to terrorize them and capture the ship and its cargo. We don't want to spill blood for a sunken ship and cargo, especially the ship, if we decide to take it. So it's best if we can scare them into cooperating. And they usually do. You'll see."

Peter nodded slowly, thinking, *Not soon, I hope!*

"Now, how 'bout another tune?" Bartholomew began playing a few chords. "One of my favorites; it's called 'Yankee Doodle.'"

Tarot: THE SEVEN OF CUPS

Revelation: Scattered energies
in many dreams and desires.

⁓

Jacques's visit, short as it was, made Marguerite quite animated. The following day, against Sheila's advice, she insisted upon getting up early and taking on her responsibilities as a plantation owner's wife. After breakfast in bed—two slices of cane syrup–soaked *pain perdu*—she made a couple of changes to the cook's dinner menu. Bounding out of bed, she enthusiastically selected a favorite, light-colored frock to wear. Meanwhile, Sheila continued her warnings.

"You're not well enough, Marguerite. You need more rest. What's the hurry? At least another week, now . . ."

Marguerite ignored Sheila's admonitions and hummed to herself as her maid tightened her corset. The conical stays pressed her breasts upward, and although her waistline had not quite returned to its prepregnancy shape, the newly popular empire style would camouflage her midriff nicely. She stepped into the dress and twirled around with a smile.

"See, Mother? Good as new! I'm ready to help Jacques with the plantation."

"You do look lovely, Marguerite, but there's no need to rush into things," Sheila repeated. "The most important task you have is to make sure you're strong and healthy to become pregnant again."

"I'm fine, and my husband needs me! If you could have seen how sad he was to see me still in bed . . . Bless his heart, he did not want to wear me out, so he did not stay long, but I know he misses me. We are a team. I must not let him down! I know you have overseen the domestic responsibilities during my recuperation, Mother, and I thank you. But I'm ready and able now."

Sheila seemed to grasp that Marguerite was determined to take on her duties, so she did not argue any further.

"In fact," her daughter continued, "I think we shall have a party. It's been so long since we've had laughter in this house. Yes—a fine celebration! The men will hunt, the women will play tennis, and at night we will all dance. We'll have a feast: fried oysters, pheasant, quail, salads, and fruitcake. Oh, won't that be fun, Mother? Jacques will be so pleased. I can't wait to tell him!"

Marguerite danced out of her bedroom, eager to find Jacques. She spotted him outside, behind the main house, with his servant Tobias, watching some workers build a new row of slave cabins.

She stopped to observe her husband and slave for a minute. With their hats on, they were almost identical from behind. Both were close to six feet in height, slim, and brawny. The two also had a sort of vibrant energetic aura, which was very apparent during their animated discussions. And, she thought, each was handsome in his own way. Jacques had reddish-blond hair topping his tanned complexion and complemented by his remarkable green eyes; Tobias had thick, wavy, sable-colored hair; a lustrous, dark complexion; and large, burnt umber–like eyes.

They had grown up together; Tobias's parents had been house slaves for Jacques's folks. The boys were inseparable as playmates. Tobias also learned how to read and write with Jacques; the tutor found both students capable, competent, and competitive, and the fact that they challenged each other enhanced their performances. Tobias also had a flair for numbers, as well as farming. After Jacques's parents passed away, the young master often conferred with Tobias when planning additions to or changes in the plantation.

And, Marguerite thought, like a brother, Tobias had been there for Jacques when his parents had passed away, and, of course, when the baby had died. Jacques had no siblings; how fortunate, she thought, that he had Tobias.

Master and slave were now comfortably talking and nodding to each other. Jacques smiled at something Tobias had pointed out.

"Jacques!" she called out. "Hello!"

Jacques said something to Tobias, and the slave nodded and headed toward his quarters, which were above Jacques's office.

"Marguerite! What a surprise!"

His wife hurried to his side and drew her arm through his. He leaned over and kissed her cheek. "You look very pretty today, dear; you must be feeling better!"

"Yes, darling, I feel wonderful and am ready to resume my role as plantation mistress. And I have the most marvelous idea: let's have a party! I know you're busy with these buildings and the planting, so Mother and I will take care of all the arrangements."

Jacques hesitated for just a moment and then said, "Marguerite, that's a splendid idea!" He added, "But you're right—this is a busy time of year. The men are still positioning the seed stems into the furrowed ground."

"Look!" He pointed first to the slave cabins and then beyond, to the toiling field hands. "We're planning on a bigger yield, which is why we need more housing for additional slaves. Before harvest, I must acquire more hogsheads for the raw sugar, as well as barrels for the molasses. And, of course, we're building a new sugar mill, so we need to get more animals to power it. Tobias and I are sure that sugar will be Louisiana's next big crop. Cotton will still be strong, of course, because of the cotton gin, but . . ."

He stopped for a second, noticing the look on Marguerite's face.

"Now, darling, don't pout! Of course you'll have your party; it's a grand idea. But I won't be able to help you very much. Remember that running a plantation is a year-round business. Especially this year, with the expansion, I have to watch my crop prices, my slaves' numbers and needs, and the water level. But I'm certain you and your mother will give the finest party Louisiana has ever had!"

"Oh, Jacques," she said. "We will indeed! Thank you, my darling." Then, wiping her brow, she added, "My, it's so warm and muggy out here!"

"Yes, it's been a very hot and uncomfortable summer this year. You should probably stay inside with your mother."

"You're right, Jacques. I love the way you try to take care of me. Well, I was just going to the kitchen to make some changes for our dinner with the head cook. I'll send a cold drink out for you."

"Thank you, darling. Oh, and send one out for Tobias, too. We'll be in my office."

Tarot: THE TWO OF WANDS

Revelation: Riches; fortune; magnificence;
a new venture full of potential.

—⁓

The *Dorada* made its way from the Gulf of Mexico to the Mississippi River Delta and landed on Grand Terre, a mid-size island with smaller islands around it.

"It's beautiful, isn't it?" asked Bartholomew. "We have shrimp, crabs, oysters, and fish in the water; frogs and turtles in the marshes; rabbits, squirrels, and deer in the forest; and ducks, geese, and other water birds all around."

"Great! Although we've had better fare than the English Navy provides, I'm tired of salted sea rations!"

"And, I'm happy to say, there are lots of women ashore, some of them young and not yet spoken for."

"That sounds better yet!"

A number of ships were already anchored. Farther up the beach, Peter could see cottages among the palm, pine, and oak trees, festooned with Spanish moss that gave the scene an ethereal beauty.

Not quite so fragile-looking were the flamboyant pirates walking about. Many of them wore red-and-black-striped blouses, pantaloons, boots, and bandannas. Cutlasses, knives, swords, and earrings flashed in the sunlight.

"How many people live here, Bart?"

"There are about a thousand of us privateers, and many have wives and families."

"Since they're not at sea, um, acquiring commodities, what does everybody do?"

"There's plenty of work here, Peter; besides delivering the goods, we need to store them in one of the forty warehouses. Of course, that takes a lot of sorting, cleaning, and categorizing. We have merchandise from all over. Besides Europe, we have goods from Mexico, South America, and the West Indies; slaves captured from slave ships; and sugar, spices, rum, silverware, cloth, fine china—luxuries of all kinds. Everything the people in New Orleans could wish for, we have it!"

"You mentioned slaves again. . . ."

"Sometimes we have several hundred of them in the pens, called barracoons. We feed and exercise them there until the auction. Lafitte's Blacksmith Shop in New Orleans is always busy making shackles and chains."

Bartholomew changed the subject and pointed to a large house. "Look over there," he said. "That's Captain Lafitte's home. And on the west end you can see our fort, armed with cannons."

"Are you worried about being attacked?" asked Peter.

"No, we're pretty safe here. To the north, we're surrounded by miles of bayous and reedy marshland; the grasses are even taller than you! You don't want to go swimming, because of the alligators and water moccasins." He laughed at his own joke. "On the open water, we have our ships, of course. Also, Lafitte has been storing away arms, ammunition, and cannonballs in various places. Again, I don't think we'll ever be in danger, but one never knows."

Peter nodded, wondering what this new situation would be like. Penshurst seemed very far away.

Bartholomew broke into his thoughts. "So, we're able to take our goods to New Orleans in pirogues, through a water route made up of bayous, lakes, and the Mississippi."

"How do you know where the land ends and the water begins?" Peter asked.

"Experience," answered Bartholomew. "Many of those bayous turn back upon themselves, cross and recross, and finally end up in a cul-de-sac. Men have fallen ill, gone missing, and died in Barataria. It's perfect for our needs, though."

"As long as you don't get lost. . . ."

"Just don't go out by yourself until you know your way around; it can be disorienting."

"And the weather? It must be ninety-some degrees here."

"Probably is. This hot weather is typical for the end of summer. Next month it will start cooling a bit; it's milder in the winter, mostly in the fifties, with a fair amount of rainfall—five or six inches each month. Sometimes thunderstorms. Lots of fog and humidity. Just leaving your house in the morning and walking a few feet away, you begin to perspire. A lot. It's not like where you came from."

Bartholomew waved to a couple of the burly buccaneers onshore. "Come on," he said to Peter. "Let's get you acquainted."

To be sure, Peter thought, *Penshurst is very far away.*

Tarot: THE ACE OF WANDS

Revelation: The beginning of an enterprise.

⁓

October 1813

This month was special, for it hailed the start of the social season for free women of color. This was also the time when many young girls' destinies were designed and determined, for it was in October that the wealthy quadroon matrons sponsored the grand Bal de Cordon Bleu on Rue de St. Philip, specifically to make permanent arrangements for their daughters with well-born Creole men. These settlements, called *plaçages* in French, were sometimes referred to as left-handed marriages.

This evening, along with the other mothers, Catherine Caresse sat on the side of the warm ballroom. All were attired in elegant evening gowns, slowly fanning themselves, sipping champagne, and nibbling hors d'oeuvres. And, like the other older women, Catherine was appraising the white males milling about in their snowy, ruffled shirts and dark, fitted suits. Some men were smiling, having just won money from gambling on the first floor of the building. Several of the older, more portly gentlemen were red-faced from having climbed the stairs to the ballroom in the heat of the evening. Regardless of their age, Catherine noted, many of them had eyes on her sixteen-year-old daughter, who was dressed in her finest, ivory silk dress, her petite waist defined by her whalebone corset and cinched with a brilliant green ribbon, her slender neck adorned with one beautiful emerald.

And why wouldn't they be watching my daughter? thought Catherine. *Suzanne is the loveliest girl here.*

Suzanne looked even more beautiful in the flickering candlelight, like a butterfly shimmering. Her green eyes shone out from under her fluttering, dark lashes, her copper-colored curls delicately framing her honey-colored, heart-shaped face.

I must remember to compliment Hortense on the wonderful way she dressed Suzanne's hair, thought Catherine.

Turning her attention back to the males, Catherine, herself a beautiful free woman of color and the former *placée* of a green-eyed plantation owner, considered the suitors' credentials.

The tall privateer, Mr. Lafitte, was there; his eyes, too, were locked on Suzanne's winsome figure. Catherine coolly assessed him.

Wealthy: yes. All six feet of him quite handsome: yes. But his own class, white Creole society, does not yet accept him in their parlors or at their social events. No, he is not suitable for my Suzanne. My daughter's lover must be a wealthy young Creole from a highly esteemed family. He will promise paternal recognition of future children, supply a fine home in our Quadroon Quarter—complete with a cook, a maid, and an errand boy—and continually provide sufficient money for the education, prosperity, and safekeeping of his second family.

And, of course, Catherine's scheme included negotiating a healthy payment for herself for arranging this *plaçage.* Just as Catherine's own mother had successfully marketed her at a quadroon ball, so, too, was Catherine merchandising Suzanne to guarantee her a secure future.

Catherine recognized another man, younger than the famous privateer, the handsome, light-haired son of a local plantation owner. His name was René Bonet, and he was eagerly making his way to Suzanne's side while she was already flirting with several admirers. The new young man said just a few words to her and extended his hand. Catherine watched as Suzanne responded with delight, her dimples fully on display. Then she daintily took his hand, smiled up at him, and proceeded with him to the dance floor.

Yes, this René is the perfect match. And now, Catherine thought, *it is Suzanne's task to charm her way into this young man's heart.*

Catherine herself would then make her way into his pockets.

Tarot: THE DEVIL

Revelation: Facing darkness;
perceiving the untamed.

⁓

Millie wanted out. They all did. Every working girl she knew would give the rest of her teeth for the opportunity to leave the profession. The career lasted only fifteen years at most, and then nearly all the girls were dead by age thirty—besides the universal scourges of smallpox, influenza, typhus, and cholera, plus the epidemics of typhoid and yellow fever, there were the accompanying risks of the trade: venereal disease, battery, and murder.

A very few had escaped and learned to be seamstresses or procured jobs in a dance hall. But, no other employment opportunities were available, the remainder had to continue working in the only profession they knew.

Millie's maternal family had been here in the "business" since 1720. Her great-grandmother had had the choice to remain imprisoned in France or be exiled to Louisiana. As a working girl, she had chosen the latter and settled in La Nouvelle-Orléans. Most of the importees were smugglers, thieves, and beggars. Her new neighbors and customers were the dregs of society.

Almost one hundred years later, this miserable life continued in the brothels. The customers were of all sorts: sailors, gamblers, boatmen, workingmen, and wealthy merchants. It was the population of a vibrant and growing city, clamoring and shrieking in a dozen different languages.

Most of the working girls could not refuse any customer, no matter how repulsive, obnoxious, or violent he appeared, and no matter what disgusting demands he might make. When pushed against the wall, his face in hers, expelling heavy breath evocative of rotten fish, mirroring perversion and debauchery, she had to consent. Or starve.

Luckily, though, because Millie's mother was the madam of the "house," her customers were the least offensive. Millie had built up a clientele among which, although she didn't look forward to any of their arrivals, some had become not friends, and certainly not romantic lovers, but likable enough, given the circumstances.

They also seemed to prefer her because of her fastidiousness. Unlike her peers, she was very tidy and clean and insisted that her customers also be washed themselves. Her mother had taught her how to incorporate this into her "routine," insisting that it helped prevent disease. "You don't want any stinking body in your bed," she had counseled her daughter.

Millie also kept a supply of sheep's-gut condoms on hand, building that into her repertoire of titillating tricks. Of course, because they were expensive, she reused them. One lasted an entire week before disintegrating into shreds.

Naturally, she protected herself further by inserting inside her the rind of half a lemon, including some of its acidic flesh, as a homemade cervical cap. It wasn't foolproof, but . . .

Millie could hear her next client clambering up the stairs from the ground-floor saloon. She played her own personal guessing game: Would he be a sailor, a gambler, a boatman, or perhaps . . . The good news was that he hadn't stumbled yet. That might mean that he was not drunk.

She heard his boot steps on the landing outside her room. *It's showtime*, she thought. The door opened.

"Hello, Millie," said the young seaman. "Do you remember me?" He had an eager, hopeful smile on his face.

Millie recognized his type; like the rest of Jean Lafitte's Baratarians, he wore a red-and-black-striped shirt overhanging his breeches. His leggings were tucked into tall, dark boots. The glint of a gold earring in his right ear caught her eye. But he did not have the thick beard and mustache that most of his cohorts sported. He hadn't had the time to grow them in yet. This pirate and Millie were probably the same age.

"Why, of course I do, honey," Millie replied softly. "You're my . . ." She was going to utter some inane endearment, such as "handsomest man" or "favorite dear heart," when she actually did remember who this client was.

"Pete!" she responded with a smile. The young man grinned broadly when she called out his name. He had seen her only a few times before. However, she remembered even more about him as he quickly removed his clothing and prepared to jump into her bed. "Uh-uh-uh!" she said. "First some suds for my favorite seaman!"

She had privately nicknamed him the Gabber. He was new to Barataria. He had told her on his first visit that he was lonely, and she understood; hers was a lonely life, too. They had talked the whole night. She chuckled to herself, remembering their conversation:

"Just a few months ago, Millie, after having a few drinks with friends in Penshurst—"

"Penshurst? Where's Penshurst?"

"It's southeast of London. Ann Boleyn grew up there."

"Ann Boleyn?"

"King Henry the Eighth's second wife. He had six of them altogether. I'll tell you about them another time."

She had smiled. "Sorry for interrupting, Pete. You're just so interesting! Please continue."

It had been his turn to smile. "Anyway, I went outside for a couple of minutes, and I was hit over the head, kidnapped, and forced by a press gang to join the Royal Navy."

"Were you in any battles?"

"No, because several weeks later, I jumped overboard and swam to an island, but then Lafitte's privateers picked me up."

"You're lucky they didn't take your clothes and kill you. They could have made you walk off the gangplank!"

"They don't really do that. If they want to get rid of you, they just throw you into the ocean. Because I'm a carpenter, though, they gave me a choice of joining them or dying. Lucky for me, they always need carpenters. Actually, I kind of like the life of a privateer."

"But isn't it like the Royal Navy?"

"Not at all. On the Navy ship, the captain was both dictatorial and sadistic, and the cat-o'-nine-tails was in frequent use. Plus, the King rarely pays his sailors."

"No wonder you escaped! And the pirates?"

"Ahem, yes, the *privateers*"—Peter had emphasized the last word—"are very democratic. We elect the captain, determine whether someone should be punished, and how. And we divide equally the value of any goods captured."

"What rules do the—ahem—privateers have?" she had asked with a grin.

"Well, we can't bring any females aboard when we're setting sail, for one thing.

"Is that because we're the enemy?" she had asked, twirling a lock of his hair in a provocative manner.

"No," he had answered, drawing her in closer. "You're the prize. And besides, Millie, you wouldn't like being a privateer.

We sometimes run out of food and water, and anyone caught having an open flame around the powder room is put to death. Aside from that, though, it's a good life. And spending time with you makes it even better!"

Each time Peter visited, he told her more stories from his homeland. Millie heard all about the Tudors, the Romans, and King Arthur and his knights. Peter even described the Cornish pasties his mother used to make. He talked all night, after "business" was through, and he paid her well for her time.

Millie didn't mind; in fact, she found Peter's stories wonderfully diverting. They transported her away from her small room, with its barred window and stale smells of smoke and liquor. She especially liked his pirate adventures (although he insisted on calling himself a "privateer"), including his spying exploits (which he referred to as "intelligence gathering"), his smuggling escapades (he alluded to them as "importing missions"), the attacks and sometimes bloody brawls ("struggles," he said), and the plundered spoils (which he spoke of as "resources" or "assets").

To Millie, these feats were titillating. Peter did not mention (although Millie knew it) that if the English captured him and his mates, they'd be executed. But no other career could give him access to a potential fortune: gold, silver, silks, spices, and—Millie thought, best of all—freedom.

"I'm very happy to see you, Pete," she said seductively, finishing the preparations for his bath. She crooked her finger at him, smiling. "Come on over here and let me wash off all your worries. Then you and me can get wild tonight! How does that sound?"

Splash!

Tarot: THE TEN OF CUPS

*Revelation: Attainment of the heart's desires;
ongoing and permanent contentment.*

⟞⟋

Free men of color were rare and were actively wooed by women with discontinued "secondhand marriages" who coveted a legal union and were dogged in pursuing the few available males.

Miguel Plicque was one of these free men of color. His mother had been a beautiful African, finely featured, the color of tobacco, with dark, liquid eyes. Her owner had been a Creole colonist.

Upon giving birth to Miguel, she and her son were emancipated and maintained by his Creole father in the Tremé neighborhood of New Orleans. As was the tradition, Miguel was sent to France to be educated and apprenticed in a trade like carpentry or baking. He developed his artistic talents and returned to Louisiana to become an ornamental plasterer.

Miguel was happy with his life. As a thirty-three-year-old bachelor, he had many social invitations from unattached, free women of color. Most of these invitations were what he termed all-inclusive. But he had no intention of tying himself down to just one woman; he told friends that he was like the Lord: "I love them all!"

Tonight he was having dinner at Madame Caresse's home.

Catherine was one of his favorites: She was beautiful, successful, and self-assured. She also provided a fine meal with wine. However, he hadn't slept with her. Yet.

Her daughter, Suzanne, was staying with a friend. Miguel was happy about that; Suzanne craved her mother's attention and was quite sullen, even pouted, when Miguel came over. Now that she had been promised to René, she would be moving into the house the young Creole man was preparing for her, and Miguel could spend more time with Catherine. Alone.

Of course, there was the maid, Hortense, who also seemed to be annoyed when he showed up. Although Miguel suspected that was just the way Hortense was, tonight he was going to try to win her over. Another conquest.

Miguel livened his step up to Catherine's house, carrying a large bouquet of flowers and a box of pralines. Hortense opened the door and, as he expected, scowled at him.

"Hortense!" He smiled. "*Belle soirée*, isn't it? These are for you!" With a flourish, he presented her with the box of candy. "Brown sugar for a Brown Sugar!" he added.

"For me?" The maid's eyes widened, and she actually smiled. "Well, for heaven's sake. How nice! *Merci beaucoup!* Do come in, Monsieur Plicque; do come in! I'll tell Madame Caresse that you're here."

Miguel noted that, while hugging the candy box, Hortense practically pirouetted to the back of the house.

Catherine came into the parlor to greet him. "Miguel, right on time. I'm happy to see you, as is Hortense. The candy was very thoughtful of you."

He bowed, handed her the flowers, and beamed. "And the bloom on your face, Catherine, puts these poor blossoms to shame!"

Catherine looked at him, then burst out laughing. "Thank

you, Miguel; they're charming. And so was your poetic effort. Excuse me while I find a vase."

Overkill, Miguel, he said to himself, watching her go into the dining room. *Slow down; you don't want to make her suspicious of your plans for after dessert.*

"I hope you're hungry," she called out. "We're having crawfish étouffée for dinner. First, though, we'll eat some raw oysters. Hortense just got them at the market."

Raw oysters? That Italian lover Casanova's famous aphrodisiac? Fabulous! Miguel joined Catherine in the dining room with another huge smile on his face. He noted the bottle of champagne on the table. *A further good sign. I'll just keep on pouring.*

Rubbing his hands together, he said, "Yes, I'm ravenous. And it sounds wonderful! I'm sure we'll have a delicious night."

Catherine looked at him and cocked an eyebrow but then smiled and said, "I suspect it will be most pleasurable, Miguel."

It was indeed. Much later, having been pleased and fully sated, Miguel was now in her walnut bed, sound asleep, even slightly snoring, lying naked on his back next to Catherine.

As the full moon shone through the window, Catherine considered Miguel closely for several minutes. Unlike her first lover, who was tall and thin, Miguel's dark and compact body was finely chiseled, typical of that of many free men of color. He was boyishly handsome, and he knew it.

As a plasterer, he was always in demand. His decorative moldings were renowned throughout the city for their artistic, innovative designs and their quality and durability.

She knew Miguel was skillful in other ways, too. Always quick-witted, he could flatter even the most resistant old crones in the city. Women of all colors were attracted to his twinkling eyes and his ready smile. A wink in their direction, and they were smitten, eager to run their fingers through his thick, silky hair.

Many of his clients' wives found excuses to watch him work. They plied him with freshly baked croissants. And wouldn't he like a little coffee to go with that pastry? He would flash his grin, offer another compliment conveying appreciation and pleasure (and, for himself, personal amusement), and continue his work. For he always had plenty of that.

Catherine was fully aware of his flirtations and his lovers, including his most recent previous affair. However, she, too, had her own special talents, and she enjoyed his company, and tonight she had a plan.

Satisfied that Miguel was not likely to awaken, she reached under the mattress for her hidden piece of silk string. She extended the strand out along his member, then multiplied that length by nine. Carefully following the specifications passed down to her through her maternal lineage, she tied nine knots in the string, whispering the words "You are now bound to me in love, Miguel." Each knot signified a specific element she wanted included in her spell: passion, commitment, communication, support, trust, comfort, appreciation, strength, and satisfaction.

Catherine then smiled to herself and set aside the string to wrap around her waist. She turned to look at the slumbering man. "You will never love another woman, my dear," she whispered softly. "I've just made sure of that!"

Tarot: THE HIEROPHANT

Revelation: Bondage to societal conventions.

~

I t was a beautiful, brisk November morning for her adventure. Millie took the trousers and shirt from their hiding place in her cedar chest and put them on, then slipped her feet into shoes meant for a young lad. She gathered her long auburn hair up into a bun and stuck it all into a tight-fitting boys' cap, then tiptoed downstairs from her room and outside to savor the sounds and smells of New Orleans.

From Dauphine Street, she headed toward the wharf, passing hawkers going from house to house, peddling their wares to the women leaning over their galleries. Reaching the riverfront, she gazed out at the water.

Before the Embargo Act, the port had been busy. Scores of plank-built flatboats from as far away as Pittsburgh, Pennsylvania, had floated west on the Ohio River to Cairo, Illinois, where the Ohio merged with the Mississippi, then south to New Orleans. Each had been able to transport up to a hundred tons of cargo into the harbor. Longshoremen had bustled about, conveying sacks of grain, bales of cotton and buckskin, barrels of whiskey, and crates of other goods up and down the gangplanks, to and from the warehouses, ready to be loaded on oceangoing vessels.

Not anymore. The merchandise was now all trapped;

jammed into the city by the embargo. Millie felt as if she were just like those goods: a valuable commodity, but stuck.

She dreamed once again of escape. But how? And what could she do to support herself? Yes, there was always a demand for those in her line of work, but she would have to start at the bottom. Too dangerous.

Heading to the French market, she picked her way carefully down the banquettes. These wooden sidewalks were made from some of the lumber from the dismantled flatboats. But the lack of flatboat lumber left gaps in banquettes where boards had rotted away and hadn't been replaced; this was yet another casualty of the embargo.

Passing one of the bakery shops, she felt the heat emanating from the ovens and stopped to watch the black men already sweating over the kneading troughs. She inhaled deeply. What a heavenly fragrance! The gorgeous baguettes had thin, crunchy crusts enveloping soft, fluffy middles. *Pain de boulanger: fantastique!*

She walked quickly past the butcher shops, also called flesh markets. They were almost completely enclosed, with only a door and a window, yet the odors emerging from them were disgusting, and flies and filth were visible on the floors, the walls, and all the dead carcasses hanging from the racks.

Most of the small carts were already set up at the curbstones and unloaded. Americans, Creoles, Cajuns, free people of color, Indians, and slaves were ready to do business. Farmers' eggs; eggplants; hunters' fowl; rabbit, squirrel, fish, and alligator meat; handmade cheeses and sausages; and bottles of wine were prominently arranged to be eye-catching, and all, insisted the merchants, were the best quality.

Millie stopped at a little stall with a table and ordered chicory coffee. It arrived in a small white cup on a saucer. Perched on a stool, she savored her drink, watching people in the market-place. Women of all colors were selecting produce, filling their baskets with onions, garlic, and peppers. *A gumbo for tonight's supper*, she thought. Taking another sip, she watched as some of the workmen took a break and snacked on sweet-potato pies or rice cakes.

She cherished her time here. No one gave her a second look. On a couple of her previous trips she had passed clients, but they did not recognize her. It was her adventure, an escape of sorts. It was rebellious, independent, a thrill. And she hated to go "home."

Tarot: THE ACE OF CUPS

Revelation: Embarking on the journey of love.

~~~

The lovely, young free woman of color had a mission. Tonight was the beginning of her "left-handed marriage," and the weather promised to be sultry—perfect for passion. Yes, she had been instructed about how to please her handsome young man. As well as being chaste, she was willing. She was the perfect virgin.

Although she was dressed in a simple muslin dress, her lustrous reddish-blond curls mostly concealed by the required tignon, her beautiful features attracted attention. They always did. But she was unaware of the appreciative glances aimed her way, so intent was she upon her purpose.

She carefully picked her way through the marketplace, dodging the mangy dogs looking for scraps and ignoring the goading vendors calling out their produce. She was unmindful of the sight of dead chickens hanging head down from the racks, the squawks of the live ones in their coops, or the smells of the unwanted fruits and vegetables rotting on the spattered ground. She was aware, however, of her left shoe, in which she had placed a lock of René's hair, tied with her own pubic hair. The spell was in place.

She mentally reviewed her shopping list: oysters from the fish market; two white candles from a shop on Decatur Street;

and fresh flowers, dill, cloves, and champagne from the French market—all necessary for tonight's ceremony. Her mother's servants—young Scamp, recently acquired from Lafitte's auction, and the housemaid, Hortense—normally did the marketing, but these specific items, for this particular spiritual rite, needed to be chosen with ultimate care.

Love, luck, and protection, she thought, *will be mine, thanks to Maman's tutelage and the patron* loa *of New Orleans, Erzulie Dantor, the goddess of love.*

Finally stopping at a stall for some sugar, she took out her money. The merchant accepted her picayunes and handed her a penny change. She looked at it, nonplussed.

"Why, what is this, sir? Did I not give you the correct amount?"

"You did, mademoiselle. But this is one of those American coins," he said. "And because there's a shortage of copper since the war began, they're rather scarce. But it matches your shiny hair. You should have it—perhaps for good luck!"

"Well, I shall treasure it, then. *Merci!*"

"Will you be making some pralines with that sugar?" asked the merchant.

"No," Suzanne replied with a slight smile, "but something else just as sweet!"

Love, luck, and protection. So far, so good.

Tarot: THE QUEEN OF SWORDS

Revelation: Sadness, and faith in high ideals.

~

Another soft and beautiful day, with the rich scent of jasmines padding the November air. Again disguised as a young lad, Millie walked briskly toward the French market, avoiding the little boys "sword fighting" with sticks, and smiling at the small girls playing with dolls.

She made her way around the noisy men and older boys surrounding the cockpit. Males of all colors were yelling and cheering in their disparate languages for their favorite rooster. *Those poor gamecocks*, she thought. *All bloody, and fighting until one dies.* Although Pete had told her that cockfighting was the oldest spectator sport in the world, she did not understand why all these men—French, English, Spanish, German, even Choctaw— thought it amusing. *Well, it's one thing they all have in common!*

She noticed the old women clustered in small groups. *They're probably grousing about aches and pains, or gossiping. And some of them are laughing! It must be nice.*

Then she stopped to look up and admire the spires of St. Louis Church in the background. A priest was on the steps, talking to a Creole family, the mother holding a baby. *Maybe making baptismal arrangements . . .*

"Millie? Is that you?"

Panic. Someone recognized her. She felt a tap on her shoulder from behind. She whirled around with alarm.

"Millie! It's Pete! What are you doing here, and why are you dressed like that?"

Thinking quickly, her heart beating rapidly, she tried to smile and say, in her best working-girl character, "Well, a girl's got to eat, Pete!"

Peter shook his head. "You don't look like a girl in that getup, Millie! And I don't see any food you've supposedly been shopping for."

He continued gazing at her, a mixture of surprise and amusement on his face. "Hmm. I've been telling you my stories, and here you are with a much better one!" He chuckled then and comfortably, gently, took her hand and led her to a bench at Rose's, a popular coffee spot.

After ordering two cups of chicory coffee and beignets, he said, "So? Tell me what you're up to."

Peter looked sincerely interested, but Millie was not accustomed to trusting—him or anybody—and was not about to share her most private experiences.

"I would rather not, Pete. You'd think it's silly. Can't you just forget you saw me here?" She tried to divert him. "Tell me instead what *you're* doing these days."

Peter continued to study her. "No, no, no—not so fast, there!" He chuckled again. "I want to know what's going on, and no, I can't forget you, Millie, no matter where you are or how you're dressed. You ought to know that by now! And by the way," he added, "you're the prettiest boy around here."

"Oh, *sacré bleu*," she said, trying to think of another way to distract him. Cradling her coffee cup, she picked it up to sniff its delightfully pungent aroma, then took a sip. Looking up again at Peter, she found him still gazing softly at her, and she felt her reluctance melt away.

"Oh, all right then." She paused, putting her cup down. "But only if you keep my secret!"

"Of course you can trust me—always." He reached for her hand and stroked her palm.

"I come here to the market to get away from all the pimps, the thieves, the murderers, and, yes, the whorehouses in my neighborhood. I like to watch all the nice, clean-looking people here, think about what their lives might be like, pretend I exist in a different world."

"And what would that world be like, Millie?"

She moved her hand away from him and picked up her sugary beignet. "Oh, you'll think it's absurd, Pete."

She nibbled an edge of the fried pastry, looking up at him for several seconds to be certain that he wasn't mocking her.

He wasn't.

Lowering her eyes, she chose her words with care. "I would like to be a normal woman, Pete. Someone who could shop, meet and greet friends, laugh and share gossip, and then go home to make a nice oyster stew for my husband, who loves me for who I really am."

Millie looked up at Peter again, suddenly feeling uncomfortably exposed and vulnerable. She was surprised to see the tender expression on his face. As he reached across the table (*Is he going to take my hand again?*), he knocked over her coffee cup, spilling the hot liquid and, she realized, spoiling the mood she was (*surely?*) imagining.

"Oh!" She jumped up, composing herself quickly. "Well, look at that! Thank goodness nothing broke!" She purposefully placed the empty cup back on the saucer, without looking at him.

"And," she added, with a quick glance up at the sun, "it's getting late. Thanks for the coffee, Pete; hope to see you soon!"

And before he could say anything, she gave him a "professional" wink and bounded away.

Tarot: THE ACE OF PENTACLES

Revelation: Perfect attainment, rapture, bliss.

~

Ouah! Or, Suzanne thought, *as the Yankees would say, ooh là là! Last night—what a night!* She fairly skipped along the wooden sidewalks toward her mother's home, recalling every luscious moment of her first entire evening with René Bonet. And he had promised to come back again tonight!

Rapping on Catherine's door, Suzanne heard Hortense shuffling across the cypress floorboards.

Hortense will love hearing about it, too! Suzanne smiled as she thought of sharing her euphoria with the older woman.

Hortense was like another mother to Suzanne; she had helped Catherine raise her. Catherine had procured the maid through her *plaçage* arrangement, the year before Suzanne's birth. Hortense's bedroom was one of the two small rooms in the rear of the house. Once used for storage, it was perfect for the maid's needs. There was enough space for the narrow bed and a small dresser; plus, it adjoined Suzanne's childhood chamber. The servant was often at Suzanne's bedside to comfort her after bad dreams, calm her during storms, and feed her and nurse her when she was ill.

Also, along with her household responsibilities, Hortense had been charged with watching over Suzanne to make sure that she completed her lessons assigned by the Ursuline nuns.

Of course, Suzanne had gradually become aware that Hortense was covertly educating herself. The intelligent woman had also become quite adept in her teaching skills, having the ingenuity to make assignments more interesting for Suzanne. *Those were such happy times*, Suzanne thought. *We both enjoyed learning!*

And now Hortense had another student; she was teaching Scamp to read, write, and do sums. Catherine, too, encouraged the young boy to study, although educating slaves was not customary.

Despite the fact that Scamp was bright, Hortense complained that he was not quite as enthusiastic about learning as Suzanne had been. And so Hortense fretted over his lack of concentration on the lessons she prepared. She worked even harder on creatively developing lesson plans, and her motivating techniques, from sweet treats to promising more time to read additional stories to him, were meeting with success.

And the many hugs she gives that boy! Hmph! Suzanne recognized the slight envy she was feeling, for Scamp had replaced her in Hortense's life. She also strongly suspected that some of Scamp's alleged lack of enthusiasm was merely to gain more attention from Hortense. *Yes indeed, he is bright.*

Suzanne's musing ceased when Scamp opened the door. "I got it, Madame Hortense! It's Mademoiselle Suzanne! And she looks beautiful! As usual!" Now addressing Suzanne, the boy said, "I sure did miss you last night, Mademoiselle Suzanne. It's way too quiet here without you around! But did you have a good time with Monsieur Bonet?"

Suzanne's heart softened upon seeing the young boy looking up at her adoringly with his big, velvety brown eyes. "Yes, I did, Scamp. And I'm not that far away. You could come and visit me!"

At that moment, Hortense walked into the parlor, hands on her hips and a frown on her face. "Now, Scamp, I know you haven't finished your math exercises yet. You get right back to that assignment!"

"*Oui*, Madame," he said, slowly retreating to the rear of the house. "Maybe tomorrow I could visit, then?" he turned to ask Suzanne.

She laughed. "*Oui!* But only if Madame Hortense says it's all right."

"I'll do all my chores and my lessons quickly and perfectly tomorrow! Absolutely! In fact, I'll start now! Hurrah!" And he hurried off.

"That boy. Moves real fast when he wants to. Otherwise . . . But look at you—why, you're positively glowing! So?"

Suzanne flushed. "Mmm, *oui*, Hortense, last night was so . . . *magnifique!*"

"Enough said; I'll tell your *maman* you're here. I know she's eager to hear how you and Monsieur Bonet got along. And so am I!"

Catherine came into the room, gave her daughter a quick kiss, and then said, "Well?"

"Oh, Maman, René is the most wonderful man in the world! He's thoughtful, kind, and gentle. And he's smart! We talked all through the night. Well, much of the night, anyway." Suzanne blushed then, thinking about her previous evening's activities.

"Yessss? So, your first night together was satisfactory for both of you?"

"Oh, my, 'satisfactory' hardly describes it. He . . . it . . . everything was wonderful. Perhaps I did not even need to hide the scented bags of ribbons!"

"Maybe not, my dear, but with the measures you have taken, and thanks to your prayers to the spirit of love, Erzulie Freda, you can be confident that René will always cherish you and give you everything you need."

Suzanne answered with a smile, "I only want him to need me!"

Tarot: THE QUEEN OF PENTACLES

Revelation: An intelligent, thoughtful woman
uses her talents generously.

~

With her husband busy overseeing the new sugar mill's construction and her mother visiting a neighbor's plantation, Marguerite ordered a carriage brought to the front of the mansion. She instructed the driver to take her to the Rue de Rampart in the city. No need to give the directions to the specific house; they had been there before.

Upon arrival, she bade the driver to wait. "I won't be long."

At the door, she said to the maid, "Hello, I'm here to see Madame Caresse. I hope she's in?"

"Yes, madame; please come in and sit down. I'll get her for you."

A few minutes later, Catherine entered the parlor. "Madame de Trahan! How nice to see you again! It's been over a year since . . ."

"Ah, Madame Caresse! A pleasure to see you also. Yes. Over a year." Marguerite was nervously wringing her hands.

"You're looking well."

"Thank you. But . . ."

"What is it, Madame de Trahan? You seem troubled." Catherine said gently. "How can I help you?"

Marguerite sighed. "Ah, Madame Caresse, as you may recall, my husband and I tried for a number of years to have a child.

That's why I sought you before. The tincture was wonderful; I became pregnant shortly thereafter. But the baby died at birth."

"Oh, I'm so sorry, madame."

"I would like to have some more of your elixir."

"Why, of course! I'll get some now."

Returning with a small vial of powdered black cohosh root steeped in brandy, Catherine reviewed the directions.

"As you may remember, you are to take ten drops every day with juice. Did you have any stomach problems when taking it before?"

"No, and, again, the tonic worked like a charm."

Catherine laughed. "There's no magic involved in this remedy, madame; the Native Americans have been using it for years. But if you're interested in the supernatural, you might petition St. Anthony of Padua to help you become pregnant. And then invoke the help of St. Gerard Mejella; he's the patron saint of expectant mothers."

"Thank you, Madame Caresse. I'm very grateful."

"You're welcome, Madame de Trahan. Success be with you!"

Tarot: THE TWO OF CUPS

*Revelation: Agreement and cooperation where
an existing relationship has undergone difficulty.*

~~

1814

The house servants removed the dinner plates from the table
and brought the decanter for the wine. Jacques poured two small
glasses of Madeira. Marguerite saw that he was in a very favor-
able mood. This was good.

"How are the party plans coming, dear?" he asked.

"Mother and I think the best time to have it would be around
the middle of September. The weather won't be too warm and
humid, and rainfall will be at a minimum. What do you think?"

"Yes, the weather will be perfect, but that's why the harvest
may be under way. However, I'm sure I can squeeze in some
time for the festivities."

"Of course you must, Jacques! You're already working such
long hours," she exclaimed.

"Ah, yes, Marguerite, so far, no problems, but it is too early
to tell about the next six months." He leaned back thoughtfully
in his chair, hands clasped behind his head. "Not enough rain, or
too much rain. Insects, disease, and of course a hurricane could
make all the work for naught. Right now, the green shoots are
pushing up through the ground and the field hands are at work
getting rid of the weeds that are trying to choke the new growth."

"We must ask St. Benedict for a bountiful harvest! But this has been a glorious spring so far, don't you agree, dear?"

Her husband looked at her oddly and said, "Well, yes, Marguerite; after all, it is March! And soon the sugarcane will grow thicker and stronger."

"Yes, thicker and stronger, dear," she repeated.

Jacques gave her a look that indicated he was beginning to suspect that this conversation was not about sugarcane. But he continued, "The levee has been reinforced, I have enough hogsheads, and Tobias and I figure our workforce is now large enough to handle the hoped-for yield. We have prepared as best we can; however, all is in the hands of God."

"I understand, Jacques; when you grow only one crop, you risk complete success or complete failure."

Jacques tilted his head and searched his wife's face, seeming not quite certain where she was leading him. She continued to sit across the table from him with a small smile on her face, and he changed the subject.

"Wonderful dinner tonight, dear; Cook makes the best gumbo in Louisiana, and you know how I love her spicy chicken soup. Sometimes I think you're trying to fatten me up." Jacques patted his stomach.

Marguerite laughed. "Jacques, you never gain weight. But I need to!"

He looked across the table at her and raised his eyebrows. "Women rarely say that, Marguerite. Whatever do you mean?"

She rose from her chair, and walked over to his. Standing directly in front of him, she cupped his chin in her hands and gazed lovingly down at him. His green eyes widened and looked back at her in surprise.

"Marguerite, what is it? You're behaving in a very unusual manner!"

"Darling, we have each other and our beautiful home. And I do love you so much."

"Yes, I quite agree," Jacques said, shaking his head and looking uncomfortable. "In fact, I should get back to the office right now to work on the accounts, to make sure that we continue to have this lovely home."

He started to get up, but Marguerite grabbed his hands, forcing him back down. She knelt in front of him and looked up at him imploringly.

"Marguerite? What . . ."

"Jacques, it's time. I want to try again. You have to come to my bed. I know you've been afraid of hurting me since the baby died. But please!"

"Well." He said the word slowly and patted her head, as if she were a child. "Now, Marguerite, do you think that everything is, uh, mended?" He thought a moment and added, "I couldn't bear losing you."

She took his hands again and gently kissed each one. "The doctor said it's all right. I am in good health, and he assured me that I am perfectly capable of bearing another child. Please, Jacques!" She was begging him, tears running down her cheeks. "Come tonight! I miss you so much!"

He gazed at her for a couple of minutes, not saying a word. Finally, he agreed: "All right, Marguerite. Tonight."

Still holding his hands, she laid her head on his lap. "Oh, my darling, thank you!"

Tarot: THE MAGICIAN

*Revelation: Having skill that takes power
from above and directs it to possibilities.*

—

One might have expected the popular, handsome, and charming Miguel Plicque to continue enjoying his philandering ways, but now he desired only Catherine Caresse. Quite passionately! He ascribed it to maturity.

Catherine knew otherwise. They were happy together, and with Suzanne now taken care of by René Bonet, Catherine had married her plasterer. Life was good, she thought.

Having finished a light supper, Catherine and Miguel were sitting in the garden, each sipping a glass of wine and enjoying the late-June sunset. The vibrant bougainvillea vines covered the walls, their flowers glowing in the softening light. Their vigor reminded Catherine of her daughter. Suzanne visited almost every afternoon, full of news about René's nightly visits to her home. Although she delighted endlessly in detailing René's many thoughts and convictions, today's visit had been brief. She had asked Hortense for cooking instructions, borrowed some cayenne pepper, and then rushed home to prepare a chicken fricassee, one of René's favorite meals.

Catherine smiled to herself. Suzanne had never taken an interest in food preparation before; she'd been quite content to leave Hortense alone in the kitchen. Now, however, she was asking Catherine's maid for favorite recipes. Although René had provided her with a competent cook, Suzanne wanted perfection. For René. Because *he* was perfect.

Well, Catherine had to admit that because of René, Suzanne's interests and proficiencies were growing. And, like the bougainvillea plants, she was blooming. But they seemed to be only René's interests, as well as his opinions and concerns. She was no longer her own person.

In more ways than one! Catherine thought. She smiled at her private joke. *Yes, this "secondhand marriage" has quite changed her.*

Then she sighed, caught Miguel's eye, and smiled again. Although she missed doting on her daughter, she loved her new married life with Miguel. And these were cherished moments the couple shared: sometimes intimate, other times merely exchanging neighborhood news, but always relaxed and satisfying.

Miguel smiled back at his new wife. He also relished this time; while he supplied much of the gossip, Catherine usually astonished him with her analysis of people and situations.

The topic he was about to broach now, however, was delicate. *Tread softly, Miguel,* he told himself.

"Suzanne is quite in love with René, isn't she?" he said, topping off her wine.

"Yes, she is," said Catherine. "She is very happy. By the way, Miguel, what do you think of René?"

Her question caught Miguel by surprise. Catherine had never asked his opinion about anything regarding Suzanne—probably because Catherine believed her daughter was perfect. He, on the other hand, considered Suzanne self-centered, spoiled, and stubborn, and he suspected she was also impulsive. But he would never tell that to Catherine. And René Bonet, too, Miguel thought, might be somewhat reckless. But he didn't want to upset Catherine, so he chose his words carefully.

"Well, René is young," Miguel said diplomatically, after sipping a bit of his wine. "Full of himself and his ideas, inexperienced and thus presumptuously confident—you know the sort."

"Ha! Pompous, you mean!" Catherine hooted, and swallowed the remaining liquid in her glass. "I quite agree! But Suzanne thinks he's brilliant."

Miguel looked at his wife with surprise. He couldn't believe it: Catherine actually admitted to a chink in Suzanne's *amour.* Must be the wine. And yet she was looking back at him directly, with clearheaded candor in her eyes. And expecting him to say something.

He continued cautiously. "Ah, yes. She thinks he's brilliant," he repeated. "And I'm sure that he appreciates her thinking that. All men do!"

He smiled as she laughed again. Then he said, "Actually, though, some of René's notions are quite interesting. For example, he likes to quote Thomas Jefferson's writing in the Constitution that 'all men are created equal.' I find that astonishing, because that just goes against all the ideas he grew up with, as a white man."

"Oh, I'm sure his parents aren't too pleased with his notions—that is, if he's foolish enough to expound on them at family gatherings." Frowning, she held up her empty glass and he leaned over and poured some of his wine into hers.

"He's just too intense, overzealous," she declared.

"He's young, Catherine. And, again, I think some of his arguments are valid."

"Hmph! Suzanne says he's also against slavery. And, of course, now she is, too. Why, my daughter never gave slavery a single thought before she met René!"

"Well, I've seen his type before—excessive enthusiasm for a cause," said Miguel. "But I suspect he'll change his tune if he has to actually stand up for what he professes to believe in."

Catherine sighed as she again drained her glass. "Well, as long as it's all just talk. And you're right—I doubt very much that he'd give up his Creole society in order to demonstrate his convictions to terminate slavery. He'd have too much to lose. His family, friends, position—no. Right now, as you say, he's young. But eventually his family's norms, the habits and instincts he basically inherited, will prevail. As they should."

She settled back into her chair, apparently relieved that "it" was settled, and surely "everything" would turn out favorably.

"Of course, dear," Miguel agreed, silently congratulating himself for his tactfulness. "Basically, René is a good man, treats Suzanne well, makes her happy, and that's all that counts."

Miguel took the last sip of his wine. Catherine had gotten him off track, talking about René, so he gingerly approached his issue again, tying it into their previous conversation. "I was thinking, though . . . René's going to break Suzanne's heart when he marries a Creole woman."

"Yes, that is possible," agreed Catherine.

"Mmm, yes. Uh, Catherine, when Suzanne's father married, how did you react?"

Catherine tilted her head and looked up at her husband. She thought for a moment, then said, "I accepted the situation, had even anticipated it. He told me when he met his soon-to-be bride that he would be completely faithful to her.

"By that time," she continued, "I had already given birth to Suzanne. My daughter became the main focus of my life. And although her father never visited me again, he honored his *plaçage* commitment. I never wanted for money, and Suzanne was provided with the best education possible."

"It doesn't sound like you were that upset."

"I was not in love with him, Miguel." Smiling, she reached across the table to take his hand.

"So, it would be best if Suzanne has René's baby as soon as possible?"

"She is already with child," Catherine acknowledged.

"What! How did I miss her announcement?"

"She does not yet know. She is only in her first month."

"Then how do you . . . ?"

Catherine merely smiled.

"By the way," she said, returning to the previous topic, "because Suzanne's father did not request my company, I had more time to improve my skill."

"Ah, the 'skill,'" Miguel mused. *Another sensitive topic.* "We're not talking about your healing potions or midwifery here. It's that *other* skill."

"Hmm?" Catherine looked at him questioningly.

"Like knowing that your daughter is with child before she does. And having some sort of a connection with spirits. I have never really asked you about it. Actually, sometimes it scares me. Some say it's a freakish power. Do you feel that way about it?"

Catherine took some time before answering. "It is a gift, Miguel, and needs to be treated with care. I believe that it has helped many people in a"—she paused—"in a fitting way."

"How did you know . . . when did you realize . . . what's it like?"

She laughed. "Hard to describe; it's like feeling a different kind of energy. Like an internal sparkling. And I inherited it from my mother's side. It skipped her, but her *père* had it. Grand-père recognized that I had the gift when I was born. He helped prepare me for its uses."

"Does Suzanne have it?"

"No, but her baby might!"

"Whew! I just can't imagine. I mean, the mysticism, the magic, the otherworldliness of it all . . . I know you would never use it to cause harm. But do you ever find this power frightening?"

"No," she said, "but sometimes it's painful."

Tarot: THE THREE OF SWORDS

Revelation: Misfortune, strife, sorrow, separation.

~

August 24, 1814

Tarnation seize me if I don't get these valuables to safety! Dolley swore to herself.

Through her spyglass, Mrs. Madison could see the British cautiously making their way northwest up Pennsylvania Avenue. However, there was no organized resistance to oppose them. There were only carts crowding the other streets as people left the city with what they could carry of their precious personal property.

Dolley paused for a moment, not only to gather energy and courage, but also to assure her servants that they would all escape safely. Then she moved quickly through the rest of the executive mansion, looking for other treasures she might rescue.

"Jean," she called out, "how are you doing?"

"We can't get it down, Mrs. Madison!" answered the doorkeeper. It was apparent from his tone that he was unnerved, and the First Lady did not blame him. After all, the soldiers who were to guard the President's Mansion had already fled, right along with the citizens of Washington, DC.

"I'll be right there, Jean!"

The First Lady hastened into the dining room, concerned about the giant portrait of George Washington hanging on the wall. The doorkeeper was on a stepladder, trying to remove the picture.

"It simply won't budge, Mrs. Madison!" he said.

"Get a hatchet and chop the frame apart," she instructed. "Then just pack the canvas. Is the wagon ready?"

"Yes, ma'am," said Mr. McGraw, the gardener. "Everything is set to go."

"All right, then. Start loading these things, and I'll be with you soon."

After gathering her bonnet and cloak, she went to a window and pulled aside the red velvet curtain to peer outside. She could see her servants carefully stowing the portrait, along with silverware, costly vases, and the president's papers, into wagons.

Jemmy will be glad that at least I was able to save his documents, she thought, referring to the President by his childhood nickname. The valuables were to be taken to a farm, out of reach of the enemy.

Dolley glanced back at the dinner table, set for forty guests. She and her personal servant, Sukey, had gone to the market two days before and had filled their baskets for tonight's elaborate celebratory dinner. Wine was cooling on the sideboard, and joints on spits were sizzling in the fireplace. Her husband was scheduled to return home victorious from a battle in Bladensburg. But there was no victory and the American forces had scattered. She was certain that, even though he was still in Maryland, he could now see the flames of Washington burning. President Madison would realize that there was no home to come back to.

"Ma'am, the British will be here soon. We must clear out immediately," Sukey called out.

Dolley nodded and slipped a few small pieces of silver into her handbag. Taking a last look at her recently decorated residence of six years, she walked briskly out of the gray sand-stone mansion with her head held high. Then the President's wife climbed into the waiting carriage and did not look back.

That night, Dolley tried to rest at the encampment, filled with other Washington citizens. They could see the glow in the night sky and smell the smoke rising from the city.

The servant posted outside her tent asked to enter.

"Come in, Jean," Dolley said. "Have you heard any news?"

"Yes, Mrs. Madison. We received confirmation that the enemy reduced the executive mansion to cinders. They looted the place first, ma'am, even ate the dinner you had prepared and drank your wine—and then burned the house. The Capitol Building, the Supreme Court Building, and the Library of Congress are also ablaze." He shook his head in dismay. "I'm sorry, ma'am," he added.

Thunder cracked, signaling the start of another late-August storm. A torrent of rain followed, pelting the city.

"Well, now. A storm! A horrible ending to a terrible day."

"Ah, this downpour will drown the fires, Mrs. Madison." The doorkeeper tried to lessen the woman's anguish. "The British camp will be a slushy mire, and they'll probably hurry back to their ships."

"Have you heard anything about the wagons we packed?"

"The country's valuables have been delivered and are safe in the house."

"Well, that's good news, anyway." Dolley gritted her teeth. "How I wish General Washington were still alive, Jean; the Redcoats would never have been able to reach shore. How dare they destroy our capital! We must exact revenge!"

Tarot: THE SEVEN OF WANDS

Revelation: Courage in the face of opposition.

~

September 1, 1814

"President Madison? Mr. Francis Scott Key is here to see you."

"Send him in, Edward," Madison said.

The thirty-three-year-old Virginia lawyer nervously entered the President's makeshift office.

"Sit down, Mr. Key," said the President. "What can I do for you?"

"Well, sir, the British have arrested my friend Dr. William Beanes. He's being held on one of their ships in Baltimore Harbor. His 'crime' was capturing their stragglers after they had burned Washington."

"He's a hero, in my book," said Madison.

"I quite agree, sir. But he's quite elderly and his friends and neighbors are concerned about him. I'd like your permission to go to the British flagship and negotiate his release. I will also deliver some letters from our British prisoners. Many of them state that we've treated them with kindness. They may be influential in getting my friend back."

"That sounds like a good incentive, Mr. Key. I'll arrange to have a sloop flying a flag of truce take you to their vessel. And good luck to you on your mission of mercy!"

Tarot: THE THREE OF WANDS

Revelation: Foundations laid, optimistic
possibilities.

⁓

Jean Lafitte's business venture in New Orleans, begun in 1809, was designated as that of a blacksmith, but everyone knew it was a front for the lucrative smuggling of slaves and captured merchandise.

Peter often came into the city to work at the smithy, for it was also the perfect spot for barrel making. Containers were always needed. Sturdy, tightly sealed barrels, casks, and kegs were used for essentials: sugar, beer, wine, rum, and brandy. Also, for ships going out to sea, the barrels held preserved salt meat, cabbage, biscuits, and water.

Peter was also appreciative that the perfect place for applying his carpenter's skills by day was also close to Millie's brothel, where he delighted in applying different skills at night.

He liked making Millie happy. He found that she really enjoyed having the back of her neck softly kissed while, at the same time, he stroked the curve in her waist. Not rushing (although at times he wanted to), he kissed and nibbled her knees, then worked his way back up to licking her ears. He talked to her throughout all the caresses, complimenting her beautiful body. And he always made sure of her ultimate sexual pleasure first before achieving his.

Although he assumed it was just business to her, his visits were special to him.

In fact, however, Millie looked forward to Peter's visits, which were becoming more and more frequent, and she did not conceal her delight when he came through her doorway this evening. He was wet from a late summer rain, but she helped him remove his bandanna, striped shirt, and pants and hung them over the drying stand, where they would stay until morning.

After a long soak in her tub and a brisk rubdown with fleecy towels, Millie wanted to make sure Peter was comfortable in her bed.

"Time for a back rub!" she said.

Peter sighed with pleasure as he turned over on his stomach. "Thank you, Millie! I am a little sore from today's work."

As Millie proceeded with strong strokes going up from his pelvis on both sides of Peter's spine, she said, "Pete, I love it that you always make me feel so special. I do believe you are my very favorite, um, boyfriend!"

"Well, you're my favorite girl, Millie! Actually, you're my only girl. Mmm. That feels so good!"

As Millie worked her thumbs in small, deep circles around his shoulder blades and moved up to the base of his head, she said, "Your muscles are really tight, Pete. What's making you so sore?"

"Making lots of barrels. Seems the rumors we've heard are true. My countrymen plan to capture New Orleans, which is very important to Louisiana's economy. I think they want to keep this territory for themselves, or maybe return it to the Spanish."

"That's horrible, Pete!" Millie cried indignantly. "But wait . . ." She suddenly stopped the massage, sat up, and crossed her arms.

"What's wrong?"

"Your 'countrymen'? Just whose side are you on?"

"I would guess I'm on your bad side now, Millie, with that remark. I should have said 'my former countrymen'!"

"Well, that's better." With her fists, she began softly pummeling his backside. "And how do you know the rumors are true?"

"Well, just a few days ago, some Royal Navy officers from the brig *Sophie* stopped to visit Jean Lafitte at Grand Terre," said Peter. "They had a letter from Colonel Nicholls giving Lafitte a choice: either we Baratarians can help them invade Louisiana by guiding them through the swamps and assisting them in attacking the city, or the British will destroy us because of our privateering enterprises against their ships."

"So they want to use Barataria as a point of invasion? They'd be coming at us from all of the swamps?"

"Right. And they'd use our boats and ships, as well as our gunners and fighters. They also offered Lafitte thirty thousand pounds to help them."

"Thirty thousand pounds!" exclaimed Millie. "Is he going to do it? Help the British?"

"We've been discussing the offer for several days now. The money is very tempting, but I don't think Lafitte is keen on the terms," answered Peter. "He's a slaver; plus, he would have to stop smuggling and give up all his ships to the British. Then what would he do? I can't see him becoming a farmer."

"That's for sure!" Millie said with a laugh. She stopped her patting, stretched out beside him, crooked her arm, and held her head up with her right hand.

Peter rolled over on his left side, mirroring her position. "No, he really thinks of himself as an American; Louisiana is where he's made his fortune, and he wants to continue his livelihood here."

"Even though Governor Claiborne incarcerated his brother Pierre in that wretched calaboose and would love to put Jean away, too?" asked Millie.

"Fair point," agreed Peter. "But aside from the governor, Lafitte does have political friends in high places. In fact, I suspect Pierre will not be locked up much longer."

"But back to the British bribe—the Baratarians are preparing for battle?" asked Millie.

"Yes. Some time ago, they began stockpiling flints, gunpowder, cannonballs, and, of course, cannons, so we're ready for whatever happens. As far as the British 'offer' is concerned, Lafitte told them that he needed a couple of weeks to think about it."

"So, you are all discussing it?"

"Yes. It's a lot of money, and we'd be battling the Royal Navy. On the other hand . . . But, Millie, you must not tell anyone about this!"

"It's very exciting, your life, Pete. And I do worry about you, especially if you get involved in warfare."

"Truly?"

"Why, of course, Pete! And I think you know that. Now, turn over so I can finish your back rub."

Peter saluted her, with a frown on his face. "Are you sure you're finished on this side, ma'am?"

Tarot: THE KNIGHT OF SWORDS

Revelation: Turbulence is possible.

⁓

On the final evening of Marguerite's weekend party, the house servants were clearing the dessert dishes from the rosewood table and taking them back through the courtyard to the kitchen. Marguerite, Sheila, and Jacques were in the front of the mansion, bidding their last guests a good night.

"This evening's dinner was absolutely delicious," said their friend Henri. "You have a fine cook!"

"Thank you; she was quite expensive, but worth it," replied Jacques. "Good cooks always are, you know. She is teaching two of our younger females to do the peeling and chopping in the scullery. Eventually, they will also learn her other culinary skills."

"Do you have any young house servants who have the physical stamina to make soap? Our laundress is getting on in years and losing her strength," said Claudia.

"No, but our laundress, who was also very costly, is excellent. She knows how to expertly remove stains, and she is willing to work on her day off. Most of our slaves like to go into the city on Sundays, but she is saving to buy her freedom. We will be willing to send her to you—but only until the baby arrives."

"*S'il vous plaît!*" said Claudia, "And *oui*—when *le bébé* arrives, you will definitely need her skills every day!"

After the laughter subsided, Claudia continued, "Your china is so exquisite, Marguerite! I love the cornucopia motif on the large plates—so symbolic of your hospitality. But surely you don't allow your servants to wash your good dishes!"

"Absolutely not, Claudia; Mother and I will do that chore ourselves tomorrow."

"It should take us a good part of the day," added Sheila.

"I will be thinking of you tomorrow, then, as I begin reading Voltaire's *Candide*. Thank you so much," said Claudia.

"You're welcome. I was happy to get this latest version; it's illustrated with seven drawings by Jean-Michel Moreau le Jeune," said Marguerite.

"I know the story well," said Jacques. "Voltaire's satire has angered many, but to me he's a hero."

"Speaking of writers, is Donatien Alphonse François de Sade still in solitary confinement at the Charenton insane asylum?" asked Henri.

"I should hope so. Such appalling books! It's been ten years now since he was transferred there from the Bastille, and I do hope he never escapes!" declared Sheila.

"Indeed. And to continue on in only good taste, do tell me, Jacques, how did you obtain such wonderful wine?" asked Henri.

"The French wines are from a small importer, who usually deals in iron products but happened on a cargo of wine rescued from a ship that had sprung a fatal leak," Jacques replied.

"*Alors*, I must admit that such a lucky importer is a valuable asset to our community!" said Claudia.

"Indeed he is!" agreed Sheila.

Henri turned back to the host. "Jacques, in addition to the wine, everything else was perfect: your plantation provided superb hunting, your cook's kitchen accomplishments were delectable, and the company, of course, was so very enjoyable.

We must get together again soon at our townhouse before your baby comes!"

"An early celebration would be lovely. What do you think, Henri? Perhaps in late October or November?" asked Claudia.

"We'll plan for early November."

"I look forward to it!" said Sheila. "I've loved these get-togethers among friends and neighbors ever since I was a little girl. I must say, however, that although our friends remain the same, our neighbors have changed quite a bit since Louisiana flew the French flag."

"Yes," said Henri, "many changes have occurred, especially since the Yankee traders began residing here."

"At least they're not moving into the Vieux Carré," said Sheila.

"No—no one will sell to them. So one of those Northerners bought up the Livoudais plantation and divided it into parcels, and the Yankees are building their mansions there."

"And their odd-looking houses are surrounded by gardens that anybody can see!" cried Sheila.

"*Oui*, the Yankees are newcomers, but they respect our culture. After the Louisiana Purchase, President Jefferson himself assured Sister Marie Theresa, of the Ursuline sisters, that their institution could continue to govern itself without interference, and that the US government would protect their property. I believe we are fortunate to be part of the United States," said Henri.

"I agree," responded Jacques. "Our countrymen in Canada are treated as serfs by their English conquerors. But I am afraid, with our new country at war, we will be facing even more adjustments soon."

"Another positive reason we are fortunate to be part of the United States. As France's navy is not equal to England's, she could not defend her colonies in the new world."

"I expect you're correct, Henri," said Jacques. "I have heard rumors. New Orleans probably should be preparing for a British attack, although I'm at a loss for how to go about it."

"What we need is a strong, experienced leader! *Que Dieu nous aide!*" said Henri.

Their carriage pulled up, and a coachman opened the door. Bidding a final goodbye to his hostesses, Henri kissed the women's fingertips. "Thank you, Marguerite and Sheila, for such a wonderful weekend, full of dancing and dining."

"*Salut*, and safe journey home!"

"*Au revoir!*"

"A final glass of champagne, my dears?" asked Jacques, as the carriage pulled away.

"*Oui!*" they both responded.

"To the library, then. We'll have it all to ourselves."

The house servants had finished cleaning the dining area, gathered firewood for the following day, and returned to their quarters behind the mansion.

As they entered the small room, Jacques said, "Ah—calm and quiet."

The three sat in a comfortable silence, each reflecting upon the long weekend, as he poured sparkling, sweet wine into three crystal flutes. Then he held up his glass and toasted them. "It was a splendid party, ladies; you outdid yourselves!"

"Thank you, Jacques. It did go well! I think Mother's favorite part was the dancing. Am I right?" Marguerite asked.

Sheila answered, "Oh, my, yes! The musicians, especially the fiddlers, kept up such a wonderfully fast tempo! I love the way the Acadians play."

"How about you, Marguerite?" asked Jacques.

"My favorite was showing off the new sugar mill and making candy from the molasses. I am so proud of you and your modern construction!"

"We owe our success to Etienne de Bore and his vacuum-pan invention. Thanks to this new continuous-boiling process, Louisiana has seen a surge in sugar production. It is as important as Eli Whitney's new version of the cotton gin!"

"I did want to ask you, darling, about what Henri meant with his comment about more adjustments in the future?" asked Marguerite.

"Well, dear, you know how you have been complaining about not getting any of the latest fashions from London and Paris?"

"Yes, President Jefferson signed that ill-advised Embargo Act in 1807, forbidding imports from France and England. My friends and I have been very irritated about that."

"Hear, hear!" added Sheila angrily. "Why, if it weren't for that dear man Mr. Lafitte, I would not even have enough coffee grounds to color my hair!"

"Many people have had to do without, my dears. And then this war started, and now the country has sunk into a severe economic depression. The US treasury is empty. We cannot import goods, nor can we export anything, either. Because the English navy has blockaded our seaports from the Atlantic Ocean to the Gulf of Mexico, our goods and crops are lying in piles and rotting in barns or on the wharves. We have heard that the capital city is in ruins and the war has gone badly for the American forces. And now there are rumors that a huge British fleet is headed in this direction to attack our city."

"Attack New Orleans?" cried Sheila. "Why, that's dreadful! I can't imagine yet another flag waving over my wonderful city. And the British are just such an odious sort."

"Yes, and their battle cry says it all: 'beauty and booty.'"

"That's an odd slogan," said Sheila. "Whatever does it mean?"

There were a few moments of silence while husband and

wife decided how to delicately explain it. Finally, Marguerite said, "Well, Mother, I'll have to be blunt: 'beauty and booty' basically means 'rape and pillage'!"

"Well, I never!" said Sheila. She thought about Marguerite's words for a minute, then said, "Excuse me. It was a wonderful party. Good night, now." She walked outside into the back courtyard and headed toward the kitchen.

"Mother, are you all right? The dishes can wait until tomorrow," said Marguerite, hurrying after her.

"Why, of course I'm fine, dear," replied Sheila. "I'm just going to get some very sharp knives; it seems we may need them. This is my way of preparing for the coming 'adjustments'!"

Tarot: THE SIX OF WANDS

Revelation: Public acclaim; growth in the arts.

~

September 20, 1814

"Come in, Edward. You look happy today! What's that you're waving in your hand?"

"It's a poem, Mr. President, and you're going to love this! Remember Mr. Key's visit a couple of weeks ago?"

"Yes! He went to Baltimore to negotiate Dr. Beane's release from the British. Do you know if he had to abort his mission because of their attack on Fort McHenry?"

"Mr. Key was able to get the doctor's release, but the British would not let him leave until after the attack. He watched the entire bombardment from the ship in the harbor."

"That must have been a miserable time for him, Edward. He was no doubt anxious not only for his friend, but for himself, too."

"Yes, and it wasn't until dawn on September fifteenth that Mr. Key finally saw that our flag was still flying over the fort. Which brings me to the poem . . ."

The secretary handed President Madison a paper. "Here's a copy, sir. It's called 'The Defence of Fort M'Henry,' and Mr. Key published it this morning. Everyone is talking about it!"

James Madison read the poem and then looked up at his secretary. "It's a very good poem indeed, Edward! I especially like 'the land of the free and the home of the brave.'"

"Yes, sir. Some folks are even singing it to the English tavern song 'To Anacreon in Heaven.'"

"Well, I doubt it will become popular, Edward," answered the President. "That tune is so very difficult to sing!"

"Couldn't agree more, sir."

"So! The tally thus far for the British: Washington ruined, but Baltimore almost unscathed."

The President thought a moment and then continued. "That leaves one more target, way down in the South, Edward."

"I suspect you're right, sir. The Redcoats are heading for New Orleans."

Tarot: THE KNIGHT OF CUPS

Revelation: An enticing proposition; a summons.

⁓

September 21, 1814

"Catherine?" she heard Miguel call for her from the front room. He had just returned from the market, where he frequently met with friends for coffee and news.

"Catherine," he called again, "it's happening! The British are getting closer, and General Jackson is coming to protect us. And he wants me to help him!"

Catherine came inside from her garden, thinking about her husband's fondness for exaggerations.

"Oh?" she called back, with amusement. "General Jackson has specifically asked for Miguel Plicque to help him save the country?"

She stopped when she saw her spouse, alarmed by the look on his face. Miguel was exhilarated, and she had to fight the panic starting to develop inside her.

War . . . danger . . . injury . . . suffering . . . her husband . . .

"But, Miguel," she said, choosing her words with care, "you said just the other day, when the bakery owner Jean Daquin tried to recruit you, that you would not join."

"I know, *chérie*. But that was because the free men of color were not given the same rights as the white volunteer soldiers. Remember? Governor Claiborne did not even want to arm

Major Daquin's battalion. He was afraid that they would take aim at the white Louisianans."

"How ridiculous!" scoffed Catherine. "Claiborne certainly does not know much about the citizens of our city. I do wish Jacques Villeré had won the governor's election instead. It's unfortunate that the Creoles split their votes between him and Jean Destrehan."

"True," agreed Miguel. "If free men of color were allowed to vote, Villeré would have won. He has a very good reputation for settling disputes."

"That said, if women could vote, Villeré would have been elected by a landslide!" she countered, laughing.

"Well, if you can foresee women voting, I might run for governor myself!"

"One can only dream, *chéri amour*. But," she continued, getting back to the disquieting issue at hand, "what's different today? What changed your mind about joining the battalion of free men of color?"

"Well, General Jackson is on his way here and probably heard about all the British getting ready to attack New Orleans. So, when he was passing through Mobile, Alabama, he issued an emergency proclamation."

Miguel's smile widened. "He's calling free blacks 'brave fellow citizens' and promising that if we enroll, we will be paid over one hundred dollars and be awarded 160 acres of land. That's the same amount that the white soldiers are getting!"

"And do you believe him?"

Miguel took both of her hands gently in his. "*Oui*. And I must do this. I did not know the situation is so critical. We are all in danger: my city, my country, my family, and, most important, my beloved wife. The English are the enemy; I am a citizen of the state of Louisiana, of the United States of

America. I will defend you with honor. And you'll support my decision?"

Catherine looked up at him. She could see that he was unafraid, perhaps even looking forward to what he saw as a heroic adventure. She, however, although proud of her husband's patriotism and courage, was also conscious of an unnerving apprehension building in her stomach. And plans for a protective spell were swirling in her head.

He was still gazing at her, hoping for her approval.

She smiled slightly and nodded yes.

Tarot: THE EIGHT OF SWORDS

Revelation: A dilemma;
fear of acting in a confrontation.

~⁓

Peter was seeing Millie at least once or twice a week now. Although neither mentioned the brief encounter in the French market, there was a different quality to his visits: his touches were caresses; his kisses were tender. He was attentive to her, solicitous of her thoughts and ideas. He cared for her! To say this was irregular was an understatement. Bizarre, even; peculiar, certainly. But nice. This was a puzzling enjoyment that she had never before experienced in her life.

"Millie?" She heard him call out and then ascend the stairs.

"Hey, Millie," he said at the doorway, holding some parcels, including flowers, a pot of cooked shrimp, and a baguette. "I thought you might be hungry."

"Pete," she said happily. "Thank you! I haven't had an opportunity to go to the market today. I so appreciate this."

They sat together, quite relaxed, at the small table in her room, shelling the shrimp, sponging up the sauce with the bread, and sipping ginger beer.

"Mmm. This is wonderful. Now, what's new with my favorite privateer?" she asked.

"Oh!" Peter replied, as he licked his fingers. "Lafitte's furious with General Jackson. Here, we offered to help defend New

Orleans, and Jackson had the audacity to call us 'hellish banditi'! Then that Commodore Patterson actually attacked us. Us! Our homes and our families in Barataria! After we volunteered to help him!"

"Oh, my," said Millie, as she helped herself to a slice of honey-flavored cake. "Tell me more."

"It happened just a few days ago, on the sixteenth, at dawn. We were caught off guard. Lafitte wasn't there, but he told us to have our cannons ready. We saw the fleet approach. But we were expecting the British. Lafitte was so sure that his offer to help defend the city would be accepted that he never thought the Americans would attack. There were the invaders: a schooner of war, six gunboats, and some barges. We were shocked, but since Jean Lafitte had ordered us to resist any American strikes, it became a free-for-all. Most of us made it out; I jumped into a canoe and headed north, toward the marsh, where they couldn't come after me."

"Oh, Pete! I'm so glad you're safe!" Millie said, and she meant it. "How many didn't get away?"

"About eighty men were captured, including Dominique Yu, Lafitte's half brother."

"What happened to them?"

"They're imprisoned in the cabildo's calaboose now."

"Another Lafitte brother at city hall's jail? Why, people get executed there! I know Pierre Lafitte was able to escape, but your luck might come to an end, especially for eighty Baratarians!"

"I'm sure that won't happen to our men; we'll get them out somehow." Peter looked grim yet resolute.

"Is there more bad news?" Millie asked hesitantly. She had stopped eating and looked at her privateer with concern.

"It was just such a shock, Millie. We were caught off guard!" Peter pounded the table angrily. "So then the Americans raided our warehouses. Jean Lafitte said that the goods Commodore Patterson and his men stole from us were worth quite a fortune. They took all our schooners and then burned our buildings." Peter shook his head glumly. "Barataria was destroyed."

"Oh, Pete, I'm so sorry. Will this be the end of Lafitte's business ventures?" Millie asked, her eyes growing wide.

"Bloody hell, no! Of course not, Millie!" Peter said, seeming surprised by her question. "It'll take more than that to stop the Baratarians; you can be sure of that!"

Peter wiped his mouth on his sleeve, held out his hand, and added, with a suggestive smile, "Now, let's you and me get down to our own business undertaking."

Tarot: THE QUEEN OF CUPS

*Revelation: the beloved woman
who acts on her dreams.*

~~~

October 1814

It was the middle of autumn, and, although Suzanne was almost
six months pregnant, she was hardly showing. The first trimester had been easy—very little nausea. She had lots of energy and
was exuberantly gathering baby items—everything from blankets to burping cloths.

René frequently came to the Rue de Rampart cottage he
provided for her. She loved cooking for him, and afterward they
spent the evenings discussing ideas. She was intoxicated with his
viewpoints, making them her own.

"Maman," she had said the previous week, "René says that
slavery should be abolished. He believes that all men are equal!
Isn't that amazing?"

"I suspect the plantation owners don't agree with him,"
responded Catherine.

"Well, he has had a number of arguments with his father.
But René says that it's a moral issue. His reasoning is so noble!"

Two weeks before, Suzanne had told Catherine that René
had criticized the Catholic Church. "He said that years ago Père
Antoine was sent to establish the Spanish Inquisition here in
Louisiana."

"Hmm, I do remember hearing something about that," Catherine commented.

"René said that people should be able to practice whatever religion they want. But Père Antoine was sent here to New Orleans to arrest people who had ideas the Catholic Church did not approve of. Then they would be tried as heretics."

"But Père Antoine did not arrest anyone, Suzanne. In fact, he is well loved by all of his parishioners."

"Well, anyway, René said that the pope should not have approved the inquisition and that it was wrong to conduct the investigations. He is so intelligent, Maman! Don't you agree?"

"That René is so intelligent, or that the inquisition was wrong?"

"Well, both, of course! Oh, I just love listening to him— so many ideas, so many thoughts. And he says that he enjoys talking to me as well."

"Yes," said Catherine, "I imagine he does find you most agreeable! And what does he say about your baby?"

"He's thrilled!" Suzanne gently kneaded her abdomen and continued. "He loves to put his hand on my tummy, and he's felt the baby kick. We don't have a name chosen yet, but he's sure it's a boy. Maman, we're so happy together!"

This morning, Catherine was recalling these sorts of conversations as she waited for Suzanne's daily call.

"René said . . ."

"René thinks that . . ."

"René believes . . ."

"He's so fascinating!"

"He's always incredibly thought-provoking!"

"He's just amazing!"

Her daughter's happiness was most important to Catherine, so, rather than debate René's views or question his ideas, she just listened to Suzanne prattle on, without concern.

But today was different. Because of a disconcerting dream the night before, Catherine had a sense of foreboding about her daughter's visit. A premonition. She heard the knock, and then the door opened.

"Maman!" Suzanne called out to Catherine as she stepped into the house. "I have wonderful news!"

Catherine steeled herself as she walked to the front room to greet her glowing daughter.

Wonderful news, she repeated to herself. *Then why am I worried?*

Yet she couldn't shake the adverse feeling.

Catherine greeted her daughter with a kiss. Yes, Suzanne was radiant. And excited. But the mother still was apprehensive that something was not quite right.

"Oh, Maman! I am about to tell you the most marvelous announcement!"

Catherine tried to steer the conversation in any other direction.

"Good morning, my darling! You look wonderful! In fact, you are positively glowing! Is the baby kicking today yet? By the way, I have another baby blanket from our neighbor Jeanette. Would you like to see it? How about some coffee?"

"Maman!" This time, Suzanne sounded annoyed.

"Yes," sighed Catherine, no longer able to put off the inevitable, "and what is your news?"

Her daughter dramatically curtsied to her mother before replying. "Maman, meet the new Madame Suzanne Bonet. René and I are married!"

Tarot: THE KNIGHT OF WANDS

Revelation: New and questionable proposals,
possible adventurous departure.

———

"How could they?" Catherine was still reeling from Suzanne's marriage announcement. "What were they thinking? And Père Antoine—why didn't he talk them out of it? I know he wants his parishioners to value him, but he is well aware that the Code Noir is still in practice—that brown cannot marry white!"

"Now, Catherine," soothed Miguel, "they're young, they're in love—maybe it will work!"

"Nonsense. She may be over three-quarters white, but here in New Orleans she can't pass as _blanc._ I'm certain René's family has already disowned him! They have broken a precept; it's an appalling scandal. René will never be forgiven. He will not get any Creole clients, and our people do not need bankers. They will not even be able to afford the little house down the block! And now, with the baby coming—"

"René seems to be a smart fellow; perhaps he has a plan about how this will work."

"Oh, he has a plan, all right," she said disdainfully. "After the baby is born, he wants to take them upriver to St. Louis, where many people do not talk about their background."

"Where would René get that idea?"

"If you remember your history—back in 1769, Monsieur Christoval de Lisa came with Governor Alejandro O'Reilly's entourage, when Louisiana was ceded to Spain."

"I have a vague recollection of learning that. And?"

"Well, Christoval's son, Manuel, who goes by the surname Lisa, married the widow Polly Charles Chew."

"Oh, yes, I remember the event because I did some work for the father on his house right before the wedding. It was in the mid-nineties. He was one of my first clients. Now that you mention it, I haven't seen the couple for a long time. Whatever happened to them?" Miguel asked.

"They moved upriver to St. Louis about ten years ago. Turns out Manuel Lisa has become a very successful fur dealer, trading with the Indian tribes of the Missouri wilderness. Seems he has gained the Indians' trust—he's the only trader some of the tribes will deal with. To get to the point, Monsieur Lisa is looking for someone to run his office and fur warehouse in St. Louis while he is off trading. He has an agent looking here in New Orleans. Must not be any trustworthy people in St. Louis. René has convinced the agent that he is just what Monsieur Lisa is looking for."

Miguel paused for a moment to assimilate all this information.

"St. Louis! Well, I suppose in such a remote frontier town, the social mores aren't as developed as those in a wealthy city like ours. I suspect even our Monsieur Lafitte could be the epitome of grace and gentility in a place like St. Louis.

"But," he continued, "I really can't imagine that Suzanne would leave her friends and you. I know she can be audacious, but surely she is against that proposal!"

"Unfortunately, she thinks it's a brilliant idea and is quite excited about it," Catherine cried. "She says they can be a family living together openly, with many more opportunities for the child."

"Sounds like something René would say," said Miguel.

"Of course!" Catherine began pacing back and forth in the room. "Because St. Louis is at the spot where the Missouri River joins the Mississippi, it has become the provisioning point for everyone who is in the lucrative fur trade and all others heading west. So they will not have to worry about money, but he has told her to imagine a different life, to forget New Orleans."

Miguel said, "Well, I have heard from the keelboatmen that even mixed-race and free black men are welcome among the coureurs de bois, the free spirits, who trade with the Indians. The boatmen say that the coureurs de bois must be able to carry, paddle, walk, sing, hit the bull's-eye, and convince the Indians to trade their valuable furs for a woolen blanket and an iron knife."

"Sounds like a rugged existence!"

"True! And a dangerous life, too, but an unrestricted one. However, it is possible, with hard work, for even a métis or a black man to advance to a bourgeois like Monsieur Lisa."

Catherine paused and then asked, "Does such an existence interest you, Miguel?"

"No, my love. I have a better life here than I ever thought possible. But I can understand the lure of such a territory."

Putting her hands on her hips and shaking her head, Catherine said, "But not for Suzanne! She would be giving up so much, and . . . and . . . I would never again see her or the baby!"

She sank down into a chair and lowered her head into her hands. "Oh, Suzanne, Suzanne, what have you done?" she sobbed.

"But wait, Catherine," said Miguel, as he gave his wife a sly look. He walked behind her and put his arms around her. "Isn't there something that you can do—you know, like magic?"

Catherine lifted her head and shook it sadly. "I have to

admit that I did consider that. Black cat hair and coffin nails are known for their ability to break up a couple."

"Well, I can get the coffin nails for you. And black cats are easy to find."

"No, Miguel. I use my gifts only for healing and protecting people I love. I could not do that to my daughter. Especially since I've given her powerful bay leaves and manroot to ward off evil. I must keep the baby safe."

Again she shook her head. "What were they thinking?"

Tarot: THE TWO OF SWORDS

Revelation: Refusal to face an imminent
situation of hostility.

~

November 1814

"Pete?" Millie whispered. They were both in her bed, but the pirate had fallen asleep almost as soon as he had crawled under the sheets. This was highly unusual.

She had dozed off, too, but his lusty snores woke her up. Millie gently nudged him.

"Pete, _mon amour_ . . ."

"_Mmmfff, ooh, ha!_" He bolted upright into a sitting position, eyes open wide. "Who's there? What do you want?" he demanded.

"Pete, it's me, Millie. We didn't do anything at all tonight; we didn't even have our discussion. You know how enjoyable I find them; plus, I have some questions."

"Oh, sorry, Millie," he said, rubbing his eyes and sinking back down onto the bed. "I guess I was more tired than I thought! November's been such a busy month, with the war and all that, and Lafitte's got us working more than usual." He pulled her down closer to him, nibbling on her ear. "What's on your mind?"

"Did you and your mates accept the British bribe?"

"No." Peter frowned and again sat straight up, crossing his arms.

He continued, "Instead, we all agreed to send the document

to the Americans, to warn them and offer them our services. Lafitte even wrote that, even though he avoids paying some taxes, he has never stopped being a good citizen."

"That's so true," said Millie. "New Orleans depends on him for many necessities."

"Absolutely! We heard that General Jacques Villeré tried to argue our case but Governor Claiborne and his committee refused to budge. They think the letters are fakes, and they insist that we just want to get Pierre Lafitte out of jail."

"Well, I can see why they might think that. . . ."

"But that's crazy! And besides, thanks to a few well-placed friends, Pierre has already escaped from the calaboose! We really just want to help!"

Millie could see that Peter now was not only fully awake but also quite agitated.

"Perhaps they'll change their minds," she said, hoping to soothe him.

"Well, I hope so!" he agreed, and then added, "Oh! And General Jackson's supposed to arrive in the city next week. There's going to be a big parade; everybody's excited about welcoming him."

"Well, maybe Jean Lafitte can talk to the general when he gets here and he'll see Mr. Lafitte's reasoning," she said.

She sat back for a few seconds to consider something. Then she smiled. "A parade, you say! This might be another outing I can look forward to!"

"I suspect you would enjoy it, Millie. Oh—but, Millie? Don't go wearing that boy costume, or you might find yourself impressed into the United States Army. And I can't have that."

And, no longer sleepy at all, Peter did what he could to impress upon her that, as his woman, she was needed right there and then. No costume necessary!

Tarot: THE KING OF SWORDS

*Revelation: Appearance of a man with power of life
and death; one with authority and military strategy.*

~

December 1, 1814

The first day of December felt frigid because of the constant
dampness, yet the residents eagerly gathered at the Place
d'Armes for the first view of their savior.

Although their relationship was still strained, Catherine and
Suzanne also waited together in the crowd for their first glimpse
of General Jackson.

"Do you see him yet?" the mother asked her daughter.

"He's surrounded by his bodyguards, so I can't . . . Oh, wait!
There he is!" Suzanne cried, moving up and down on her toes.
"But he does not look like I imagined."

"Why?"

"He's tall, but very thin and frail-looking. No real uniform
that I can see. Some sort of a cape around his shoulders."

"Probably to keep the chill and the drizzle off him," said
Catherine.

"And his army does not look very soldier-like, either. They're
not marching in ranks; they're just strolling along. No uniforms,
just guns, powder horns, and hatchets. And there aren't very
many of them!"

"Well, I'd heard that they are just like our Cajun people from the countryside, so I guess we can't expect a dignified-looking army." The older woman shuddered. "Miguel told me that some of them had fought with General Jackson in the Creek Indian War."

"Oh, yes. I know all about it!" Suzanne said, almost gleefully.

Catherine raised her eyebrows and studied her daughter. *Here we go again*, she thought. *Suzanne's going to prattle on and on about what that foolish, pedantic husband of hers has told her.*

"René said that three thousand Indians were killed in that war."

"Is that so!" *I wonder if she ever says anything to him, or if he even listens to what she has to say.*

"The Yankees killed everyone: old men, women and children."

"Oh, how awful!" *Then again, what would she tell him? The recipe to make chicken fricassee? Hmm.*

"But René also said that the Creeks, at the instigation of the English agents, had massacred families at a place called Fort Mims."

"Oh, my, they shouldn't have done that!" *But I must not criticize and must try to remain patient, so that I can convince her that this St. Louis idea is absurd. Utter craziness!*

"And René thinks that—"

"Yes, yes, darling. Of course he does!"

"But, Maman, you did not hear what I was going to—"

"Oh! Suzanne! I see General Jackson now! Oh, my; he *does* look incredibly gaunt," interrupted Catherine once again. "He just got off his horse and is being welcomed by Governor Claiborne and Mayor Girod. Can you see all of them?" She moved aside so her daughter could get a better look.

"Oh!" Suzanne said softly. "The governor and mayor look far more impressive than the general. But General Jackson looks determined, and very tough. And the people are so exuberant! I can't wait to tell all this to René!"

As the cheering continued, Andrew Jackson was escorted to his headquarters. The two women moved along with the crowd, jostling their way to Royal Street. As they pushed their way closer to his building, they became separated. Catherine waved to her daughter, and Suzanne smiled in return.

Well, thought Catherine, *at least now she'll have a story of her own to tell her husband!*

General Jackson finally appeared on the second-floor gallery, and the spectators quieted to hear him speak.

Catherine concentrated on hearing Jackson's message, which his soft-spoken congressional friend Edward Livingston was translating into French. Although the speech was brief, the people applauded; they were pleased with its content.

After the general went back inside, Catherine began looking for Suzanne.

An attractive woman next to her turned and said, "I beg your pardon, madame, but did you hear what Monsieur Livingston said?" This woman, unlike Catherine and Suzanne, did not have on a tignon, and her cloak, dress, and jewelry were very fine.

Catherine was astonished; for a Creole woman to address a woman of color in public was most uncommon. She was even more surprised upon recognizing the woman.

"He is asking all of us to unite with him to save our city, Madame de Trahan."

"*Oui?* Oh! Madame Caresse! I did not realize it was you! How good to see you again. You look well."

"As do you, Madame de Trahan." Catherine smiled. "And it appears that the black cohosh was successful!"

Marguerite nodded. "Indeed, Madame Caresse, and thank you again," she said warmly. "I am in my eighth month."

"Hmm," said Catherine. "Many women in their final trimester confine themselves in their homes. . . ."

"Yes, so my mother reminds me every day. But I am careful not to overexert myself. I am quite healthy, full of energy, and to spend these days in a bedroom when a battle is about to brew does not make sense to me."

"Yes, these are different circumstances indeed. My daughter, who is also with child, refuses to confine herself as well. Fortunately, she, too, is in good health, vigorous, and, I might add, quite stubborn!"

"I'm sure you are monitoring her movements carefully, though."

"*Oui!* Not only for her sake, but for my grandchild's."

"That's exactly what my mother says!" Marguerite laughed.

She looked back up at the remaining men gathered on Jackson's balcony. "So! According to General Jackson, all of us are to unite. Do you think he even realizes who we all are?" Marguerite gave Catherine a knowing look. "Our Creole men will certainly do their part. But surely he can't mean *everyone* here." She rolled her eyes.

Both women then scanned the crowd, which, although made up mostly of the French and Spanish Creoles, also included colorful Cajuns from the bayous, free people of color, such as Catherine and Suzanne, slaves squatting on the banquette, Choctaw Indians from upriver, and even a couple of nuns from the Ursuline convent.

"*Oui,*" agreed Catherine. "One might think he is mistranslating—that the general just means the Creoles, the Cajuns, and other whites." Then Catherine thought a moment, before adding proudly, "However, my husband, Miguel, a free man of color, has also joined the local forces. He is in Major Jean Daquin's battalion. General Jackson specifically requested our help as well."

"Excellent! It seems to me that the general will need all the help he can get." Marguerite stood on her toes to get a better look at the militiamen. She gasped. "Just look at those scruffy soldiers! Not having decent uniforms is one thing, but my goodness!"

Catherine nodded. "Most every one of them: ragged, disheveled, and undisciplined. And they're supposed to save us from the English, who have defeated the great Napoleon?"

"Well, although they do look shabby," replied Marguerite, "my husband tells me that we're lucky to have them. They're volunteers from Kentucky and Tennessee. They're hunters and used to protecting their families from Indians. It is said that they are all excellent marksmen."

"I hope so. But many of them look extremely thin and, again, poorly clothed."

"My husband also said that they have been on the trail for over a week, some of them coming all the way from Alabama. And look at General Jackson! He himself looks emaciated and in poor health. I think he should probably be in bed. Don't you?"

"Absolutely," Catherine said. "Especially in this wet weather!"

While nodding her head in agreement, the Creole continued, "He certainly isn't splendid or majestic, like the pictures I've seen of other generals. But he was sent here to rescue us from the British. Well, we know he can defeat Indians, so I guess, like he says, we had better unite and work together, or abandon our homes to the English."

And, joining the throng's chant, Marguerite cried, "Jackson has come!"

Caught up in the enthusiasm, Catherine, too, joined in: "Jackson has come!"

Several minutes later, the crowd quieted and began to disperse. Marguerite smiled as she turned back to Catherine.

"Madame Caresse, perhaps it is serendipitous that we have met here."

"*Oui*, madame?" Catherine looked at Marguerite curiously.

"Besides being knowledgeable about certain herbs, you are also well known as a healer. I've heard so much about you. You saved a neighbor's son four months ago; he had pneumonia. Raimond Fortier had such a high fever, and my friend Julia was so worried that she was going to lose him."

"Yes, I remember young Raimond," Catherine smiled. "He liked the cold, wet scarves I wrapped around his head and neck, but he did not like drinking my raisin tea. He's doing well now?"

"Oh, yes! And I did hear about your tea; he hasn't eaten a raisin since!"

Catherine chuckled. "Please give his mother my regards when you see her."

Marguerite said, "Of course." She thought a moment, and then added, "But about our fortuitous meeting today. My husband said that women are needed to help with nursing, making bandages, dressings, and such. I am organizing some of my friends and neighbors to accomplish this. Perhaps, Madame Caresse, you would consider working together with me? Your healing skills would be very much valued, as well as your knowledge of medicines and other supplies we need to acquire. May I count on you to help?"

"Certainly, Madame de Trahan. And, if you would like, I will also gather friends and neighbors from the Rue de Rampart area to support this undertaking."

"That would be wonderful!"

"Ah! And here is my daughter, Suzanne. She can assist me. This is Madame de Trahan, darling."

Suzanne turned to meet the Creole woman with a smile and a curtsy. "*Bonjour*, madame."

Marguerite's eyes widened. Interpreting the significance of the girl's tendrils of copper-colored hair, light complexion, and, most of all, green eyes, almost caused her to swoon. But she instantly steadied herself. "A pleasure to meet you, Mademoiselle Caresse."

Marguerite was still pale when she addressed Catherine. "My, do excuse me. This chill air is enough to make one faint!" She gave a wan smile.

Catherine had carefully watched Marguerite's reaction. Heedful but not surprised at the other woman's shock and discomfort, she quickly said, "I agree, and you are both in a somewhat delicate condition and should get out of this dreadful, drizzly weather. But, again, Madame de Trahan, I will be happy to assist you. As you say, we are all in this together." She turned to her daughter, "Isn't that right, dear?"

"Oh, *oui!*" began Suzanne. "My husband, René, says—"

"Right, then!" Catherine cut in. "So, how do we start, Madame de Trahan?"

The Creole woman drew a deep breath. "Père Antoine is giving us space to meet at the cathedral tomorrow afternoon. Will you both be able to join us, Madame Caresse?"

Catherine nodded. "We will see you there. Good day, Madame de Trahan."

The Creole woman smiled and left. Suzanne said, "She seemed very nice, Maman. I hope she feels better soon."

"I suspect she will in time, dear."

Catherine felt a tap on her shoulder. Turning about, she found a younger, white woman, around Suzanne's age, facing her. There was something about her, though, that seemed peculiar. Her demeanor, for one so young, was scruffy, even audacious. And her makeup—her eyebrows had been darkened with far too much charcoal, and her crimsoned lips were excessively shaped. Could she be a "woman of the wharf"?

"Beg your pardon, madame," she said shyly. "I overheard your conversation, and I would like to help General Jackson, too."

It was Suzanne who answered her. "But of course," she exclaimed. "General Jackson wants us all to participate! Isn't that right, Maman?"

Catherine nodded, although she was not certain how this girl's "skills" would be beneficial. Yet she answered, "*Oui*, I'm sure we will need everyone's help. How kind of you to offer. Do meet us tomorrow afternoon at Louis Église Street."

She almost added, "Do you know where the church is?" but the prostitute had already bowed her head, turned away, and disappeared.

Tarot: THE QUEEN OF WANDS

*Revelation: Inspiring and magnetic woman
undertaking a project.*

~~~~~

December 2, 1814

The following day, Marguerite stood on a small platform thoughtfully provided by Père Antoine and looked out at the ladies who had arrived for the meeting. Some were her friends from neighboring plantations; others were wealthy Vieux Carré wives who lived in the lovely brick houses with intricate, iron-laced galleries rimming the second floors. She gave a slight nod to Catherine and Suzanne, who had brought a few of their tignoned neighbors from the Rue de Rampart area.

Marguerite also noticed a garishly dressed young white woman, detached from any of the others, intently observing all of the other females. She seemed to be looking for a particular person. Marguerite watched with curiosity as the tawdry-looking girl finally fixed her gaze. She smiled at someone across the crowded room and then hesitantly waved. Marguerite saw Catherine's daughter enthusiastically return the gesture.

Well, well, well, Marguerite thought, slightly astonished. *We certainly have assembled quite the gumbo!*

Time to begin.

"Mesdames and mademoiselles," Marguerite said. The women,

who had been nervously chatting in their own little cliques, all turned to give her their attention.

"Thank you so much for coming. This meeting will be brief; we all require time to make arrangements. There are rumors that General Jackson will impose a curfew; we need to also take that into consideration."

"So, what needs to be done, Marguerite, and how can we help?" asked one of her neighbors.

"First, we must form committees, Claudia." Marguerite glanced down at her notes. "We shall need to provide for the wounded, and we will have to find places to care for them. The Ursuline nuns have begun readying their classrooms with pallets to accommodate up to fifty men. Sister Angelique is supervising the proceedings there. She has requested additional women to aid in tending the patients."

"My friends and neighbors will be happy to help the good sisters," called out Catherine.

"Thank you, Madame Caresse," answered Marguerite, smiling. She continued, "Also, we had better prepare private homes in the city to provide for those who need care. There may be more patients than the convent can manage. Madame Peyroux, of Three Oaks plantation in Chalmette, has already volunteered. Can any of you also help out?"

Several Creole women immediately offered their houses for that purpose.

"Next, we must find a supply of linen to make bandages, and gather clothes and blankets for the wounded. Moss must be cut and hung to dry for stuffing pillows. We'll also need bed linens, soap, food, and practical supplies, such as bowls, tumblers, and kettles. Please also donate your panniers and chests in which we can store these items. Articles that can be reused must be picked up, washed, and dried in the sun or by fire, and then delivered according to need. I will be happy to coordinate our efforts, organize shifts, and distribute supplies."

She hesitated for a moment and then delicately addressed the large group of women wearing tignons. "Madame Caresse has offered to share her medical expertise with us. Is there also someone who can work with me in scheduling the volunteers from the Rue de Rampart area?"

"I will be happy to help you, Madame de Trahan," said Suzanne. The tignoned women nodded in agreement.

Catherine looked at her daughter with surprise. "That's a big job, Suzanne! Do you think that's wise, in your condition?" she whispered.

"I am fine, Maman," Suzanne said quietly. "I have a couple months till the baby arrives. Besides, I will feel closer to René if I am doing something important for the army, too."

"Thank you, mademoiselle!" said Marguerite. "Let's get started, then. Please form into convenient groups to figure out your next meeting place, what to bring, what you might need. Let me know your results."

The women began gathering into small huddles to figure out their next moves. While Suzanne organized nursing schedules for the free women of color, Marguerite wrote down the names of Creoles who were volunteering their houses for the wounded. The leaders of the different groups also handed Marguerite slips of paper listing names of volunteers, contributions they could supply, and needs they had.

Marguerite finished writing information about the last volunteered house and suddenly realized that the room had become very quiet. Peering out at the women, she found that their upturned faces were looking back at her, mirroring her own feelings of apprehension and anxiety, along with single-minded courage. They were all worried about their men: their sons and husbands, brothers and cousins, neighbors and friends. *Brave men*, she thought, *and brave women.*

Hoping to convey her feelings of pride, as well as conviction, she said, "I believe we have an excellent start. Madame Caresse and I will be meeting tomorrow to work out some details, and we will let you all know the particulars."

The women nodded, feeling both viable and united in their cause. Marguerite hesitated, looking down at her notes. "Finally, we need a volunteer to deliver some of these supplies to the men. You will be returning with the wounded. I don't need to tell you this is a dangerous—"

"I'll do that," called out an emphatic voice from the back.

The women all turned to see who had spoken. Marguerite was surprised to see that it was Suzanne's friend, the garish girl, still standing by herself.

"My name is Millie. I will drive a wagon. I can do this!"

"Why, thank you, Millie, and bravo!" said Marguerite.

Millie smiled; she was now surrounded by applause.

Tarot: THE HANGED MAN

Revelation: A voluntary offering for the purpose of gaining something of greater value.

⁓

December 3, 1814

Millie knew Peter was coming this night, and prepared her room to be as special as possible. She had purchased candles and perfumed soaps from Judah Touro's shop and selected an expensive wine from the most exclusive store on Royal Street. She also splurged on tomorrow's breakfast, buying his favorite, Baker's No. 1 premium chocolate, for hot cocoa to accompany fresh beignets. She propped the cake of chocolate against the vase of freshly picked crimson bottlebrush blooms and then spread fragrant sheets upon her bed. Finally satisfied with her preparations, she mulled over which of her skills Peter appreciated most, for she wanted him to be in the best of moods.

It worked. All of her efforts thoroughly enchanted him, and the rest of her scheme started to unfold.

"Pete, _mon amour?_ I have a request," she began with a whisper, nuzzling his ear. "I would like you to help me."

"Of course, Millie," he answered, savoring her little nibbles. "Anything for you. Tell me what I can do,"

"Well," she said, as she perched herself up on her elbow. Batting her eyelashes at him, Millie continued, "Remember how excited you were about joining General Jackson and fighting your former countrymen?"

Peter looked a bit dubious, but he nodded and said, "Yesss?"

"So, a lot of the city's women have organized to help gather necessities for General Jackson's army."

"Uh-huh," Peter said.

"But they need someone to help bring the supplies to the battlefield and then take the wounded back to the convent where the Ursuline sisters are setting up a hospital."

"Yes, that makes sense. And?"

"So I volunteered!" She said it quickly and then felt herself glowing with pride with her announcement.

"You *what*? You can't do that!" exclaimed Peter. He sat up in the bed, crossed his arms, and regarded her with dismay. "Millie! For one thing, you don't have a horse. And, by the way, you don't have a wagon, either. Not to mention that you wouldn't know how to drive one if you did."

"True," Millie responded. She had anticipated his reaction. She reached over to uncross his arms and hold his hands. "And that's the request. Can you get me a horse with a cart and teach me to drive it? Tomorrow? Come on, Pete—you know I can do it, and you promised to help me! Please?"

She squeezed his hands gently, began kneading his palms with her thumbs, and gave him her most pleading look.

Peter cocked his head, thought for a minute, and then answered reluctantly, "Oh, all right, Millie."

She threw her arms around him and smothered his face with kisses. "Thank you, Pete! I knew I could count on you!"

"I don't like this at all, but . . . meet me at Lafitte's blacksmith forge on Rue St. Philippe and Rue Bourbon at noon tomorrow. I'll see what I can do."

"Right. Lafitte's forge tomorrow at noon!"

"Oh! And I never thought I'd be saying this, Millie, but be sure to wear your trousers."

Jarot: TEMPERANCE

*Revelation: Good management and coordination
bring about a good relationship.*

⁓

December 4, 1814

As prearranged, Marguerite and Catherine met at Rose Zabette's coffee stand in front of the cathedral.

"I am so grateful to you for your help, Madame Caresse."

"Whatever assistance we can provide, Madame de Trahan, my friends and neighbors are committed to this effort."

"Please call me Marguerite; we will be colleagues, after all."

"And I am Catherine."

The two women sat down with their tiny cups of café au lait and pastries.

"We will be asking for donations of sheets, towels, blankets, and even petticoats, which can be cut into bandages," said Marguerite.

"Good," replied Catherine. "For the best results, please see that all contributions are washed in boiling water and dried in the sun, before storing them in panniers that have been cleaned with ammonia."

Marguerite raised her eyebrows questioningly but agreed. "All right," she said, and then she smiled. "And here is my list of the Creole women volunteers and their city homes. Each one has indicated what kinds of supplies she can provide, and those who are underlined will also be prepared to care for the wounded in their homes."

"Thank you," Catherine said, looking at the list. "I have a list of volunteers who have offered their services to nurse at the Ursuline convent. My daughter, Suzanne, is setting up a timetable."

"Excellent! I will alert Sister Angelique, who is supervising this project."

Catherine smiled. "I recognize the name; I believe she was one of Suzanne's instructors when she was attending the Ursuline school."

"Your daughter, she was a good student?"

"*Oui*, when she was interested in the subject."

Marguerite smiled. "We also must provide information for Millie, the young woman who volunteered to drive the wagon. She will need to know how many patients each place can accommodate, as well as which supplies should be distributed and where."

"Suzanne will be happy to figure it out; she has a good head for numbers and organization."

"Like her father," said Marguerite.

There was an uncomfortable pause, as both women looked down at the table.

"Yes, like Jacques," agreed Catherine.

"This is awkward; please forgive me. I did not know— Jacques has never mentioned his relationship to you or Suzanne."

Catherine smiled. "I'm not surprised," she said. "Please don't feel ill at ease about the past. Jacques and I were both young at the time, but we knew we weren't in love. We did enjoy each other's company, though, simply as good friends."

"Were you upset when he stopped seeing you?"

"I understood his reasoning; he didn't want the complications of two families. Life as a new husband and running the plantation by himself was difficult. But he fulfilled all of his *plaçage* obligations and, I might add, was generous in his provisions for us. Suzanne has been well educated, and I have always had enough money to develop my healing skills, as well as take care of our home. In fact, thanks partly to your husband, I have a nice bank account for myself!"

"Mother, businesswoman, knowledgeable in medicines and herbs . . . You are a remarkable woman, Catherine!"

"Thank you. I'm grateful to have been blessed in many ways."

Marguerite continued, "And I know that you have experience in caring for patients . . ." She paused. "Plus, I have also heard that you are a midwife!"

"Yes, I have delivered many of the babies of free women of color." Catherine looked around at the passersby. "They are my friends and neighbors. Now I'm even midwifing for their daughters."

"So I've heard—your reputation for successful birthing is well known."

Catherine cocked her head and asked, "Are you concerned about your baby's birth, Marguerite? You appear to be in very good health."

"I am. And I can feel the baby's movements. Which is good, right?"

Catherine nodded.

Marguerite continued, "I want so desperately to give Jacques a son. But my time is running out. I tried for years to become pregnant, but it just didn't happen. That's why I came to you for the black cohosh. Both times! But the doctor said that, given my age, this might be—in fact, he said it *should* be—my last pregnancy. And now, with this awful war going on . . ." Marguerite put her chin in her hands and slowly shook her head.

"Oh, you poor dear," said Catherine. "I'm sure everything will be all right. But I agree with your mother: You do need plenty of rest before the 'big day.' And try not to become stressed. I know that's a tall order, given the circumstances."

"True, but just doing my little part in coordinating our efforts takes my mind off other worries. I actually feel invigorated and productive. Buoyant, even."

"Wonderful! And perhaps the baby can feel your optimism and will come out smiling."

"Wouldn't that be something?" Marguerite laughed. She became serious again and gazed at her new friend with a slight frown.

"What is it, Marguerite? You seem anxious now."

The Creole didn't answer at first; she appeared to ponder her next words carefully. Finally, she said, "Catherine, would you deliver my baby?"

Catherine was shocked. "Marguerite, I don't think—"

Marguerite quickly continued. "Please. Except for organizing these lists, I have thought of little else. You see, my old physician passed away two months ago. And, as you know, most of the other doctors are tending to the troops. Now, my friends have told me that you've successfully delivered a number of their plantation slaves' babies. They say you have other competencies also."

Catherine raised her eyebrows. "Are you sure they were referring to my midwifing skills?"

"Well, yes." Marguerite, more relaxed, almost chuckled. "I have heard of your spiritualist abilities. But I have seen you at Mass, and I remember that you also suggested, when giving me the black cohosh, that I petition St. Anthony and St. Gerard for help. I believe in them, and I believe in you!"

"Yes, but—"

"So please, Catherine. I will be staying at my friend Claudia's city home on Rue de Louis, near to your residence. Our plantation is too far away and unsafe, with the British coming and all. I promise to get plenty of rest. You will be monitoring the patients at the convent, but when my time comes, I could go to your house. I know it's a huge inconvenience and an even bigger favor, but I would forever be in your debt. . . ."

"Hmm." Catherine looked at the Creole woman with sympathy, concern, and, to her own surprise, warmth. "You seem to have given this a great deal of consideration. And I agree it's a reasonable plan. Yes, I will be happy to midwife you, Marguerite."

The white woman reached out to clasp Catherine's hand. "Thank you, my friend. You have already erased much of the stress!"

Catherine smiled. "When your time comes and you arrive at my house, you will be with Hortense, my maid. She is quite experienced and has helped with deliveries many times. She will send for me, and then we'll welcome your son together."

Tarot: THE QUEEN OF PENTACLES

*Revelation: The emergence of a strong,
sensual woman who uses her talents well.*

———

Millie was excited. She was in the front of Lafitte's black-smith forge on Rue St. Philippe, looking around for Peter, hoping that he would not disappoint her. She knew he disapproved of her volunteering for several reasons, the risk factor being the most significant, and she found his concern for her very endearing. He was becoming quite special to her, and that idea, while unusual for her to feel, was not unpleasant.

Finally, she saw Peter approaching, leading a fine-looking sorrel mule.

"I'm pleased to see that you're wearing your trousers today, Millie. You'll find they're more convenient for what you're planning to do," he said. "This is old Bella. Now, just stroke her on her head—don't pat her. Good. She'll be better for you than a horse; she has more endurance, and, like a donkey, she's patient and sure-footed."

"Oh, Pete, thank you; she's fabulous! Hello there, beautiful Bella!" She ran her hand lightly over the mule's forehead.

"Because she's a mule, the troops won't want to ride her. But she's strong and can pull a loaded cart. She's not real fast, but you don't want to go too quickly anyway, because that aggravates the wounded."

"Well, she's perfect, just wonderful, and you're wonderful, too, Pete!" Millie beamed.

Peter blushed as he handed her Bella's reins. "All right, then. I'm glad you're happy. You can keep her in the stables on Rampart Street; I've already arranged it with Monsieur Lafitte. Now, I just have to teach you a few things, and you'll be on your way. The first is getting her harnessed up. It's important to adjust her straps and fittings correctly. Remember, you're always to be in control."

Peter found that Millie learned quickly, and after she had hitched Bella up to a wagon that he had gotten from Lafitte's storehouse, they both climbed in for her first driving lesson.

"You're doing well," he said, as they sat down. "Remember, most accidents occur when securing the harness to the cart, so be careful."

The mule bobbed its head up and down and gave a little whinny. Both Bella and Millie seemed eager to get started.

"Can we go now? Do I just say 'giddyap'?"

"Sure," he said, "and continue talking to her if you want."

Millie clucked to Bella and was delighted when the mule set off with a steady pace. "Good girl," she said.

"Bella is well trained," Peter said. "She won't have any problems crossing streams or traveling through woods or fields."

While Peter gave directions, Millie drove Bella around several blocks. And although he complimented her on the way she handled the mule, he also was firm when she made small errors, and insisted she repeat certain maneuvers. After an hour's ride, he suggested they head back to the stable. It was then he noticed that Millie had a huge grin on her face.

"What are you smiling at?" he asked.

"Do you see how pretty Bella's reddish-brown color is in this sunlight?" Millie said. "And I just think her rear end is so cute!

Look how rhythmic it is, swinging back and forth. I've never noticed that on a mule before."

"Uh-huh," said Peter. "I'm glad you're having fun. But I still don't like you doing this, Millie."

"I know, Pete. But I'll be careful. And, for once, I feel proud of what I'm doing."

"Just remember, the most important command is—"

"I know, I know," she interrupted. "It's 'Whoa!'"

Peter sincerely wished he could use that command on her.

Tarot: THE KING OF PENTACLES

Revelation: Acumen, character,
and courage can lead to success.

~

"Sit down, Edward, and tell me, do you think Andrew Jackson will be able to save New Orleans?"

"Yes, Mr. President. The general is an excellent commander of volunteer troops and appears to thrive when the odds are against him. He is shrewd and will not shrink from the British."

"Yes, so he's already demonstrated."

"There's quite a story about him as a boy, sir, one that explains his drive and determination. I first heard it from one of my Irish aunts, who used to be a traveler. And the general has been quite forthright in his account."

"What happened?"

"Jackson was a messenger boy for a South Carolina partisan unit in the Revolution. While he was staying at a farmstead, an Irish gypsy read his cards. He still remembers her predictions, which were rather frightening."

"What did she say?"

"She told him that the most important battle of his life would be influenced by foreign forces in a strange landscape where the trees had beards. It was supposed to be close to an old city in a new country. She said he would command men who wore the skins of animals, and others whose bodies were covered in ink;

151

many would not speak his language. And there were going to be three unusual but crucially valuable women, one of whom, a brown woman wearing a kerchief over her hair, would cure him. And then an outlaw would ensure his victory."

"Pretty gruesome for a boy to hear," said Madison. "So, he was a courier for our country. Did he personally experience any battles with the British?"

"Yes. Right after the tinkers left, British soldiers attacked the farmstead, looted the premises, and smashed whatever they couldn't take. Then the king's officer demanded that Jackson clean his boots. The boy stubbornly refused. The man unsheathed his saber and slashed at the youth's face. Although Jackson defensively threw up his left arm, the sword was quicker; his forehead and hand were both lacerated. He still bears the scars."

"I can understand why he hates them so."

"It gets worse. The assailants tore off the boy's shoes and then marched him forty miles through the miserable, rainy weather, without hat or coat, to the squalid Camden Prison Camp, where he contracted smallpox and almost died."

"But he didn't, and we're grateful for that," said Madison.

"Indeed," said the President's secretary. "But the trauma inflicted that stormy day intensified his hatred for the British. Someday, some way, he would get revenge. Because you know, sir, the cards don't lie."

"Ah," mused Madison, "if only we could see into the future ourselves, Edward. Getting back to General Jackson, though, I understand his wanting to retaliate; still, I do find him quite loud and opinionated."

"That's not a bad thing, sir. His troops have great faith in his battle skills and his concern for them. If he's victorious, he will be the only army hero of this war."

Tarot: THE THREE OF PENTACLES

*Revelation: Skill, mastery, and hard work
in art and labor.*

~

December 10, 1814

"I'll be right back, Scamp. I hear someone knocking on the front door. You work on these numbers, now."

"I could answer it, Madame Hortense!"

"No, you have your mathematics to do!"

"Awww . . ."

Hortense smiled to herself as she went toward the front parlor. *That boy,* she thought. *I just know he's peeking around the corner, trying to see who it is!*

She herself wondered if it might be someone in need of Catherine's midwife services. She hoped it would not be an emergency; Catherine had arrived home only a few hours earlier, after tending to a birth. Today, Hortense knew, her mistress had planned on helping Suzanne finalize the shifts for the free women of color volunteering at the convent/hospital. But Catherine needed sleep and Hortense was reluctant to awaken her. Until she opened the door.

A soldier, very dignified, stood at attention at the entrance.

"Good morning. Is this the home of the healer Madame Catherine Caresse?" he inquired.

"*Oui,*" Hortense replied nervously.

"My name is Corporal Rufus E. Madden, and Major General Andrew Jackson has instructed me to summon the presence of Madame Caresse at the general's headquarters. She is to come with me as soon as possible, and she should bring her medical bag."

"Yes, of course," said Hortense, now thoroughly alarmed. "Come in." She ushered him into one of the front rooms, in which a fire was flickering in the fireplace. "Please sit down while I get Madame Caresse for you." Then she called out, "Scamp, I know you're behind me! Why don't you get the corporal some coffee?"

"Thank you, Madame, but there is no time for that."

Having heard the commotion from her back room, Catherine was already awake. She was astonished by Hortense's announcement but quickly put on a simple cotton dress and twisted a tignon about her head, knotting it on top.

The soldier, upon seeing her enter the front room, rose and bowed slightly.

"Madame Caresse," he said.

She nodded and said, "Corporal Madden. Can you give me any details—perhaps about when I might expect to be home again?"

"Yes, madame," answered the corporal. "I will be taking you back around suppertime. Shall we be on our way?"

"*Oui!* And may I bring my young assistant?" She nodded to Scamp.

"Of course," Corporal Madden agreed. While Catherine put on her cloak, Scamp grabbed the medicine bag and dashed out the door.

Once outside, Catherine said, "I'll take the medicine bag now, Scamp." She smiled. "And it was so nice of you to hurry, which I'm sure Corporal Madden appreciates, but I'm also sure Madame Hortense will save those math problems for you to do after supper."

"I reckon so, Madame Catherine," the boy said, handing Catherine the medicine bag.

Corporal Madden offered Catherine his arm and escorted her the short distance to 106 Rue Royal. Catherine did not ask him any questions, nor did he volunteer any information. They both had somber expressions as they quickly walked toward Jackson's headquarters. Scamp, however, skipped along behind, delighted to be part of this extraordinary occasion.

Inside the building, Catherine broke the silence.

"Corporal Madden, why did General Jackson summon me?" she asked the soldier. "I know there are doctors in the military, as well as some older, retired ones in our city."

"Yes, one of our men is treating him now: Dr. Morell," said the soldier. He hesitated and then added, "But you have to understand that the general does not have a real high opinion of the so-called 'educated' man, and that includes doctors." He paused again, as if deciding whether to continue.

"And why would that be?" prodded Catherine.

"A year ago, back home in Tennessee, he was shot in the arm in a duel and bled profusely. Because they feared gangrene setting in, almost every doctor in Nashville wanted to amputate the arm, but General Jackson refused. And he did get better; a month later, he was commanding troops again."

"No wonder he's called Old Hickory," said Catherine.

"He's tough, all right, physically and mentally." The soldier continued, "But he distrusts wealthy, academic types. He is a self-made man: at the age of twenty, he got his license to practice law, moved west of the Alleghenies, and, not too long afterward, was made the US attorney general for the Tennessee territory. He became a judge and then served in both the House of Representatives and the Senate."

Corporal Madden took a breath and then continued, "Andrew

Jackson regards the common man as intelligent and capable." The soldier then smiled. "That's why he has such a devoted following."

"And Dr. Morell?" she asked.

"He seems to be a good doctor, and the hospital surgeon, Dr. David Kerr, who travels with the troops, agrees with Dr. Morell's diagnosis and recommendations. However, the general wants another opinion, and many of the local citizens recommend you highly. It seems that not only do you practice midwifery, but you can relieve symptoms of other conditions as well."

Catherine let that statement pass without commenting. Instead she asked, with a bit of incredulity, "And the general will listen to a female healer?"

"The general would listen to the devil himself if it would make him feel better."

Tarot: THE PAGE OF PENTACLES

Revelation: Reflection; knowledge;
respect for new concepts.

⁓

Catherine was surprised when Corporal Madden presented her to the general. As she had guessed, Andrew Jackson was tall, just over six feet, and extremely thin—actually frail-looking. She suspected he did not weigh more than 140 pounds. He wore his coat loosely on his narrow shoulders, probably to camouflage his spindly frame. Although he was only in his midforties, his face and neck were wrinkled like peach pits, and his reddish hair, which he combed back from his forehead, was turning gray. His famous steel-blue eyes were even more prominent in a pale complexion pitted with pockmarks, and a long, chalky scar ran from his forehead to his left cheek.

He stood up and, with a wan smile, said, "Welcome to my headquarters, Madame Caresse." He sat back down on the sofa immediately. She suspected he needed to conserve energy.

The general continued, "These are my aides, Colonel Robert Butler and Major John Reid. They will be happy to assist you with whatever you may need. I will meet with you and the doctor in about ten minutes."

"Yes, of course, General," replied Catherine.

She nodded to the men and then looked around at her surroundings. A number of Jackson's officers were gathered nearby at an end of the long table, bent over maps of the Gulf Coast region and arguing quietly.

Jackson listened intently to the opinions, nodding his head. Then he said, "Men, we are fortunate to have Major Latour's maps and charts. For instance, I did not realize the river runs in a long east-and-west loop here at the city. I suspect that the British will be coming at us from Lake Pontchartrain to the north or from the east along the river. So we must plan accordingly."

The general took a deep breath, and it was very apparent to Catherine that he was suffering.

Corporal Madden led Catherine over to the other end of the table, where an older, somewhat portly gentleman was by himself, leafing through some documents. He looked up as they approached and had an obvious scowl on his face.

"Who's this, Madden? The slave to scrub the dishes in the scullery? You know she doesn't belong in here!"

Catherine bristled. How dare he!

Rufus Madden didn't miss a beat. "Madame Caresse, may I introduce Dr. Morell. He has been caring for the general for the past few days. And, Dr. Morell, the general himself has summoned Madame Caresse, the well-known New Orleans healer, to assist you in your duties."

"Harumph," sputtered Dr. Morell. "Yes, so *you* are the renowned Madame Caresse. I have heard something about your, ahem, skills."

Again, Catherine decided not to ask him to elaborate on which abilities he referred to.

The physician continued, still grimacing, "Do come with me to somewhere we can discuss the general's health without distracting everyone else."

He ushered her to an unoccupied room and said, "Here, we won't be disturbed either! I expect the general to join us shortly."

"So he said, Doctor," she replied.

He seemed to be studying her. "You may find our topic somewhat embarrassing to ladies." Then he said, obviously dubious, "Tell me: Have you had much experience in treating dysentery?"

"Yes, I have," she said evenly, meeting his gaze without hesitation. "I suspect my patients have gotten it from drinking stagnant water or eating contaminated food. New Orleans has plenty of both."

"Indeed," said Dr. Morell. "Hmm. I've also noticed that many of our troops seem to come down with flux when they've slept outside in wet weather."

"I presume General Jackson has done a lot of that," she responded.

"Yes, well"—he continued to look at her with distrust—"dysentery is known as the Soldier's Disease, and the general has it. Whatever the cause, you can be sure that I have been giving him the best professional treatment possible. I studied at the Harvard School of Medicine, after all. I don't know why he would have misgivings about my procedures and, of all things, send for a 'healer,' an unknown woman—"

At that moment, Andrew Jackson strode into the room. "Ah, I see you two have met!" he said.

Dr. Morell did not respond, so Catherine replied, "Yes, we have, General. Now, I do have a few questions to ask, if you don't mind?"

"Certainly, Madame Caresse. That's why you're here."

Dr. Morell gave a snort of disgust, which Catherine ignored.

"Do you have abdominal cramps and bloody stools?" she asked.

"Yes, along with pus and mucus," the general replied.

"Uh-huh. And how have you been treating him?" she asked the doctor.

Dr. Morell straightened up and announced disdainfully, "The general eats a bowl of grits and some toast in the morning, then has a little rice later on, along with brandy."

"Ah, the brandy is the best part—quite fortifying!" the general said, chuckling.

"And just what would you recommend, Madame Caresse?" Doctor Morell asked skeptically.

Instead of replying directly to the doctor, Catherine addressed Jackson. "You need lots of fluids, General, but let's not make it all brandy."

Andrew Jackson actually roared with laughter at that.

"Ah! A sense of humor! How refreshing—don't you agree, Dr. Morell?"

Dr. Morell just scowled.

Catherine continued, "I'd like to start you on some teas. Chamomile is good, and I also have some peppermint oil in my bag. We can mix in some powdered-wood charcoal. I have found that to be very effective. Plus, we will add lemon juice to boiled water."

"And for my food? Something tastier than grits and rice?"

"I will add garlic to your diet, although I don't think that's what you had in mind."

"Hmm, no—not what I was hoping for. Anything else?"

"Yes, General. You will get some relief by sitting in about three inches of cold water for five minutes. I highly recommend it."

"I don't think that's going to happen, Madame Caresse," said the general, with an amused expression, "but the rest of your remedies are very doable. All right, then—I'm sure the good doctor here will be happy to help you any way he can. Isn't that right, Morell?"

The "good doctor" grunted.

"Again, Madame Caresse, welcome to my headquarters."

And Andrew Jackson, with a grin on his face, strode out the door, into the other room.

Catherine looked at Dr. Morell. He looked at her. Silence. Finally, the physician shrugged his shoulders in resignation.

"All right, Madame Caresse. Whatever it takes to make General Jackson well again. He doesn't complain, but you can see that it's taking its toll on his body. He's lost weight, and although he's fatigued, he seldom sleeps. Instead, he's quite restless and keeps going by sheer willpower and a lot of stubbornness."

"Yes, that's obvious." Then she smiled, attempting to placate the doctor. "But I'm certain that if we both stress the bland diet you prescribed, increase his fluid intake, and try to persuade him to rest, our efforts will be successful."

Dr. Morell's reaction startled her—he was actually giggling!

"I beg your pardon, Madame Caresse, but the notion of General Jackson sitting in three inches of cold water for five minutes is most preposterous!"

She laughed, too. "Yes, I guess that was too much to ask for. But he *would* find it soothing!"

Catherine called out to her young servant, hovering in the corner. Scamp jumped up and ran over, eager to become involved.

"All right, Scamp," she said. "You are to take care of General Jackson's waste. No one else is to use the same chamber pot. Ask the soldiers where the latrine pit is and dump it there. Don't just throw it out the window! Then I want you to scrub it thoroughly each time, with soap and hot water."

The boy rolled his eyes. "*Oui,* madame," he said.

"Also, I want you to notice if the contents of the pot change. Pay attention to the color and smell, and whether there is any blood in the stools. You are to tell Dr. Morell or me if the feces are different. Do you have any questions?"

Scamp had wrinkled his nose as she was giving the directions, but he shook his head negatively.

"No, madame. Just like I did for Messieurs Dubois and Fournier. They had dysentery, too!"

"Good." She smiled and patted him on the head. "Make sure you wash your hands thoroughly with soap and water afterward. Now, stay out of everyone's way, but keep me informed!"

After Scamp darted out of the room, Dr. Morell cleared his throat. "I'm curious, Madame Caresse . . ."

"Yes?" Her eyebrows rose.

"Regarding your concern about matters of cleanliness," he said—rather politely, she thought.

"Midwives are trained to clean their hands and their instruments thoroughly before birthing a baby," Catherine informed him. "That is my standard procedure when treating other patients as well."

The physician nodded, so Catherine continued. "I also heard from one of my clients that Napoleon, too, was fastidious when it came to his own hygiene and demanded that French hospitals keep the patients neat, warm, and clean. The patients seemed to do well."

"Why, yes," exclaimed Dr. Morell. "Our army's surgeon general, Dr. James Tilton, was very impressed by the French system and most appalled by the lack of cleanliness in our American hospitals."

"Well," said Catherine, "good sanitation obviously eliminates some filth and odors, so I can't see how it hurts."

"Interesting," replied Dr. Morell, almost grudgingly. "I do apologize, Madame Caresse, for having doubted your abilities, and I look forward to working with you to improve the general's health."

Tarot: THE FIVE OF SWORDS

Revelation: A threat is possible.

~~

December 12, 1814

Andrew Jackson expected the British to strike New Orleans by marching overland from Lake Pontchartrain, to the north, up the river from the gulf, or to Lake Borgne, just southeast of Lake Pontchartrain.

The lake approaches did not seem likely, though. First, the entire British army would have to be rowed in small boats across the miles of hazardous open water, as the lakes were only six to twelve feet deep and filled with sand bars—impossible for the English fleet, with its heavy cannon. Then they would have to be further transported to the city through bayous, streams, and canals.

Nonetheless, Naval Lieutenant Thomas ap Catesby Jones, who commanded two hundred seamen in five small gunboats, was assigned to guard the entrance to Lake Borgne and report on any sightings of the British. Jackson also ordered that all of the marshy outlets that connected the lake with the city be blocked with felled trees.

It was with some surprise then, that Naval Lieutenant Jones's flotilla spotted the fleet of British warships on December 12. Word was sent to Jackson that the British fleet had appeared. Jones was ordered to observe their movements from a safe distance. For two days, the Americans watched as the British armada passed the Chandeleur Islands, as well as the Dog and Ship Islands, and finally anchored near the mouth of Lake Borgne.

General Jackson, however, was not concerned; he suspected it was merely a ruse. He still concentrated his meager forces in approaches from the north and east.

Tarot: THE EIGHT OF WANDS

Revelation: Hope, love, and action.

⁓

Millie had never been invited to someone's home. Yet Madame Bonet had urged that they meet at her cottage. Perhaps it was because she was pregnant and therefore it was easier than traveling to the convent, but still! And Madame Bonet—Suzanne—also insisted that they be on a first-name basis. Like friends! Millie had never really had a friend. . . .

Walking along, Millie took great pleasure in observing and savoring the neighborhood's details. Rue de Rampart was lined with wood and stucco cottages, richly painted in maroons, greens, royal blue, and mustard yellows.

She walked up the steps and onto the porch. The overhang not only sheltered her from the slight mist but also made her feel insulated from her usual world. She hesitated at the entry door and then knocked lightly, worried that it would not be answered.

The door swung open, and Suzanne greeted her with a big smile. "Hello, Millie! I'm so glad you could come. Let's sit in the dining room. My servant Hazel is getting us some refreshments."

Millie suddenly felt shy—a unique experience for her. She held out a bouquet of anise and lavender. "These are for you, Suzanne. They help to combat the bugs. Not that you have any, of course!" She flushed with embarrassment.

Suzanne laughed. "We all have bugs, Millie! What with

165

keeping the front and back galleries open for cross-ventilation, there's no way around it. At least there aren't so many in December as in the summer!"

She held the flower bunch up to her nose. "I love their perfume! I'll have Hazel scatter these around the house. Thank you so much!"

Millie was noticing the home's layout. It had two equal-size rooms in the front and two in the back. The front and back shutters were unfastened, their openings providing cool breezes throughout the house.

How different from Millie's stifling space in her mother's "house." The first item one noticed when entering Millie's room was the bed, opposite the doorway. There was a window over the bed, but she couldn't open it, because of inside bars that prevented anyone's entering or leaving. A tub was by the small fireplace on another side of the little room, along with a small table and two chairs. The fourth wall held a large mirror. That was also where she placed her trunk, which held her clothing, linens, and utensils. The accommodations were just large enough for eating, sleeping, bathing, and, of course, business. No, Millie thought, she would never be able to reciprocate with an invitation to her abode.

Millie's thoughts returned to the present as Suzanne led her toward the back of the house, saying, "And we do grow the citrus trees and roses outside in the back to help overpower the odor on the street, but the insects are constant. My *maman* believes that they can actually make you sick. She's quite rigorous about keeping everything clean."

Now in the dining room, Millie noticed a cookpot hanging over charcoal in the fireplace.

"Mmm. Something smells delicious," said Millie.

"It's my version of jambalaya. Hazel and I made it out back

in the kitchen. I'm just keeping it warm now. My husband, René, loves it. So do I, of course. I'm taking some over to my *maman*'s after our meeting. Would you like some to take home with you?"

Millie was flabbergasted. "Why, I-I-I . . . ," she stuttered.

"It's settled, then. I'll have Hazel put some into a small pot for you."

"Well, thank you," Millie said. "That's very generous of you."

"I should be thanking you!" answered Suzanne. "You are so brave to be going to the battlefield! I admire you so much."

"Well, I just want to help. And, honestly, there isn't much else I can do!" said Millie.

"We're all doing what we can, Millie."

Hazel entered the dining room with a tray of cookies and a pot of coffee. Suzanne waited until the servant left.

"Maman's upset because I'm organizing the scheduling. She's afraid that it will be too strenuous at this time." Suzanne patted the slight bulge around her waistline.

"When is the baby due?" asked Millie.

"I have another couple of months to go, and I'm healthy as a . . ."

"Mule?" suggested Millie. Then she laughed. "Sorry, that just popped into my head. I just met the mule that I'll be driving to the battlefield. Her name is Bella, and she's in extremely good shape."

Suzanne laughed, too. "All right, mule it is—although I don't think mules can get pregnant. Anyway, I have lots of energy and a good head for planning. Plus, in my own way, I'll be doing as much as I can to keep my René safe."

"It sounds like you love him very much," said Millie.

"Yes, I do. I never knew anyone like him; he's opened up a whole new world to me. Do you have anyone special in your life?"

"I believe I do, Suzanne," Millie said, thinking of Peter. "And he's done the same for me: opened up a new world, a fresh way of thinking. Oh, my!"

"You're blushing, Millie," said Suzanne. "You must tell me about him the next time we meet. But right now we need to get down to this all-important venture of ours."

She drew some papers toward her; they were neatly organized, showing columns and rows. Some listed names, shifts, duties, and places, while others had inventories for equipment and medical supplies to be recorded.

"It's just a guideline for now," said Suzanne, "easy to change if necessary. But it's a start. And here's your section—what to fill in, where to go, et cetera. Does it make sense to you?"

"Yes, this looks very thorough to me," said Millie, studying the list. "You do have a good head for details."

"I enjoyed organizing it—it helps to make the time go more quickly until my husband comes home. So, you think this will work?"

"Yes, thanks to your organizational skills, Bella and I will be ready to help win this battle."

"Good! It's too bad that René isn't home right now, so I can't introduce you to him yet. But let's go over to my mother's house with the jambalaya. You'll meet Miguel, her husband. Unfortunately, Mother is not home now, either; she's actually at General Jackson's headquarters."

"Oh, my! Why?"

"My *maman* has very special nursing skills. She's a midwife, and she also knows a lot about the curing properties of herbs. She makes medicines to heal many different ailments." She continued, "General Jackson has a recurring case of dysentery, and my mother was summoned to restore his health."

"Do you have those same doctoring skills?" asked Millie.

"No, I help her sometimes, but haven't inherited her particular gifts. We are alike in many other ways: we're both organized, good listeners, and, I have to add, stubborn!"

"You are fortunate to have such a wonderful mother, Suzanne." Millie smiled wistfully.

But, not wanting Suzanne to pity her or, even worse, ask about her own maternal line, Millie threw back her shoulders and managed a look of determination. "Well, we had better win this war, then, before your baby shows up!" she said.

"Absolutely. The sooner, the better, because René and I have so many other things planned!"

Suzanne gathered up her papers and handed Millie her duties. Just then, her servant came in bearing two containers. "Ah! Here's Hazel with the jambalaya. Let's go!"

Tarot: THE SEVEN OF SWORDS

Revelation: Precarious effort; partial success.

~

December 14, 1814

The safe distance General Jackson had prescribed wasn't safe enough, for, unfortunately, the British had also detected the presence of the American gunboats.

Through his spyglass, Lieutenant Jones could see a squadron of almost fifty barges entering Lake Borgne. As the British rowed closer, the Americans noted small cannons mounted on the bow of each barge. The Americans also became aware that these barges were filled with heavily armed British seamen and were heading directly toward them.

Ideally, Jones would move his flotilla westward into the lake and then north, drawing the enemy into the Rigolets, a shallow strait that connected Lake Borgne to Lake Pontchartrain. There, the guns of Fort Petite Coquille could support them. But Lieutenant Jones's boats were dependent on wind. There wasn't any. Not even tossing unnecessary items overboard helped their situation. His dismayed seamen watched as the British barges continued rowing straight at them.

The Americans courageously did their best against enormous odds. But after two hours of artillery fire, cannon smoke, barges smashing into gunboats, and hand-to-hand combat, the battle ended with the American gunboats captured or destroyed, ten men killed, thirty-five wounded, and most of the others taken prisoner.

Rather than trying to negotiate the zigzag channel of the Mississippi, the British had gained a shorter, direct route to New Orleans. The answer to where the British had planned the location of the invasion was obvious. Now, the question was when.

But Lieutenant Thomas ap Catesby Jones had delayed them.

Tarot: THE KNIGHT OF WANDS

Revelation: Conflict and departure.

~

December 16, 1814

Corporal Madden arrived to escort Catherine to Jackson's headquarters. As usual, she was ready, and she immediately began plying him with questions.

"Is it true?" she asked, as she grabbed her medicine bag. "The British have landed and are soon going to march on New Orleans? The whole city is in shock!"

"Yes, they've landed. But General Jackson has everything under control," he assured her. "However, right now we have new circumstances for you."

"Oh?"

"Dr. Morell and a navy purser have gone to the British fleet. Their mission was to care for the wounds of American captives from the gunboat battle. We have just received word that our injured are being treated well but the British will not allow the doctor to return. He himself is being held prisoner on the HMS *Gorgon.*"

"Oh, poor Dr. Morell. I'm so sorry! So . . ."

"What that means, Madame Caresse, is that we're depending upon you to cure the general."

Tarot: THE TWO OF PENTACLES

Revelation: Risk taking and stamina may lead to rewards.

———

December 18, 1814

Two men traveled across Lake Borgne and arrived at a fishermen's village located at the mouth of Bayou Bienvenue. They were Lieutenant John Peddie and Captain Robert Spencer, officers of the British army and navy, respectively. These men typically wore red, which would have attracted negative attention from anyone sympathetic to the American cause. Now, however, thanks to obliging Spanish fishermen, they dressed in the regional attire of blue shirts and dark, coarse canvas trousers.

The British spies negotiated with a couple of the fishermen to guide them to a plantation along the edge of the Mississippi. Their mission: to plan the best clandestine approach inland for two thousand troops to move from their ships, now anchored at Pea Island in Lake Borgne. Their goal: to establish a base camp and prepare for a quick surprise invasion and seizure of the city of New Orleans.

"What do you think?" asked Peddie quietly, as they floated in the pirogue down Bayou Bienvenue. "It's pretty shallow here, I'd say maybe only six feet deep and one hundred yards wide. Do you think we can move our men through this bayou?"

"It's not ideal," answered Spencer. "I'm not liking the dankness of the swamp."

"And don't forget all the wildlife," added Peddie, as another alligator lying on a log slowly turned its head to observe the pirogue gliding by. "But the bayou is navigable and this eastern route is not protected. According to our guides, all the other bayous have felled trees blocking any approaches."

"Yes," said Spencer, brushing a spider off his shoulder. "The Americans probably expect us to attack them by land from the north. But I think General Keane will agree that this unobstructed bayou is the best way to go."

The Spanish fishermen continued rowing the British scouts most of the way down Bayou Bienvenue and then punted with long poles through the much shallower Bayou Mazant. They reached the canal of the Villeré plantation, less than ten miles below New Orleans. The Englishmen noted the firm footing afforded by the roads running along the canal's banks.

"This is ideal for us," said Peddie. "The levee protects the area from the river. We can ferry the troops across Lake Borgne to the mouth of Bayou Bienvenue—that's about thirty miles—and then they can row another six miles to Bayou Mazant."

"You're right," agreed Spencer. "Once they reach the path onshore, though, that will take them to the Mississippi, and then it's onward to New Orleans."

The two men stepped out of the pirogue and continued their exploration of the cultivated area on foot. They spied on the main big house, along with the smaller cabins, outbuildings, pigsties, and poultry yards.

Spencer nodded enthusiastically to Peddie. "I think we've just found our new camp," he whispered. "Beauty and booty!"

Tarot: THE STAR

Revelation: Hope, significance, and encouragement.

⁓

Under the laws of Louisiana, Sundays and holy days were days of rest for all residents. So, on Sundays, although required to attend Mass at the Catholic church, slaves were afterward free to move about the city as they pleased.

Some chose to hire themselves out for the day, because under the laws they were allowed to keep their savings. Middle-class whites and free people of color who did not own slaves but needed help with laundry, house cleaning, or maintenance were grateful for this source of labor, even if it was available only on Sundays. It was not unusual for a slave who chose to work on these days to save enough to buy his or her freedom. Many masters were amenable to such a transaction, as it allowed them to free a middle-aged slave and purchase a younger one.

Most slaves, though, chose to attend the weekly Sunday afternoon celebration in Place Congo.

And Sunday, December 18, one week before Christmas, was no different.

Several hundred black people, both free and slaves, gathered on the old parade ground located west of Rampart Street. Here, they anticipated participating in sensual dances that provided a sense of solidarity, as well as honoring and preserving their traditional African culture.

While awaiting the arrival of their queen, friends, family, and neighbors exchanged greetings and gossip at the provisional market or in small clusters throughout the grounds. Included in everyone's discussions that day was speculation about the imminent British invasion. Once the ritual began, they would pray to their *loas* for the protection and safety of New Orleans. Most had already implored various Catholic saints at Mass in St. Louis Cathedral; now it was time to include their voodoo counterparts.

Hush.

Soundlessly, the crowd gathered into a unified oneness, a large spiral, each individual facing its center, expectant, reverent, and somber, knowing their queen had arrived.

The majestic-looking spiritual leader seemed to flow through her people as she silently proceeded to their nucleus, solemnly cradling the body of a sizable snake, as if presenting an offering. The queen's large, almond-shaped cobalt eyes calmly acknowledged her people as she passed; her sensuous, blood-red lips were upturned. Her constituents bowed their heads.

As a free and affluent black, the queen wore a lustrous ivory silk tignon that set off her polished ebony face and enveloped most of her gleaming dark hair. Her large gold earrings and bracelets glistened in the sunlight, and, like her female congregants, she had on a loose dress. This garment made it practical for the ceremony's twisting, turning, and twirling movements. It, too, was a creamy white and was embellished with ribbons, shells, and little bells, which jingled when she moved.

A small gathering of spectators was assembled on one side of the square. Some of the Creole women had on the newer-fashioned high-waisted, empire-silhouette chemises. Others had tightly laced themselves into corsets that, although uncomfortable, displayed their waistlines. All wore petticoats decorated with ruffles or lace; these could be seen when the outer gowns were lifted.

These women and their male companions did not intend to participate in this ritual. In fact, just a few months ago, they would have complained about the loud music and what they considered lewd dances and songs. Today, though, was different. Today, they recognized a singleness of purpose: blacks and whites, in their own ways, were praying for safety and protection. General Jackson was demanding unity; their survival depended upon it.

On the opposite side of the square, a black man squatted and held his single-headed drum between his knees. Another sat astride his percussion instrument, hunched, ready to slap his palms and fingers on its drumhead.

The queen came to a standstill. Soundless seconds passed. She elevated the snake and slowly raised her face toward the sky. More silent seconds. Suddenly, her head dropped down. The drums and rattles commenced, setting the women to trilling a single tone, which gained momentum.

At first, the queen's feet and shoulders did not move but every other part of her body does. Then, as the blending of exuberant energy reached a crescendo, a spirit took control of her body. She swirled forward with extraordinary speed and agility. Her followers joined in the sacred dance. Her snake, symbolizing rebirth, the interconnection between heaven and earth, seemed to smile, swinging and swaying with the queen's tempo.

With rhythmic chants, the congregation whirled about in a circle, following their spiritual leader, gyrating with passion. The singing, dancing, and drumming continued, until the queen was certain that all invocations to the deities were made, all petitions were addressed, and appropriate animal sacrificial offerings were proffered.

Quiet again.

The ceremony concluded solemnly, and all of the people departed, trusting in a greater strength.

Whether that strength was the queen, a *loa*, the Christian God, or even General Jackson, faith and hope were abundant.

Tarot: THE TOWER

Revelation: Conflict; reaching the boiling point.

~

It was a crisp, lovely morning, and since Corporal Madden was not expected for another hour, Catherine and Suzanne were relaxing in the dining room, having coffee and beignets.

"How are you feeling, Suzanne? Perhaps you should rest more, stay home, not go to the convent so frequently."

"I'm fine, Maman. And I look forward to those trips. I feel like I'm contributing to the cause, especially since René's so busy with his training."

"And have you and Sister Angelique worked out satisfactory work assignments?"

"For now. But we know it's all subject to change, as Madame de Trahan keeps reminding us. That woman really gets on my nerves."

"Madame de Trahan?"

"*Oui.* She makes me feel strange. She's not threatening or anything, but when she thinks I'm not looking, I know she's staring at me."

"Probably because she's older than you and is amazed that you're so young and capable."

"I'm sure that's not the case; she just never smiles and seems to always be ready to say something to me. . . ."

"I have not noticed her staring at you or anyone. But perhaps

179

she's not accustomed to chatting with younger women—just with older females, like me," Catherine said lightly.

Her daughter scowled at her. "That's probably because every time you're around her, you just seem to fawn over her! Is it because she's a Creole aristocrat and her husband's a wealthy plantation owner with scores of black slaves?"

Catherine took a few moments before answering. She wanted to appease her daughter without revealing past history, but Suzanne was making this difficult. Finally, she said, "I admire her, Suzanne, for taking on this job, especially in her condition."

Suzanne was not mollified. "Well, how about me? And *my* condition?" she said petulantly.

"You know I'm very proud of you, Suzanne. And you also know that I'm quite vigilant in watching over you, especially in your condition! But Madame de Trahan is older than you and farther along in her pregnancy. Plus, I've agreed to help her when the time comes; that is why I am attentive to her."

"Well, I still think there's something odd about her watching me all the time; Millie's noticed it, too."

"Um, yes. About Millie . . ."

"What about her?"

"Well, I simply don't think you should be a friend to a woman like that."

"A woman like what, Maman?" Suzanne glared at Catherine, as if daring her to say something.

The look on Catherine's face should have made words unnecessary, but Suzanne was feeling contentious and repeated, "A woman like *what*? One who volunteers to risk her life to take supplies to our troops?" Her voice grew louder as she leaned across the table.

"Yes, well . . ."

"A woman who will transport our injured back to the convent

to be cared for?" And louder yet: "Just maybe one of them will be Miguel or René! Have you thought of that?" By now Suzanne could surely be heard in the street. "And you don't think I should be her friend?"

Suzanne sank back into her chair and glowered at her mother. "I am honored to have her friendship!"

"Suzanne, dear, I don't want to quarrel. But your friend Millie is a prostitute; she lives in a bordello!"

"I know that, Maman!" Suzanne thought a moment and smirked. "But she's a white prostitute. You should be pleased about that."

Controlling her temper, Catherine responded, "A harlot's a harlot, even if she's the Queen of England."

"Millie can't help it, Maman. She doesn't want to, um, 'do it.' But it's either that or starve. And you have to admit that she's brave, Maman, and she's also intelligent and considerate!" Suzanne paused a moment and then added, "Besides, René likes her, too, and so does Miguel!"

"Of course they do!" Catherine smirked. "They're men. She's young and alluring in that *fille de joie* way of hers, and . . . and . . ."

"Maman!"

Catherine stopped. She had lost her composure, and she struggled to calm herself.

"I'm sorry, Suzanne. That was wrong of me to say. Let's both try to be tolerant of each other's associates. Agreed?"

Suzanne just nodded grimly, got up, and stalked out of her mother's house.

Tarot: THE EIGHT OF WANDS

Revelation: Haste, hope, and movement toward a goal.

~

December 21, 1814

Millie smiled as she recognized Peter's gait coming up the steps quite quickly. Preparing herself in a welcoming (and captivating) manner on the bed, she was stunned when he barged through the door, flushed and breathless with news.

"Millie! It's happening! Jackson accepted Lafitte's offer! We're going to fight the English!"

"Finally!" said Millie, patting the space she'd created for him next to her on the bed. "What made him change his mind?"

Peter did not take her hint. Still standing just inside her door, he continued his report animatedly. "Well, Jackson knows that his chances are thin without our help; he needs every man he can get. And we Baratarians have the cannons and the skilled artillerymen. But, most important, Jackson does not have enough flints for his volunteers' muskets, and we have barrels of them."

Millie noticed that Peter no longer considered himself English; he was absolutely Baratarian. A British Baratarian pirate. Quite an identity!

Peter went on, "Our skill with artillery is much greater than the Redcoats'. In other words, we have the will and the power to help. Jean Lafitte is with General Jackson right now at Pierre

Maspero's coffee house on Chartres Street. They're planning a strategy to beat those Redcoats. Isn't that fantastic?"

Then he stopped, seemed to really see her for the first time, and said, in a softer tone, "Gosh, Millie, you look beautiful."

"Thank you, Pete! Why don't you join me?" She gave him a wink and patted the vacant spot on the sheets again.

Peter hesitated, then walked over to the bed and bent down to give her a tender kiss on her cheek. "Love to, Millie, but I can't stay. I'm to meet with Dominique Yu; we need to collect and deliver the weapons and ammunition to General Jackson. I'm off to fight the war!" And with that, he dashed out her door and down the stairs.

Tarot: THE PAGE OF PENTACLES

Revelation: Gathering energy and respect for new ideas to fulfill needs.

→

Corporal Madden was ready to walk Catherine home after a long day.

"Come on, Scamp!" she called out. The boy reluctantly left one of the soldiers, who had been teaching him a card game, and slowly trailed his mistress and her escort.

Corporal Madden observed, "You seem to be fond of the boy."

"Yes, I am," replied Catherine. "He's been with me a little over a year now. When I purchased him, I learned that he had just been orphaned. His parents both died, probably from dysentery or cholera, when being transported across the Atlantic. Poor lad. He actually witnessed their bodies being tossed overboard. He had some horrible nightmares about the crossing."

"I can't imagine." The corporal shook his head. "Does he talk about the other details?"

"Not anymore. And his nightmares have ceased. But when he joined us, he was terrorized and confused and, of course, grief-stricken by the death of his parents. He did describe, after his capture, being crammed into a windowless and airless dungeon on Africa's coast until he was sold to a European company. That's probably where his parents became ill."

"And the trip over here?"

"He estimates that it took about ten weeks. And he remembers women shrieking, and the groans of the dying, as well as the overpowering stink of sickness."

"Terrible thing for a boy to go through."

"*Oui*. But he's plucky, and I have found him to be cheerful, as well as a good worker. He learns quickly, and I am training him in the art of healing. Like my maid, Hortense, he will be able to support himself when I give him his freedom."

"Oh? As a healer?"

"That's my hope! Some time ago, there was a slave named James Derham, owned over time by three different doctors in Philadelphia. Then he was sold to Dr. Robert Love, a surgeon here in New Orleans, who needed an assistant. James learned from all of his doctor owners. He was able to purchase his freedom and practiced medicine here for both white and Negro patients."

"Is he still alive and practicing?"

"Unfortunately, after you Yankees purchased Louisiana, because he had not attended medical school, he was not allowed to continue his practice and left the city. My dream is for Scamp to succeed in Dr. Derham's place."

"Scamp is very fortunate to have you as a mentor. I think you're a wizard, Madame Caresse! I have already seen the general's health improve, and I believe it is due to your healing skills." The corporal looked at Catherine with admiration.

"I am happy to be of service, Corporal Madden!"

As they walked past the cathedral, he commented, "Other situations seem to be improving also."

"Oh? What are you referring to, Corporal?"

"The good citizens of New Orleans seem to be a little more accepting of us Yankees these days."

Catherine chuckled and said, "You're right! We're fortunate to be part of the United States. If we had remained part of France, we would, with Napoleon's defeat, have become an English colony, like Canada—and I would not be allowed to practice my profession, or, even if I was a man, allowed to vote."

"I couldn't agree more! That's what our War of Independence was all about! Yet, although we all have the same goals, I still detect some aloofness toward the Yankees. Why?"

Catherine thought a moment. She did not want to offend the soldier, yet to deny that there were differences would be to insult his intelligence.

She took a deep breath and said, "When the Yankees first arrived in New Orleans, it appeared to us that they were, um . . . well, they acted like conquerors. They were impatient, and their manners were atrocious. We called them the quick-walking and talking Yankees."

"Most of that is true," Corporal Madden said, with a broad smile. "On the other hand, we were told that all you people are haughty and indolent and that you're only interested in dancing and fencing; plus, you don't speak English!"

"And very few of the Yankees could speak French, and fewer tried to learn. We, however, were expected to know their language and were treated with suspicion when we spoke French in their presence. Now we are becoming bilingual, mostly out of necessity!"

"Yes," agreed Rufus, "a good example is Mr. Jean Lafitte. I've heard that he speaks four languages."

"Indeed, he does have his admirable qualities," agreed Catherine.

"Oh? I really don't know much about him—just that he has a reputation of being quite a, um, rascal, shall we say?"

"Rascal—*oui*! But also an astute businessman, as well as generous to his 'employees.' If a Baratarian loses an arm or leg,

Lafitte will give him extra money. If the pirate—or, should I say, privateer—is killed, his family receives financial help."

"Very commendable. And smart, too!"

"*Oui,* Lafitte's men are as devoted to him as yours are to General Jackson."

"And now the privateers are considered heroes"—the corporal smiled—"along with our backcountry volunteers."

"*Oui!*"

"So tell me, what are some other Yankee traits that set us apart from you? And are we fitting in a little bit more since we got here?"

"Hmm, well, I must say that the volunteers from Tennessee and Kentucky are now much more at ease with us, and polite," she said.

"Uh-huh!" said Rufus. "That's good. But can you explain?"

"Well, like you said, your soldiers are a disparate group," agreed Catherine, nodding her head. "When your people came," she continued, "some of their behaviors shocked us."

"Like what?"

"They bathe in the Mississippi without any clothes on! We find this very upsetting."

"They are bathing, after all," the corporal responded. "Really, Madame Caresse, aren't you normally naked when you take baths?" He looked at her with a playful smile.

"Correct," said Catherine, taking his mischievousness in stride. "But we find it more suitable to bathe in private. The same goes for relieving oneself in public; that, too, is not acceptable!"

"Hmm, yes; our officers have gotten quite a few complaints about that. I'm afraid that many of our men are from rural places, where the social graces are quite different from yours. But they have been ordered to be more selective when choosing a relief station."

Catherine tried not to sound sarcastic as she responded, "That is good news indeed!"

They had reached her cottage. Corporal Madden turned to face the woman and smiled. "I now understand, gentle lady, why you would think that our men are a bit wild, but when it comes to this battle for your homeland, they're here for you!"

"And we are grateful to them, Corporal Madden." She smiled back at him. "I did not wish to offend you. We are very happy to have Yankee Doodle come to our town!"

Tarot: THE TOWER

Revelation: Danger; unforeseen catastrophe.

~~~

December 23, 1814

It was just after noon, two days before Christmas, and Hortense was quietly humming to herself as she polished Catherine's silver. The house was quiet; Catherine and Scamp were at General Jackson's headquarters on Rue Royal, and Miguel was at Place d'Armes, training with Major Pierre Lacoste's battalion of free men of color.

Hortense refused to dwell on the city's problems; instead, she was happily considering the ingredients she would need for preparing the Reveillon dinner. On Christmas Eve, the family would go to St. Louis Cathedral for midnight Mass and, because they had fasted, would return for a marvelous, table d'hôte feast. Hortense planned on making her famous turtle soup, followed by oysters, egg pudding, and a veal roast. A brioche and a fruit loaf would be served for dessert.

Hortense also looked forward to the weeklong festivities following Christmas. The New Year's celebration meant putting gifts under the new-year tree. And in the coming years, once Suzanne's child, sure to be bubbly and perhaps even boisterous, was born, the season would be even more high-spirited.

Hortense smiled to herself. She enjoyed the preparations, for, although she had relatives on some of the plantations, she considered this her home and Catherine, Miguel, Suzanne, and Scamp her family. Catherine was good to her, had subtly encouraged her to learn to read, taught her healing skills, and, as she had promised, emancipated her several years earlier. She was gratified to continue working as a paid servant for this benevolent woman.

A frenzied knocking on the back door interrupted her reverie.

Hmph! she thought, annoyed that someone was intruding upon her quiet afternoon. The knocking continued, turning into a louder pounding.

"All right, all right," Hortense yelled, "I'm coming!"

When she opened the door, her eyes widened with astonishment. Her cousin and his wife, house slaves from the Villeré plantation, stood there, quite dirty and disheveled, and obviously exhausted.

"Andre! Claire! What are you doing here?"

Andre responded. "The plantation has been captured by the Redcoats, Hortense! It happened this morning, around ten thirty. They had Monsieur Villeré under guard."

"We were in the kitchen house," added Claire. "We were able to get away while the English were busy stealing the tableware and emptying the wine cellar."

"Oh my goodness!" cried Hortense. "You must have been terrified!"

"At first, but it soon was clear that the Redcoats weren't interested in the slaves; we have nothing worth stealing," replied Claire.

"We saw Major Gabriel Villeré escape, too. He leaped through an open window, then jumped over a fence and ran across the fields, toward the cypress swamp," added Andre. "Meanwhile, the English were running after him, and one of them was yelling out to 'catch him or kill him!'"

"Oh!" said Hortense, wringing her hands. "This is dreadful news!"

"We don't know what happened to Monsieur Villeré. I hope he got away!" said Andre.

"Well, what about your escape?" asked Hortense.

"We were walking here as fast as we could, when we met two soldiers, a Yankee and a Creole. They were on horses and were riding to our plantation," said Andre.

"We stopped them and told them what we told you," added Claire. "The Yankee soldier, he turned his horse right around and raced off toward the city."

"The Creole gave us this gold piece," said Andre, showing Hortense the coin. "He said that we'd done a great service for our country. Then he headed for the plantation!"

"You suppose he was going to fight all those English by himself?" asked Hortense.

"By the time he gets there, the British will probably be so drunk on free wine that he most likely could!" responded Andre.

"We didn't know where else to go, Hortense! Do you think Madame Catherine will let us stay here for a while?" asked Claire.

"I suspect she'll be happy to have your help," replied Hortense. "But first we need to go to General Jackson's headquarters and make sure that he knows about all this! Allons!"

Tarot: THE EIGHT OF PENTACLES

Revelation: A difficult career decision must be made.

~

Meanwhile, at Jackson's Rue de Royal headquarters, the staff members were quietly exchanging news, studying maps, or writing letters home. It was one thirty, and, along with his early-afternoon meal of rice and ginger tea, Catherine gave the general a small amount of water, into which she had stirred a tablespoon full of powdered charcoal.

"Another dose, General," she said, handing him the black liquid.

"Thank you, Madame Caresse. It seems to be helping my cramps."

"I am happy to hear that, sir," she said. "And when you finish your tea, I want you to relax, possibly take a nap."

"Perhaps I can afford a nap right now," said Jackson as he obligingly sipped Catherine's concoction. He was just settling his angular body down on the sofa to get some rest, when Corporal Madden burst through the door, obviously with disturbing news.

Jackson immediately sat up, eyes wide open. Madden addressed the general.

"Three men to see you, sir. They say it's urgent!"

"Well, show them in, Corporal!"

Major Gabriel Villeré was the first to enter, followed by

Colonel Denis de Laronde and Major Howell Tatum. They were all quite shaken and mud-stained.

"General Jackson, sir!" Major Tatum saluted. "The British are less than seven miles away from New Orleans. Major Latour and I were appraising the bayous in the area, when we met a number of people fleeing toward the city."

"They have taken over my father's entire plantation!" said Villeré. "It happened just this morning. They captured me and then turned our home into their headquarters."

Jackson didn't say a word; he just stared at Major Villeré.

"Luckily," the young man continued, "I was able to escape. I met with my neighbor Colonel de Laronde, and—"

"We rowed across the river and then came here by horse as quickly as possible!" finished de Laronde.

Catherine noticed the cuts and bruises Gabriel Villeré had on his legs, and briefly considered tending to them with a milk-and-bread poultice. She quickly changed her mind about treating the major's wounds, though, as she saw General Jackson's face blanch and then turn crimson, his body taut with alarm.

Focusing her attention solely on her patient, she admonished, "General! You need to relax!"

Jackson ignored her, leaped up from the sofa, and paced back and forth angrily. "Curses!"

Major Villeré looked down at the floor, obviously distressed. The general continued pacing. No one said a word. They were hoping that his legendary temper would dissipate somewhat as he considered the situation.

Finally, Jackson stopped and looked again at Tatum. "Where's Major Latour?"

"Sir," Tatum began, "Latour continued toward Villeré's plantation to spy on the British."

At this moment, Major Arsène Latour rushed in, saluted,

and spoke. "Sir! I was able to get within two hundred yards of their camp. The Brits have made their headquarters at Villeré's house, and between sixteen hundred and eighteen hundred men are bivouacked a mile north, at the boundary of the Lacoste plantation."

Jackson nodded his head. "Good work, Major. Anything else?"

"I noted also that they appear to be extremely tired and hungry."

The general looked at the other three men. "Tired and hungry. Good. We must stop them immediately; they cannot come any closer to the city."

Again, no one spoke.

Thinking to himself for a couple of moments, the general narrowed his eyes, put his hands on his hips, and looked around at his hushed staff.

"All right, then," he declared, his mouth twisted into a grimace. His staff stared back at him, wondering what exactly the general was thinking was "all right."

A few more seconds passed in total silence. And then Andrew Jackson drew himself up to his full height, took a deep breath, and furiously pounded his fist on the table. "We will attack them tonight! Sound the alarm. Send for all of my aides. And God help us!"

He paused, reached over for the carafe, and poured himself, his staff members, and Major Villeré some brandy. Holding up his glass, he seemed to be infused with a new strength and vitality as he proclaimed, "By the eternal, they shall not sleep soundly on our soil!"

"Hurrah!" his staff agreed with fervor.

Catherine, too, believing in her general's competence, obligingly gulped down her drink with gusto.

At that moment, the alarm cannon was fired, alerting the army and citizens that the enemy was near. Catherine's household, Andrew Jackson, and the general's staff were now not the only ones who knew about the British approach; all of New Orleans was on notice.

Tarot: THE NINE OF WANDS

Revelation: Preparedness to meet the challenge.

⁓

As his aides responded to the alarm, gathering about in keyed-up clusters, Jackson pushed the nervous young Major Villeré into a smaller chamber.

"And just how did the British manage to reach your plantation?" the general demanded, his arms akimbo.

Gabriel Villeré hesitated, then admitted, "They must have used Bayou Bienvenue, sir."

"Blast it, man!" Jackson fumed at the Creole. "I ordered all the bayous to be obstructed! That included the one by your plantation! You will be court-martialed for this!"

"Yes, sir. Sorry, sir. I didn't think . . ."

"No, you did not, Major!" and Jackson stormed out of the smaller room.

As additional men crowded into the headquarters, the tension grew more acute while Jackson quickly analyzed advice from his top aides and then spit out orders.

Jean Lafitte recommended an attack from the left bank of the river, opposite the British camp. His gunners would staff the schooner USS *Carolina*.

General Coffee suggested that local plantation owners guide his men through the swampy territory north of the LaCoste and Villeré plantations. There, his Tennesseans would attack the

English from the right flank, driving the Redcoats toward the river and the *Carolina*'s cannon fire. Holding the center would be the free men of color, the city battalion, and, next to the river, the US Army artillery contingent and the Marines; they would all, at Jackson's command, proceed south and west.

Meanwhile, Catherine was making her own plans. Her assistant, his face full of excitement, was dancing with anticipation.

She pulled him over to a corner by the doorway. "Scamp, I need you to settle down," she said quietly. "Without attracting attention, I want you to hurry home and explain to Hortense what is happening. Ask her to keep an eye on Suzanne; her time is not too far away, and I don't want my daughter to overdo it. Then give Hortense this list; it has some things she can pack that you and I will need when we accompany General Jackson."

Catherine was just about to add, "Now, be careful", but Scamp had already grabbed the list and darted out the door, sure that he was in for quite an adventure.

Tarot: THE SEVEN OF WANDS

Revelation: Boldness in the face of trouble.

$\sim$

It was almost five in the afternoon as Scamp was sprinting down Rue de Toulouse toward Rue de Rampart. He passed women tugging children, hastening to their homes, and armed males of all different dress proceeding to their rendezvous locations. General Coffee's veterans were first to move through on their mounts. Then came the mix of forces. Major Jean Plauché's militia, consisting of New Orleans lawyers, bankers, and merchants, in their vivid red, blue, and gold uniforms. Captain Pierre Jugeant's Choctaws, in their buckskin leggings and hunting coats, their long, loose black hair, some with one or more feathers in a colored headband. General William Carrol's Tennesseans, looking rough and wild, clothed similarly to the Choctaws in deerskins. Major Jean Daquin's free men of color, marching in perfect order with pride. And Jean Lafitte's Baratarians, sweeping by, looking ferocious. Not since the fall of the Roman Empire had the world seen an army like this one. White, black, brown, and red. Protestant, Catholic, and animist. Of a single purpose: to prevent the enemy from reaching the city.

About an hour after sunset, Jackson led his kaleidoscope of colors on a ten-mile march down the levee that ran along the Mississippi, toward the English encampment, the shadowy cypress swamp beyond the cane fields on their left, the

Mississippi River, illuminated by a full moon, on their immediate right.

The trek past the sequence of plantations was under strict noise discipline. No talking. Orders were passed from man to man in whispers.

Along the way, women and children, waving white handkerchiefs from the windows and balconies of their houses, watched the silent army pass, aware that their husbands, fathers, sons, and brothers were marching into harm's way.

From the gallery outside the second floor of her mansion, Marguerite watched nervously. She knew that Jacques was somewhere in the mass of men, and assured herself that he could see her and that only his duty prevented him from racing to her side. And then she thought she saw him and was sure he was looking at her, as he gave a small salute.

He really does love me, she thought.

A throbbing behind her eyes began.

You think so? responded an odious voice she recognized. *Why?*

I'm carrying his child. This time will be different!

You'll lose this one, too. Face it, Marguerite—you're worthless! You're a failure!

The pounding inside her head worsened.

No! You're wrong, ogre! Stop telling me that! My husband loves me!

Did he tell you so?

Well, no, not exactly with those words. But I know he does. He's just very reserved. Always has been. A gentleman. And I understand that.

Ha! Jacques joined up with Jackson just to get away from you! The salute? That wasn't for you. It was for his house, his servants, the things he really cares about.

He cares about me, about our unborn baby, and our family. You don't know what you're talking about!

She rubbed her temples, trying to get rid of the hammering sensation inside her skull.

You're just a hollow shell, Madame de Trahan, no substance. You have his name, but really you're a blight on his life. Like mold! An affliction! Why don't you just do him a favor and go away? I can help you. For his sake, Marguerite! The voice was now wheedling.

No! No, I'm not going to listen to you! Go away, ogre! My love for Jacques will drown out whatever lies you have to say!

Marguerite shut her eyes tightly, put her hands on her ears, and shook her head back and forth. The throbbing stopped; the ogre was gone.

She felt someone embrace her. It was her mother. Sheila had also been watching the army pass, swishing her monogrammed lace handkerchief back and forth. She had noticed Marguerite's odd behavior and assumed it was stress.

"There, there, Marguerite, dear," she said, giving her another hug. Then, while massaging her daughter's back, she added, "Jacques will be all right. Don't fret! Do you need to sit down?"

Marguerite smiled weakly. "No, Mother. I just had a ghastly headache, but it's gone now."

After the troops had passed, Marguerite said, "Thank you, Mother. I guess I was so upset, I didn't realize . . . well, anyway, thank you."

"Of course, dear. This is taxing for all of us, but, again, I'm sure Jacques will come back to us soon with a victory. Try not to worry."

"Of course. I must leave now to go into the city. I just want to go over a few details with Sister Angelique. She's the Ursuline sister in charge of preparing their convent's classrooms for the wounded. Are you sure you'll be all right by yourself?"

"I won't be alone for long, dear," answered Sheila. "The other plantation ladies will be joining me soon. Then we're going to Claudia's home to prepare bandages and blankets to be distributed."

She reached down into her apron pocket and took out her scissors. "Plus, besides these," she said, as she placed the shears on a banister, "I've also got this." Sheila slipped her hand inside her skirts and brought out a dagger. "So don't worry about me."

Marguerite laughed. "Good for you, Mother! Those Redcoats have no idea what danger they're facing!"

"True! All of the ladies will be similarly armed, so why don't you join us after you see Sister Angelique? You could stay at Claudia's; she has plenty of room. It would be safer than coming back here, especially in your condition."

"That's exactly what I planned on doing, Mother. Claudia is expecting me."

"Good. Be careful, my dear, and I will see you later."

Marguerite hugged Sheila, picked up her travel bag, and, tried to look as plucky as her mother sounded. Then she began her journey west in her carriage after her husband and the rest of the army marched east.

Tarot: THE NINE OF SWORDS

Revelation: A period of doubt and worry.

~

As he marched by his own plantation buildings, Jacques turned his attention away from his family to the circumstances at hand. Questions clamored in his mind: Would he ever see his loved ones again? Would they take the English by surprise, or were they marching into a trap? Yes, the parade two weeks earlier on the Place d'Armes had given the citizens more confidence—Jackson now had about 2,100 men—but Jacques was a bit concerned about the quality of the local volunteers marching with him. Besides local plantation owners, bankers, lawyers, and merchants, he also knew that some of them were actually prisoners who had been awaiting trial, along with released criminals who had served most of their sentences. Could these untried citizen participants show the same bravado against soldiers who had defeated Napoleon's armies in Spain?

The general called a halt, forming a line on the Laronde and Lacoste plantations. They were just half a mile west of the British encampment. Orders were passed from unit to unit by hand signals and from rank to rank by whispers.

Old Hickory, looking through his telescope, made out the dark form of the schooner *Carolina* gradually approaching its position opposite the British encampment. Turning his telescope to his left, he could plainly see the enemy's campsite. Many of the English were gathered around big bonfires, no doubt to dry their clothing after slogging through the swamps. Others, whom he could not see, were probably sleeping off the effects of the alcohol looted from the nearby plantation, oblivious to any threat.

Andrew Jackson smiled to himself. How splendid for our attack!

Tarot: THE FOUR OF WANDS

*Revelation: A reward for a creative effort,
but more challenges ahead.*

⁓

As the American schooner USS *Carolina*, with seven cannons on each side, slowly and silently drifted with the current down the Mississippi, Peter could feel the thick mist forming above the river, concealing the *Carolina* from anyone watching from the far shore. The customary evening chill was accompanying the fog. It was close to 7:30 p.m., but not a light shone as the schooner made its way toward the Villeré plantation buildings.

Peter strained to see the fires that would reveal the Redcoats' camp. Gauging that the vessel had a ways to go, Peter's thoughts returned to Millie. He wondered when he could see her again, hoped that she was safe, and anticipated what she would say about the whale's tooth he was scrimshawing for her. He had wanted to do a mermaid in her likeness, but was still not having much luck with his awl dexterity. A simple dolphin would have to do—this time.

He was also pondering why he was so enamored with her. Yes, she was pretty and exuberant, but so were many of the women who lived in Barataria. Also, she was bold and a risk taker. He smiled to himself; she would have made a good privateer. Most important, though, he concluded, she reveled in freedom. Like he did. And he loved her for that. Love? A strange concept—he must think more about this.

Peter's reverie was broken when the *Carolina*'s forward progress stopped. The anchor, which had been eased into the water, hooked into the river bottom and the current swung the vessel around to face New Orleans. The ship was about one hundred yards from the British encampment at the Villeré plantation.

Peter nodded to his mates, who quietly removed the lead apron at the rear of the cannon and then took off the underlying sheepskin. Both had been placed over the touchhole to keep the gunpowder dry. A supply of cloth bags, each full of grapeshot, was nearby. All was in order.

The tampion was removed, no longer plugging the cannon's muzzle. Peter and the three other privateers plunged the powder charge down the barrel of their cannon. While Peter pushed the metal pick into the touchhole, piercing the canvas cover of the powder charge, his mates rammed home the cloth containers of grape-size lead shot. The elevation of the gun was adjusted perfectly with the wedge-shaped quoin, and the cannon moved into position, firmly secured by preventer tackle and shielded from the outside by the gun port.

They were ready.

Peter heard a voice from onshore call out to their ship. Nobody onboard breathed or answered. A couple of rifle shots from the embankment followed, but, again, no response came from the dark ship. Losing interest in the silent vessel, the few Redcoat sentries went about their duties.

Good, Peter thought. *They must think we're an English ship, or perhaps a merchant ship.*

His muscles remained taut; it was almost time to make their identities known.

Then a voice called out, "Give them this for the honor of America!"

Peter was not certain if that was the voice of Commodore Daniel Patterson or not, but the gun port opened and the rest of his gun crew stepped back. Peter took the smoldering slow match from its shielding dry bucket and ignited the fuse. He quickly stepped aside to avoid the puffing blow of flame from the vent, as well as to dodge the cannon's recoil. In an instant, the flame moved down the quill fuse and ignited the powder.

Success!

Then came a deafening roar as sheets of fire and masses of deadly grapeshot blasted from his cannon and the other six on the starboard side of the *Carolina*. Peter and the Baratarians could clearly hear the screams and groans of the shocked British as their shot ripped through Redcoat flesh.

With well-practiced vigor, Peter and his crewmates continued their bombardment, each performing like gears in a watch. Sponging, inserting, ramming, picking, aiming, firing. Every forty seconds, their cannon roared. And their prowess was creating chaos for the Redcoats. The grapeshot swept down on the Brits, around their glowing campfires, which silhouetted the startled and confused targets.

Some Brits did their best to extinguish the fires while trying not to reveal themselves to the deadly rain of grapeshot. Lying low behind the levees, others returned fire, but the *Carolina*'s high oak gunwales protected its crew from the musket shots. And the Redcoats who crawled to and hugged the embankment, prostrated but safe, helplessly heard the moans and screams of their wounded. The American onslaught continued. The British, because their heavy artillery was still in transit, could only keep their heads down.

Never did these tired Redcoats expect the ship anchored in

the river to be an armed American naval vessel. And with their amazing acquisition of the Villeré plantation, the British supposedly had the element of surprise on their side. They were unquestionably the best-trained and most experienced military in the world. Plus, battles occurred only in the daytime, certainly not at night. It just wasn't done. And yet . . .

Tarot: THE STAR

Revelation: Hope and faith.

~

While Corporal Madden guarded the outside of Jackson's headquarters on Rue de Royal, Catherine and Scamp were together inside. Catherine was sitting at the table; Scamp stood next to her. To keep her young assistant's mind occupied, Catherine reviewed some of the items she had in her medical bag and their purposes.

"Here's the catnip, Scamp. Do you remember what it's used for?"

"It can ease toothaches, and you give it to mothers for their babies when they're colicky. Sometimes you tell them just to use dill water, though."

"Good! Anything else? Think back a few weeks," she hinted.

"Oh! You gave me some when I had a stomachache!"

"Right! Do you remember any other herbs that are useful for treating intestinal cramps?"

"Yes! Teas can be made from sage, thyme, or spearmint. And the spearmint can also be rubbed on your temples to get rid of a headache."

"Well done, Scamp! Very good indeed."

Her student was smiling proudly.

"Now, what about taking care of—"

The first booms of the *Carolina*'s cannons interrupted Catherine's question.

"*Merde!*" the boy yelled out, and clung to his mistress. She in turn hugged him right back.

They held on to each other for a few moments, the cannons continuing their clamor.

Corporal Madden opened the door and stuck his head in. "You folks all right?" he asked.

"We're fine, Corporal, just a little shaken is all."

"You'll get used to it."

He shut the door again.

Scamp said, "I'm scared, Madame Catherine. Aren't you?"

"It is a bit unnerving, Scamp. But it'll be all right," she said. "The general knows what he's doing."

The boy didn't seem very convinced. He looked up at her, his eyes wide, his eyebrows raised.

"It'll be all right."

Tarot: TEMPERANCE

Revelation: Fine guidance.

~

Because he was a local planter and knew the area well, Jacques had volunteered to lead General Coffee and his troops. When the schooner *Carolina* first opened fire, the dismounted Tennessee horse soldiers were headed across the south end of the Lacoste plantation, closest to the cypress swamp, and about three hundred yards south of the swamp. They had crossed about a third of the field, when suddenly several figures rose from the ground.

Fortunately, Jacques and the startled General Coffee's staff could discern that the men were leaning on their rifles and muskets, not aiming at them. Their spokesman, Nakni, identified himself and his fellows as eight of Captain Pierre Jugeant's Choctaw scouts. He informed Coffee that the captain and all eighteen Choctaws had infiltrated the English camp. They were there, avoiding the light of the campfires, when the *Carolina* opened fire. Captain Jugeant had sent Nakni and his companions to lead Coffee's men through a gap in the English pickets. Also, Nakni had discovered that Coffee was headed directly for an English picket outpost of eighty soldiers.

Nakni and his fellow scouts trotted ahead of the Tennessean volunteers, fanning out to locate the nearest British outposts.

Coffee sent his aides with orders to the officers to swing

the column toward the river and the flashes of the *Carolina*'s cannons. The Tennesseans were to obey the directions of the Choctaw scouts, who would be posted along the line of march, and, above all, to "make no noise!"

As Nakni led the way, Jacques relinquished his guide duties but remained with General Coffee as aide and messenger, if needed.

Tarot: THE ACE OF SWORDS

*Revelation: Change in one's life; activity due to
the old order being threatened.*

~

"All right, everybody. One more time. Shove it!" commanded Sheila.

"Do try to be careful about scraping the floors, though!" cautioned Claudia.

With combined effort, the Creole women slowly pushed the heavy, ornate sofa next to the grand piano, already moved against the wall.

"Good job," Sheila congratulated her friends. "Now that we have cleared the center of the room, we'll be able to take in more wounded. We're lucky you have such a large house in the city, Claudia!"

"I'm happy to help, Sheila."

"Let's get back to sewing the quilts and pillows and cutting the petticoats into bandages. When we finish those, we can begin making blanket cloaks, shirts, and pants. It's going to be a long night, my friends."

The candles were lit, many of them in sconces in front of the multiple mirrors, providing a duplicate effect. As Sheila picked up some more fabric from the table, she glanced into the convex chaperone mirror and noted her friends' grim looks. All were familiar with the reports that the British had raided the

Atlantic coastal towns with impunity, assaulting old men, violating women, looting and burning. And now they were here.

The ladies labored on. They could hear the cannons from the *Carolina* firing east of the city. As the bombardment continued, they looked at one another, fear and apprehension now plain upon their faces.

Sheila interrupted her sewing for a moment and fingered the sheath of her dagger concealed inside her skirt. Some of the women stopped to see what their leader was doing. "Check your weapons, ladies!"

The women nodded, and all reaffirmed the locations of their defenses, touching knives, scissors, and cleavers. Some items were hidden within their garments; others had been placed conveniently nearby.

Sheila then shook her fist, saying, "And we will not hesitate to use them against those British barbarians!"

Along with the rest, Sheila heard another burst of cannon fire. Her face set with steely determination, she made the sign of the cross, took up her needle again, and ferociously stabbed the cloth.

Tarot: THE KNIGHT OF SWORDS

Revelation: Sudden changes; turbulence.

~

The balance of the American army was aligned just west of the Lacoste plantation boundary, starting at the river and extending inland for a distance of roughly four hundred yards. Closest to the river on the high road, Jackson placed the two six-pounder cannons and their crews, with a contingent of Marines in support. Next, posted from right to left, were the 7th and 44th US infantry regiments and Major Plauché's battalion of Creole volunteers, which included Private René Bonet. Holding the left flank, Miguel Plicque was with Major Dacquin's battalion of free men of color.

The continuing bombardment from the *Carolina* and the resulting confusion in the camp kept the British unaware of the American battle lines forming on two sides of their position.

At 8:00 p.m., General Jackson gave the order for the professional soldiers of the 44th and the 7th regiments to advance toward the Redcoats' camp. The two cannons were rolled forward on the high road, accompanied by the Marines. The men of the 7th were the first to reach the edge of Lacoste's plantation, where they stumbled into an English outpost. Although suffering casualties, the Yankees were able to push the Redcoats back toward their camp.

Now alerted to the American army's presence, English

General Thornton rushed every soldier he could toward the sound of the musket fire. Illuminated only by the moon, and obscured by the fog drifting from the river, the fight became a matter of firing at the flashes of the enemy's muskets and then dodging before the enemy fired at the flashes of the Americans' muskets.

As the English reinforcements arrived at the sight of the engagement, they spread to the left of the 44th regiment. The volunteer units on the far left of the American line, for unknown reasons, had not gotten the word to advance with the regular army regiment.

René, on the far left of Plauché's Creole unit, was waiting in formation with a churning stomach. Despite the cooling night, sweat soaked his hands while he listened to the gunfire and the battle cries. He silently repeated the musket loading-and-firing procedure to himself; yet again, he found it somewhat calming. The next man to his left was a member of Major Daquin's battalion; he was quietly saying the Lord's Prayer over and over. René recognized the voice; it was Miguel, his father-in-law.

Suddenly came the command to move forward with caution and not to fire until given the order. In the darkness, it would be difficult to distinguish friend from foe. René gripped his musket, and Miguel stopped praying out loud as the battalions moved forward silently over the fields of the Lacoste plantation.

René's head ached from the strain of peering into the darkness ahead. He could feel the bile rising in his throat and feared that he might not be able to contain it. Just as he was about to bend over, he heard someone shout the password, "Doodle," followed by a silence that seemed to last an eternity. Instead of the counterword, "Yankee," the next sound was a burst of musket fire and the thump of musket balls striking human bodies.

Automatically, René knelt on one knee and raised his musket to his shoulder, the ache in his head and the churning in his stomach suddenly gone. At the command *"Au feu,"* he pulled the trigger and immediately commenced the reloading routine that he had silently been repeating in his head.

A few yards to René's left, Miguel and the rest of Daquin's battalion also fired. Then came the order to fire at will.

The Redcoats, who had apparently believed that they out-flanked the Americans, now found that their own flank had been turned. They began to withdraw. Amid their confusion and the darkness, the Redcoats' musket balls flew ineffectively over the heads of the Americans. However, the Americans' aimed fire devastated the English ranks, forcing them to retreat.

The word was passed from Plauché's men to Daquin's battalion to "fix bayonets and advance cautiously." René's exuberance at having survived his first firefight suddenly evaporated as he fumbled to remove his bayonet from its scabbard and fasten it to the barrel of his musket. He had done so easily while standing still in daylight at the Place d'Armes, but now it was dark and he was walking across a field while hoping not to encounter a Redcoat experienced in fighting with a bayonet. As he stopped to complete the task, he could hear what he believed to be such encounters just in front of him. The hair on his neck stood up, and his heart stopped beating when someone bumped into his back. René was about to spin around, bayonet ready, when he heard the curse in French. Grasping the stock of his musket just behind the trigger guard with his right hand, his left hand on the breech end of the barrel, he started forward.

Miguel, who did not have a bayonet, reloaded his musket. Although he had sheathed his six-inch hunting knife, concealed in its usual place under his trousers, on his right calf, it would be of little use against a Redcoat with a musket and a bayonet. In that case, he was ready to use his musket as a club in close-quarters fighting.

Carefully, slowly, he and René began to move. After they had advanced about twenty yards, they were relieved to receive a command to halt and assume firing positions. While a few of their comrades remained standing, others knelt. But the majority lay down on their stomachs. Whatever their posture, all eyes tried nervously to penetrate the dark and fog before them. But they had readied themselves.

"As we forgive those who trespass against us . . ."

Well, no, not really.

Periodically, disoriented English soldiers stumbled into their lines, where they quickly either surrendered or died.

"And deliver us from evil . . ."

S'il vous plaît.

Tarot: THE FIVE OF SWORDS

Revelation: Facing one's own limits and
backing off before moving forward.

———

After a twenty-minute hike, General Coffee's officers called
a halt to prevent stumbling into the English before the
scouts reported back with their exact location. Almost instantly,
Nakni appeared out of the gloom. The scouts reported that
about thirty Redcoats were fifty yards ahead. Positioned four or
five yards apart, the English were facing west.

They were told there was to be no gunfire; the Redcoats
were to be taken prisoner. If necessary, tomahawks and rifle
butts were to be used to dispatch uncooperative English.

Nakni and the Choctaws led the Tennessee volunteers
silently to the rear of the English picket line. The individual
sentries were not aware of the Americans' presence until they
felt rifle muzzles pressed against their spines. This rude greeting
was accompanied by a whispered order to ground their muskets and take three paces forward. The sound of their captors'
rifles being cocked ended any hesitation or thoughts of a heroic
response.

Quickly, Jacques and thirty other men were assigned to escort
the captured English and their weapons back to the American
army's rear, at the Laronde plantation. The balance of the covering party again remained in place while the Choctaw scouts

jogged into the darkness to locate the remaining English out-post. Behind them, they could hear the main body of General Coffee's force closing in on the English camp. The thunderous volleys of the English muskets and the roar of the *Carolina*'s cannons periodically drowned out the Americans' scattered rifle shots. The distant fireworks were a sharp contrast with their own small and mostly bloodless victory.

Nakni and the other scouts finally returned, only to report that the second English picket outpost was no longer in their former location and had apparently withdrawn to the main English battle line. With that information, the remaining troops of the covering force proceeded toward the river to rejoin General Coffee.

The blanket of fog moving inland from the river had obscured the light from the full moon, causing General Cof-fee's main force to become intermingled with the enemy. Using the flashes of the *Carolina*'s cannons, elements of the Tennessee volunteers had penetrated to the buildings of the LaCoste plan-tation. Others were firing from the fields directly northeast of the *Carolina*, picking off the English silhouetted by the cannon blasts.

As the two sides mingled in the fog, hand-to-hand fight-ing ensued. The English brandished bayonets and swords, while the Americans wielded rifle butts and tomahawks. Although a bayonet or sword gave the English extended reach, a Tennessee backwoodsman and a Choctaw could throw a tomahawk or a hunting knife up to ten feet with deadly accuracy.

The battle became a multitude of skirmishes between small groups and even individual soldiers. In the fog and confusion, mis-identification occurred and friend unknowingly attacked friend.

Meanwhile, English reinforcements were arriving at the bat-tle from their beachhead on Lake Borgne. These light infantry soldiers of the 85th Regiment moved quickly to the sound of the fighting around the Lacoste plantation. There, they joined the smoke and fog–shrouded clashes hoping that they were attacking Americans.

The Tennessee volunteers had been engaged for almost two hours when a courier brought General Coffee the news that the west end of their battle line had made contact with the New Orleans militia. That meant that the English force was enclosed in a U shape, with Americans on their west and north and the river on their southwest. This intelligence reinforced Coffee's supposition that the English were being driven east, toward the Villeré plantation. He took comfort in the strategy of General Jackson, who was presently giving the famed English army hell from three directions.

Coffee sent the courier to find General Jackson and report that the English were withdrawing from his front. However, he was concerned that his men would not be sure of their targets in the fog and might soon run out of powder and shot.

Within half an hour, the courier returned with a dispatch from General Jackson ordering Coffee to slowly disengage his troops from contact with the enemy and withdraw to their original position at the east end of the Laronde plantation, adjacent to the swamp.

Tarot: THE SEVEN OF CUPS

Revelation: Emotional situation; necessary action.

⁓

A ll this time, Peter and his shipmates on the _Carolina_ kept
up their bombardment of the English camp, occasionally
changing position by playing out and drawing in the anchor chain.

Another good strike, Peter cheered to himself. _And that's too
bad. I guess._

What? "Too bad"? Where did that come from? And then he
realized he was feeling slightly guilty for the punishment being
inflicted on his former countrymen.

_Aye, I really am sorry about that, mates—although I'm glad that
your muskets have no effect at all on this schooner's thick oak gunwales!_

His internal monologue continued, _But it's just you enlisted
men I feel bad about, because you were coerced, just like I was. You
had to choose between taking the King's shilling and starvation!_

On the other hand . . .

He recalled those responsible for the deprivations and misery in the Royal Navy.

_I hope we kill every one of your arrogant upper-class officers. I
have no remorse for maiming those bastards!_

Peter remembered having begun the journey down the river;
he had vowed death over surrender. As he would not be able to
conceal his accent, capture would mean hanging or an intolera-
ble life in the English military. Neither was acceptable.

No—no guilt at all.

Tarot: TEN OF SWORDS

Revelation: Sudden misfortune; pain.

⁓

When the firing slackened on Coffee's battle front, Jackson then started the withdrawal of his main force to the Laronde plantation. First to be withdrawn were the cannons with their Marine escort, followed by the two regular army regiments. Major Plauché's and Major Daquin's battalions took up the back of the column as rear guards.

René again felt relief as his unit spread out, facing the English lines. On command, every other man, including those on both sides of René, did an about-face, moved twenty paces to the rear, halted, and did a second about-face. René and the other soldiers, holding the original position, performed the same maneuver, except they moved forty steps, passing their comrades who had previously withdrawn.

His anxiety lessened, René executed the maneuver by rote: moving the paces, halting, turning, estimating the five-minute wait.

As both battalions moved to the rear, they stumbled over abandoned weapons, discarded knapsacks, and casualties of friend and foe. Between pausing to assist their own wounded and collecting usable weapons and other valuables from the dead, the lines of each battalion became disorganized and intermingled.

Easy enough to maintain contact in the daylight. However,

now that fog and gunsmoke hid the moon, René was not surprised when a figure appeared before him; he assumed it was another member of Plauché's battalion.

Approaching his comrade, he said, *"C'est une bonne victoire!"*

Just as a sudden breeze parted the fog, René saw the fear on the man's face. At that instant, René felt excruciating pain in his stomach and the breath explode from his mouth, followed by the taste of bile and blood. Instinctively, René spun his musket around and pointed it at the Redcoat's chest and, as his knees gave way, pulled the trigger.

Tarot: TWO OF CUPS

Revelation: Arrangements made for cooperation.

⁓

Hortense heard the visitors coming to the door and opened it with a smile. "Welcome, Jeanette! We're all ready for your *enfants!*"

Jeanette stepped inside, holding her baby. Antoinette followed her quietly. "Are you sure they won't be a problem, Hortense?" asked the young mother.

"Of course not! We have Suzanne's bassinet for Pierre in the dining room, and Antoinette, the big sister now, can tell me what to do just in case I don't know. Isn't that right, Antoinette?"

The young girl gave Hortense a huge grin. "I help Maman every day!" she said.

"Good. I know I can count on you." Hortense turned to gesture to the female adult quietly standing behind her. "Plus, my cousin's wife, Claire, is here to help me take care of them," she said to Jeanette.

Bending down to look into the little girl's eyes, Hortense continued, "Why, Antoinette, you get prettier every day!"

Antoinette blushed and said, "Thank you, Madame Hortense." She held out a large basket. "Maman put everything we need in this."

"*Très bien.* We'll set it right here on this table, and you can go with Madame Claire to the dining room. I just happen to have some biscuits waiting to be eaten."

Claire smiled and held out her hand to Antoinette. "You know, Madame Hortense makes the best biscuits I've ever tasted!"

The little girl started to skip into the dining room but looked back at Hortense to say, "Oh, I know. She's the best cook ever!"

Hortense chuckled, then held out her hands to take the baby from Jeanette. "Ah, and here's *petit* Pierre! My, but you've grown so!" Kissing the child on his forehead, she added, "And I'll bet you like sweet biscuits, too!"

"There's not much he doesn't like, Hortense!" Jeanette laughed. "He has a hearty appetite. I suspect he's going to be quite big and tall, like his daddy."

"And where is his father now?" asked Hortense.

"He's with Major Plauché's battalion; I've been praying to Our Lady of Prompt Succor all day."

"As have we all," agreed Hortense gently, rocking the baby.

"I'm grateful to you for taking the children while I help out at the Ursuline convent. Especially on this late notice."

"You know us, Jeanette—always on call! It was Suzanne's idea to organize caring for one another's children; everybody is pitching in to aid the cause, and I'm happy to help. But it's so dark outside. Will you be all right walking to the convent?"

"Several of us from the neighborhood are going to walk together. We have lanterns and, just in case, a couple of brooms."

"Brooms?"

"Well, we gave all of our weapons to Jackson's forces, but in case we run into a wayward Redcoat, the brooms will look like rifles in the dark and we'll scare him off!"

Hortense laughed. "Ah—good luck to the Rampart witches, then!"

Jeanette bent down to give her baby a kiss. *"Au revoir,* my sweet *bébé,* and to you also, Hortense."

"And *bonne chance* to you, Jeanette!"

After Jeanette left the house, Hortense carried Pierre into the dining room. Antoinette was sitting with Claire at the table, and, while munching her biscuit and swinging her legs underneath the chair, the little girl was also peppering the woman with questions.

"Do you think we'll be safe? Ooooh! There goes a cannon again. That was a really loud noise! Do you think somebody got killed? What if the British capture all of us? Will I see Maman soon? All she says is"—and here, Antoinette lowered her voice to a somber tone—"'Let's not talk about that, *ma petite.* You don't need to worry.'"

Antoinette stopped chewing, stuck out her lower lip, crossed her arms, and glared at Claire. "But I *do* worry, and nobody will tell me what's happening. After all, I am almost a grown woman!"

Claire looked up at Hortense, stifling a smile. Hortense laid the baby in the bassinet and poured herself some coffee. "Your *maman* will be back by tomorrow morning, Antoinette. And we are safe—General Jackson and his troops won't let those Redcoats into our city. But we must do all we can to help him. So that means that while I take care of your little brother here, you can assist Madame Claire in making biscuits as a special treat for everyone at the hospital. How does that sound?"

"Are your biscuits as good as Madame Hortense's?"

Claire smiled. "I've never had any complaints."

Tarot: THE THREE OF SWORDS

Revelation: Sorrow; tears.

~~~

It was time for the men in Miguel's rank to turn and withdraw the forty paces. After moving half the distance, Miguel heard a faint plea.

"_Au secours! Au secours! Un médecin!_"

With his musket at the ready, Miguel moved cautiously toward the source of the sound. Scanning the ground to his left, he saw what appeared to be a pile of brush. As he drew closer, he could make out two bodies, one on top of the other. The soldier on the bottom was not moving, and the white piping on his uniform, which seemed to glow in the moonlight, identified him as English. The other man was facedown, on all fours.

Miguel, his musket aimed at the crouching figure, asked, "_Comment vous appelez-vous?_"

After a liquid cough, the voice croaked, "René Bonet."

The astonished Miguel set down his musket and moved to his comrade's side. Pushing René away from the dead Englishman, Miguel had to use all of his concentration to keep his stomach under control when he saw the blood and vomit dripping from René's mouth and the gaping wound in his abdomen. Turning René on his side, Miguel called for assistance and again began praying the Pater Noster. Within minutes, another of Major Daquin's free men of color and a Creole from René's own battalion joined him. The two free men of color carefully lifted René to a sitting position while the Creole collected the muskets. As he led the way to the rear of the American army at the Lacoste plantation, the Creole soldier also tried to find the best footing for the two men carrying René.

When they finally reached their destination, Miguel spied a wagon already filled with wounded and called out to the driver. "Do you have room for one more?"

"I think I can squeeze another one in," said the driver.

The two free men of color gently placed René inside the cart.

"René, you're going to be all right now. Just keep thinking of Suzanne and your baby!"

René opened his eyes again and gave Miguel a wan smile.

Miguel could hear the moans of the other injured troops sitting or lying in various positions in the wagon's interior. The smells of blood and vomit mixed with the scent of the straw being used to cushion the jolts of the wagon.

Miguel approached the driver.

"That last man I put into your wagon . . . ," he began. Then he stopped. "Millie? Is that you?"

"Miguel!" the driver responded. "Yes, it's me. What do you need?"

"René, Suzanne's husband, is the man I just laid in your wagon."

"Oh, *mon Dieu*!"

"He's in a bad way; he was stabbed with a bayonet. Can you get my wife from Jackson's headquarters on Rue de Royal? She's the best healer in town."

"Absolutely, Miguel. I'll pick her up on my way to the convent." Now addressing her mule, she said, "Giddyap, Bella. We've got a job to do."

Although the distance should have merited a two-hour ride, Millie was able to shave off fifteen minutes by keeping Bella at a quick clip. She arrived at Jackson's headquarters and was met by Corporal Madden.

"I'm here for Madame Caresse. She needs to come with me to the convent; her daughter's husband, René Bonet, has been horribly wounded."

Rufus Madden did not have time to hear any more; Catherine had already pushed by him on her way out. Scamp hurried after her, carrying the medicine bag.

"Millie! Where is he?"

"He was the last one on," said Millie, pointing.

The older woman rushed to the back of the wagon and saw René curled up in a fetal position. She grabbed her medicine bag from Scamp, climbed into the wagon, and made room for herself next to René. Scamp joined Millie up front as she took up the reins again and got Bella going.

"René," Catherine said, stroking his hair, noting his feverish forehead, "it's me, Catherine. We're taking you to the convent, where I will take care of you."

She removed one of the cloths from her medicine bag. René winced as she lifted his shirt and gently cleaned away some of the blood. No wonder—the wound's excoriated edges were raw, and the blood continued to flow. As she pressed René's rigid abdomen to stop the bleeding, his face contorted with pain. Her eyes teared up when she realized the damage; his intestine had been perforated.

The young man tried to say something.

"Don't talk, René. Be very still. You need to save your strength. We still have a rocky ride ahead, but we should be there in less than twenty minutes."

René nodded slightly, then closed his eyes. Clutching her

medicine bag, Catherine began her crawl through the cart, giving as much relief as possible to the other victims.

When Millie's cart reached the Ursuline convent, she pulled up next to another wagon carrying the severely wounded. Several nuns and free women of color were taking the men inside. While they transferred the wounded onto stretchers, handed out crutches, and aided those who could walk by themselves, Scamp jumped out of the front seat of the wagon and went to see Catherine in the rear.

"They're backed up here, Scamp. Why don't you see if the ladies can use your help inside with mopping up or something?" his mistress suggested.

The boy dashed into the convent, then stopped to watch the developing scene with wide, horrified eyes.

The makeshift hospital was filling up with soldiers in agony, moaning with pain, calling out for wives, mothers, or friends. The newly recruited caregivers, both overcoming their dread and concealing their instinctive reactions, displayed unflinching faces, in sharp contrast with their patients' anguished countenances. As the doctors shouted out abrupt instructions for each new casualty, there was no time to stare or cry. The women scurried from one patient to another, analyzing needs, getting supplies, stitching up gashes, wiping brows, offering water, and comforting those they could.

Père Antoine moved expeditiously from one severely wounded American soldier to another, administering absolution in Latin to the Catholics and saying an Our Father in English for those who were not. The women had seen to it that a window in each room had been opened to enable souls to depart.

Wives, mothers, sisters, and daughters were searching among the wounded for relatives and friends. Finding a loved one, they did what they could, stroking the forehead, holding the hands, whispering courage, hoping to heal the hurting.

Scamp could not move, staring at the clamorous sight that brought back such monstrous memories of the slave ship his parents had died on. He began to tremble.

Still outside, Millie climbed down from the wagon and joined the women helping Catherine lift René onto a stretcher.

"It's bad, isn't it?"

Catherine just nodded. Then she turned to the young girl and said, "Millie, thank you for getting me, and for volunteering for such a risky job. Suzanne was right—you are indeed amazing." Then, clutching her medicine bag, she followed those carrying René's stretcher into the convent.

Catherine was surprised to see her young servant boy in the hallway. His body was shaking, his teeth chattering; the hospital's commotion obviously terrified him. She stopped, laid her hand on his head, and said softly, "Scamp?"

"It's . . . it's . . . like when I came across the ocean . . . on the ship—everyone sick, everyone dying: Mama, Daddy . . ." Big tears descended down his face.

Catherine placed her hands on the boy's shoulders. "I'm sorry, Scamp; this must be awful for you. But please try not to think of that now; René and I both need your help."

He looked up at her, still teary-eyed. She dried his face tenderly with her shawl. "There, now. We'll get through this together. Come with me!" She took his hand and followed the ladies who had gently placed René on a pallet along the side of the hallway.

Catherine said, "See, Scamp? It's our René. You and I will be taking care of him, so try to ignore everything else. Just concentrate on making him comfortable. You can do that, right?"

Scamp nodded his head slowly and knelt down to look at

René. The boy glanced at Catherine, who gave him a reassuring smile. Taking the man's hand and stroking it, he said softly, "*Bonsoir*, Monsieur Bonet. It's me, Scamp. I'm going to help make you feel better."

Tarot: THE NINE OF WANDS

Revelation: Becoming prepared to meet the challenge.

~~~

Andrew Jackson's aides were gathering in his temporary headquarters, reporting that the American casualties, including those missing, totaled slightly over two hundred. They could only assume that the English had incurred considerably more.

"Dreadful—can't continue those numbers. We shall renew the battle tomorrow morning!" he said, with renewed vigor. "The men are all veterans now and will be eager to fight."

"Sir, that might not be wise," said Captain Jugeant. "The Choctaw scouts have reported that fresh troops are reinforcing the British camp."

"My men are reporting the same," added General John Coffee.

"Hmm," pondered Jackson, looking at the map. "All right, then. We will slowly withdraw toward the city. If it becomes evident that the English have committed the entire army to advance on the city along the river, we will find the best position to set up our defenses. Gentlemen, set up your picket posts and have the rest of your men try to get some sleep without the warmth of fires. Also, tell them that their general could not be prouder of their conduct in this night's battle. They have engaged the best soldiers in the world and forced them to withdraw."

The staff nodded at that, and some even smiled.

Jackson continued, "Your volunteers have demonstrated professional discipline and heroic courage. They have purchased with their blood great honor for New Orleans, as well as these United States. They can take comfort in the knowledge that the Redcoats will not find it easy to sleep with one eye open."

The general paused, looked at each staff member, and slowly nodded his head. Then, placing his hands on his hips, he said, "Gentlemen, please see to your men."

Tarot: THE FOUR OF CUPS

Revelation: Contemplation; a feeling of dissatisfaction.

~

December 24, 1814

While Scamp napped by her side, Catherine continued ministering to René's wound. The young man's eyes suddenly opened yet did not focus. His head twitched; his body shivered. He was trying to say something. "Thirrrst."

"Here, René. Try to swallow some of this."

In order to lesson his pain, she gave him a drink from a tumbler containing opium mixed in some wine. She held the cup as he struggled for breath. He sipped some, gagged, and then took a bigger gulp. She was grateful that he fell asleep almost immediately, and she was able to apply dry, soft lint compresses to the still-bleeding laceration.

One of the Ursuline nuns stopped by. Noticing Catherine's medicine bag, she said, "Hello, I am Sister Angelique. I am working in the room next door. I see you are a healer. You are taking a special interest in this one?"

"Yes, he is my daughter's husband," replied Catherine.

"*Mon Dieu.* I am so sorry. How is he doing?" asked the nun.

"I'm afraid he may not make it," said Catherine. "His abdomen was stabbed with a bayonet, then twisted like a knife. Who knows where that weapon has been before! It may have been used to roast meat or dig a British latrine. I'm very concerned about contamination."

"Of course. I suspect we will lose more patients to infection than to the actual wounds."

"Yes. Unfortunately, there's not much I can do, besides wait. My treatment is simple: keep him clean, warm, and comfortable."

"Do let me know if you need anything. In the meantime, I will pray for you both."

Tarot: THE SEVEN OF PENTACLES

Revelation: A difficult work decision must be made.

⟜

Jackson set up his new headquarters in the two-story Macarty plantation house. Located about one hundred yards north of the Rodriguez Canal, it was the site for his first line of defense. Ascending to the second floor, he was presented with a panoramic view of the Mississippi and the flat countryside. While he checked on the British movements through his telescope, his staff updated him on his soldiers' activities.

Edward Livingston announced, "Nine hundred slaves are joining the troops to help in raising the embankment. It's difficult labor; the ground is soggy, so posts have to be driven down to firmer soil. With no rocks, we have only mud to work with."

"We'll have to make it work," said Jackson. "In addition, be sure that every male in this region under age fifty comes forward and joins us here on the battlefield. After all, we're protecting their homes!"

"That presents a problem, sir: we are sorely in need of weapons."

"Then we must ask the good people of New Orleans to again search every room in their homes for muskets, rifles, swords, and pistols. Whatever they can find . . . Now, I want the work on the rampart to proceed night and day. The men can work in shifts. When it's their turn to rest, they need to do it on-site."

"Speaking of nonstop undertakings," Jean Lafitte said, "the *Carolina* has been joined by the *Louisiana*. They are continuing their intermittent bombardment of the British camp."

"Excellent! That will keep the British in place for a while."

Lafitte continued, "Also, we need to make sure that the English don't outflank the north end of our rampart by wading through the swamp. We should either post a substantial force in the knee-deep water or extend the rampart west, parallel to the swamp."

"Good idea, although I don't think the Redcoats like to get their knees wet," said Jackson. "However, concerning the rampart and Lafitte's suggestion: General Coffee, do what you can to extend the north end of the rampart into the swamp. I will see about some artillery for support. Once the strengthening of the rampart is done, we must have the slaves and men without weapons begin work on a second line."

Captain Jugeant spoke up. "General, my scouts have seen many Creeks and Cherokees in the English camp."

"Captain, instruct your Choctaws to make these other warriors their prime targets in their nightly probes of the English lines. General Coffee, same for your men. We'll teach all tribes which side they should join."

Looking down at his notes, Jackson continued, "I want a huge flag flying high near the center of the rampart; it will help motivate our men."

He looked back up and directed his gaze at each member of his staff, one by one. "Last night we gave the Redcoats reason to pause and lick their wounds. But they are not about to turn and run—at least not yet. Although our army fought like professionals, we must remember that we have encountered only the enemy's advance guard."

The officers nodded in agreement.

"Once their entire army is assembled, more than one thousand professional soldiers will outnumber us. The rampart must be built strong and high enough to make up for our shortage in manpower, experience, and equipment."

The general checked his notes once again and continued, "There's much to be done. Let's go, gentlemen." He winced as he limped to the door. Nevertheless, he took a deep breath and drew himself up to his full height, and resoluteness set in as he looked back to add, "We will make certain that the Redcoats do not enjoy their visit to Louisiana!"

Tarot: THE KING OF WANDS

Revelation: Encountering new and impassioned ideas.

⁓

Catherine opened her eyes slowly, after about four hours of rest. She had fallen asleep shortly after Sister Angelique had left. The classrooms and hallway were filled with more men on mattresses, some of them softly crying, others snoring. She noticed one man quietly fingering a rosary.

So many different men: planters, lawyers, bankers, laborers, artisans, seamen. White, brown, black, and red brought together for battle, now fighting individually for their lives.

Catherine got to her knees and bent over her patient. René's breathing was shallow, but he did not seem to be in pain. Scamp was still sound asleep. Catherine turned to gently nudge him.

"Scamp, you must awaken now. We have a lot to do."

The boy sat up and rubbed his eyes. He looked around at all the wounded who had joined them during the night, and then turned to Catherine with a questioning look.

"First," she said, "go find Sister Angelique. Ask her where you can get a clean bowl filled with water that has been boiled. Also inquire about borrowing a broom to sweep up the bloody straw."

By now, Scamp was fully awake. "And we'll probably need fresh straw, too, right?"

Catherine smiled. "You're a smart lad, Scamp. I'm grateful you're with me."

After Scamp ran off on his errands, Catherine looked down at René and found that he was awake. He smiled weakly.

Scamp returned with the bowl of water and a broom. "Sister Angelique says hello, and she would like some advice when you have a minute," he announced.

"Thank you, Scamp. You can start sweeping now." Catherine gently cleaned René's wound, noticing that his abdominal region still felt stiff to her touch. He winced as she applied a fresh dressing.

"Catherine . . ."

"There, now, René," she said, "let me get you some more medicine so that you won't be in pain." She tried to sound encouraging and soothing at the same time.

"Catherine."

"Shh, now, René. You've been hurt. You need to save your energy."

"Catherine," he repeated once again, sounding urgent, "I know it's bad, that I have not long to live. But I want you to promise me something. Please. Will you do that?"

Catherine looked into René's eyes. He knew he was dying. His breathing was shallow but labored, and talking was strenuous, but he was unflinching in his determination to extract this pledge.

"Of course, René. What is it?"

With difficulty, the dying man propped himself up on his elbows and met her gaze head-on. "It's about our baby. Our son."

Catherine nodded. She had sensed that Suzanne was bearing a boy.

"I want you to swear that you will do all you can to assure that my son is a free man."

"But certainly, René; as Suzanne's son, he will be a free man of color," she responded.

"But he is my son also, and I want him to be like me, an undiminished citizen of the United States." René's voice grew stronger. "I want my son to be able to vote, sit on juries, run for public office if he wants to, even run for president. I want him to be able to associate with whomever he chooses."

René took another gulp of air. "He cannot do that as a free man of color. That is why we were going to move north, so that our son would be genuinely free, without shame or denial of his heritage."

René paused. Inhaling was becoming more difficult. He tried to take another deep breath to continue.

"Suzanne has grit, Catherine, but I don't think she's capable of doing this on her own." Taking another labored breath and grabbing his mother-in-law's hand, he said, "Will you pledge to do whatever you can, within your power, to ensure that our son, your grandson, will be truly free?"

Catherine nodded slowly. "That is a formidable request, René, and I do not know how I might make that happen, but I will do whatever I can. I give you my word."

René sank back onto his pallet. "*Merci*. I am at peace now."

She gave him another measure of wine with laudanum and was gratified to see him doze off. She hoped that he would sleep at least an hour more without pain. She was afraid that it might be his last.

Catherine went over to Scamp, who was helping some women replace straw on the mattresses. "It's time to get Suzanne, Scamp," she said. "I believe she is at our house, helping Hortense."

Catherine paused and put her hand on the boy's head. "Scamp, I'm sorry that you must give Suzanne the bad news. Your message will make her very distraught. Warn her that René was severely injured and that she needs to be brave when she sees him. You need to escort her here and hold her arm all the while to make sure she does not fall. Can you do that, Scamp?"

The boy nodded solemnly.

"Good. I know I can count on you. Now, while Suzanne is preparing to come here, you have one more message to convey."

"Yes, madame?"

"Privately ask Madame Hortense to put some rum and cigars on my altar. They are for Baron Samedi, the loa who will help René cross over into the underworld."

Tarot: THE PAGE OF CUPS

*Revelation: A new and delicate sensibility;
being willing to serve has its rewards.*

—

It had been a long night, and today seemed even longer. Millie was driving Bella back to the big ditch. In her wagon on this trip, she had digging tools that had been rounded up in the city for building the rampart. She could hear the *Carolina* intermittently blasting at the British, and she prayed that Peter was all right.

Although she had made a couple of runs taking the wounded to the convent, seeing the suffering of her friend's husband made the conflict more intense, more personal. She was exhausted, dirty, and scared. But she also had a stronger sense of commitment. She felt a connection with her new colleagues, an awareness of belonging to this community. They made her feel worthy, and that sustained her.

Her mule whinnied softly.

"Good girl, Bella, you're doing a great job," she said to her weary animal. Then she added to herself, "And good girl, Millie!"

Tarot: THE SIX OF CUPS

Revelation: A beginning of new knowledge.

~

Sister Angelique walked in and saw Catherine sitting in a chair by René's mattress.

"How is your son-in-law doing?" she asked.

"He's not in pain, but he's fading fast," responded Catherine. "I have sent for my daughter, Suzanne. I believe you know her. She was a student of yours several years ago. She also worked with you at the beginning of this month to organize the women working the shifts."

The nun's eyes widened. "Oh, why, of course! And this is Suzanne's husband; I am so sorry," she said. "Your daughter has been such a help to us. She has incredible energy, especially in her condition. This will be quite a shock to her."

"Yes, I'm afraid so."

"When is she due?"

"Sometime in February," Catherine said. Changing the subject, she asked, "Scamp said you wanted to see me?"

"Ah, yes, I have a few items I want to discuss. Is this a good time?"

"As good as it will get, I'm afraid. René is sleeping now, thanks to the laudanum, and Suzanne won't arrive here for at least another half hour."

The nun wiped her forehead with her sleeve and sank down

on a chair next to Catherine. She took a pencil and a piece of paper out of her apron and examined what appeared to be a list.

Catherine waited, noting that the sister looked quite exhausted. A couple more minutes passed. It seemed like Sister Angelique had forgotten Catherine's presence. Catherine leaned over to her and quietly laid her hand on the other woman's shoulder, giving it a slight squeeze.

The nun put aside the list and looked up.

"I'm sorry, Madame Caresse. How rude of me."

"Are you all right, Sister Angelique?"

"Yes, thank you. But I am tired—tired and frustrated. This"—she spread her arms, as if to take in the entire building and its occupants—"is just so . . ."

"Appalling?"

"Yes. And we're so unprepared." She took a deep breath. "When we Ursulines came to New Orleans in 1723, Louisiana was part of New France. Besides teaching, we cared for the sick and injured in the military hospital."

"I was not aware of that; I knew only that you taught school," said Catherine.

Sister Angelique nodded and then continued, "That's because King Louis the Fifteenth gave the territory to Spain during the Seven Years' War. The English had defeated the French armies in Canada. By giving Louisiana to Spain in 1762, he prevented the same thing from happening here."

"Ah, yes. The Yankees called it the French and Indian War," said Catherine.

"Correct. Anyway, the Spanish authorities restricted us to educating girls and hand-stitching the priests' chasubles," Sister Angelica paused and shrugged. "Even though Napoleon negotiated, nothing changed with the return to French rule. That was

more than fifty years ago, so our nursing skills now are nonex-
istent." The nun gave a long sigh.

Catherine took the nun's hand. "Considering the circumstances, Sister Angelique, you're doing an admirable job. The
patients are fortunate to have the sisters here to care for them."

Then Catherine smiled. "Plus," she added with a slight
chuckle, "these men have the most stylish stitches ever pulled
through human flesh!"

The nun laughed. "Thank you. Why, lucky us! We may be
short of other supplies, but we do have plenty of needles and lots
of thread!"

Sister Angelique sighed again. "Please forgive me for complaining like this. I realize I am not alone in feeling frustrated,
and I know we are all very tired."

"It has been stressful, in more ways than one."

"But . . . Madame Caresse, you have had much experience
with suffering, and you know different medicines. I am hoping
that you can help us."

"Why, of course!"

The nun dabbed at her eyes and picked up the paper. "I drew
up a list of questions, but, first of all, do you have any recommendations for how we can improve our care of these men?"

"Hmm," said Catherine. "Well, most of my clients are pregnant women. However, as you know, I do advocate cleanliness
in all procedures. I have stressed that all the bandages and linens sent here should be washed in boiling water before they are
used."

Sister Angelique nodded. "Yes. We have been continuously
laundering since the first supplies arrived."

"How frequently will you be washing the patients' sheets
and blankets?"

"We nuns have our own linens and bedding washed every week!" Sister Angelique boasted. "So we'll do theirs just as frequently as we wash ours."

She noticed Catherine's frown. "Not often enough, right?"

"They should be fresh for each new patient, and if a patient soils anything, it must be replaced promptly. If you have extra beds, you can move the bedridden patient to a vacant bed, then strip and wash the used linens."

"Oh, my! All right. I'll instruct our servants to begin working on that immediately." She jotted a note on her piece of paper.

"And the hands and face of each patient should be washed off at least once daily. The entire body should be bathed two or three times a week."

"And fresh clothing?"

Catherine nodded. "And patients who can walk should be up and moving about during the day. Also . . ." Catherine hesitated.

"Yes?"

"If a patient dies, the straw in his bed sack needs to be burned."

"Yes. Well. We have been lucky to procure loads of hay for ticking."

"Good. Now, what about your list of questions?"

"I'm concerned about some of the food we're receiving. It's not cooked properly, and some men have already complained of cramps."

"Try to get the patient to vomit by using ipecac. I've used this medicine also for fevers."

Sister Angelique glanced again at her list. "What about poultices? Many of the men have leg sores."

"What have you been using?"

"We have been pounding bread crumbs, stirring in boiled milk, and adding lard. Then we smear it on the leg. The procedure is quite time-consuming!"

"An easier method you might employ to relieve pain and reduce inflammation is honey, if you can get some. Just apply it directly to the skin. You can use it for insect bites and burns, too."

After Sister Angelique wrote the word "honey," she said, "I notice that you don't suggest bloodletting or blistering."

"I certainly don't use those methods when delivering a baby!" Catherine laughed. "But you're right—I don't favor either of those treatments, although they're popular among doctors. They're used primarily for diseases, not for the wounds you're tending. Again, I attempt to treat symptoms with what I have in my personal apothecary, but otherwise I strongly advocate cleanliness, rest, and a good diet."

"I'm grateful, Madame Caresse, not only for your recommendations, but also for being able to share your spirit." Sister Angelique said, standing up and pocketing her paper and pencil. "I feel better already!"

Catherine clasped one of the nun's hands in her own and said, "I'm happy to hear that. We'll get through this together, Sister Angelique."

"Again, thank you, Madame Caresse. I'm going to the laundry right now!"

Tarot: THE QUEEN OF SWORDS

Revelation: Sadness; possible widowhood.

~

Hortense opened the door to Catherine's cottage and, seeing Scamp alone, knew at once that something was wrong.

"I need to talk to Mademoiselle Suzanne," the boy said.

Suzanne walked into the front room and looked first at the boy, and then at the older woman. They were both looking down at the floor.

"What is it, Scamp?" Suzanne asked softly.

Scamp moved closer to Suzanne and gazed up at her with a regretful expression. Before relaying Catherine's message, he reached out to hold both of Suzanne's hands.

"M-M-M-Mademoiselle Suzanne," he stammered.

"*Non! Non, non,* Scamp!"

Scamp looked at Hortense, his eyes wide. Hortense ran over to Suzanne and put her arm around the pregnant girl. "Now, Suzanne, you need to let the boy tell us what's going on."

"Y-y-you must be brave, Mademoiselle Suzanne!" he started again.

"It's René, isn't it?" She cut him off. "He's hurt!" she cried. "I can feel it; it's a pain right here!" She pointed to her abdomen.

Suzanne began sobbing in Hortense's arms. "*Mon Dieu! Mon* René!"

Hortense rocked her back and forth, murmuring "*Tout sera*

bien, Suzanne. *Tout sera bien*," yet wondering to herself if everything would in fact be all right.

When Suzanne's tears stopped, her mouth was dry and she began trembling. Turning to face the boy, she said, "Tell me, Scamp: How bad is it?"

"Well . . ." Scamp looked at Hortense, who shook her head slightly, as a warning.

"Well," he said again, wringing his hands, "Monsieur Bonet has been hurt real bad. And your *maman* thinks it would be good for you to come and visit him . . . and," he improvised, "make him feel better. I'm to take you there right now!" he finished proudly.

"*Oui*, of course! Oh, Our Lady of Prompt Succor, save my husband," prayed Suzanne, as she threw on her cloak and grabbed her bag.

"Do you need any help getting your things?" Hortense asked, opening the door.

"No, thank you, Hortense; I'll just bring an extra blanket and pillow, and perhaps the missal, to pray with him. Scamp, I'll meet you outside." She gave Hortense a hug and hastened out toward her house.

"Does Madame Catherine have instructions for me, Scamp?" asked the maid.

"*Oui*, madame."

"I was afraid of that."

Tarot: THE SIX OF SWORDS

*Revelation: A capacity for understanding
helps ease anxiety.*

⟶

Hortense's cousin Andre was in one of the carts bringing slaves to help build the rampart. Wagons from the city and surrounding plantations were also arriving, filled with beans, rice, greens, hams, rum, and more shovels, spades, hoes, and pickaxes. Along the shallow canal, workers were excavating mud and piling it around cypress logs notched and stacked in interlocking rectangles laid along the north side of the ditch.

Andre's wagon came to a halt. As he jumped down, a tall, handsome black man handed him a shovel.

"Hello. I'm Tobias, and you are . . ."

"Andre."

"Welcome to the Macarty plantation, Andre—or, as we now call it, Camp Jackson." Tobias explained, "Since time is of the essence, Major Latour is keeping the various groups working separately to promote competition. So far, the Yankee volunteers seem to be in the lead, but we slaves and the free coloreds are gaining." Then Tobias chuckled. "As you would expect, the Creoles are in last place."

Contest or no, Andre thought, *what a way to spend Christmas Eve.*

Andre headed toward a group of Negroes, whose clothes

and distasteful expressions indicated that they were fellow house slaves.

He groaned inwardly as he dug in. A shovel was not a tool he used at the Villeré plantation house. But while he was scooping up sludge, he heard some of his fellow slaves talking about being set free by General Jackson. They said that if they made a strong rampart here and two more upriver, and the English were defeated, they would be granted their freedom. The thought of one day being his own man took his mind off the mud and sweat, and Andre dug deeper and faster.

More soil was hauled in to strengthen the wall, and his group enthusiastically continued its work. They set cotton bales into the ground, to serve as solid platforms for the artillery, and spaced the cannons to cover all the fields in front of the rising rampart.

Andre started feeling a kinship with the other workers, but he was curious about Tobias, who was moving along the canal, encouraging the men and praising their work. Andre wondered who this uppity slave was.

Hours passed quickly. The men now sang as they dug in unison, scooping a shovel full of mud on the first beat, lifting with a vocal grunt on the second, throwing the mud onto the rampart on the third, slapping the mud with the empty shovel on the fourth, and then bending to repeat the rhythm. One of the slaves improvised the words and shouted them before each move, changing the lyrics with each round; then all sang them.

Finally, it was suppertime. Although red beans and rice flavored with onions and dried red peppers was not Andre's usual fare, he considered it the best meal he had ever tasted.

He could hear gunshots coming from the Choctaws and Tennessee riflemen, as they picked off the sentries around the English camp. Knowing that the Redcoats had been devouring the hams—his hams—from the Villeré mansion, he hoped the snipers were successful with each shot.

His work was over for the day. After a second helping, Andre looked around for a place to lie down. The area behind the rampart was ten feet wide, to give the sleeping shift some room. Exhausted, chilled, and wet, Andre removed his shoes and socks, stretched out, and put his head on his arms, grateful to get a few hours of slumber. Some of the men in his group were already snoring. He had heard that General Jackson, who had come by his area earlier to inspect, slept very little. Yet Catherine had said that the general needed rest because of his dysentery. Andre wondered how this would all finish: an ill and fatigued leader, an undermanned army, a powerful enemy . . .

Fingering the small leather pouch hanging around his neck, he hoped that Catherine's protection gris-gris was truly potent. Just to be on the safe side, he brought it up to his mouth and gently blew on it.

Next was his prayer to Our Lady of Prompt Succor, known for protecting those in need. Andre's petition included safety for his wife, Claire, for his cousin Hortense, and for Catherine's family, and then he thought he had better include Andrew Jackson and the army, too.

Now he could sleep.

Tarot: DEATH

Revelation: A sudden change; a transformation.

~

Scamp took Suzanne's arm and was ready to steady her, even steer her, but she did not falter as they walked quickly to the makeshift hospital. She did not say anything but seemed resolute in her mission. Her husband needed her.

At the convent door, she shook Scamp's arm away from her, strode into the hallway, and came to an abrupt stop. She could see that the first classroom was lined with men lying on beds, pallets, and simple blankets. She recognized the varying dress of the Creoles, Kentuckians, and Choctaws. She noticed the visitors, the nurses, and the priest. Some of the injured were asleep, groaning as they turned over. Others were being fed, taking medication, or having fresh bandages applied. Still others were reading or talking quietly to one another.

She had entered the room many times in the previous days, efficiently checking the supplies and genially supporting the lady volunteers. The nuns and other women had all admired her energy.

This time, she had only one purpose. Where was René?

Scamp joined her and, gently taking her hand, led her back into the hallway, where the worst cases were laid. At this moment, she fully comprehended René's critical condition. In fact, she had actually set up this placement for the terminally wounded, knowing that the hallway meant a quicker and shorter distance for removal of the deceased: it was easier to clean up, and the dying patients wouldn't upset those who were probably going to heal.

When she saw him, it took all her willpower to keep from wailing out in anguish. René was colorless; his eyes were closed, and his lips moved feebly. Suzanne started to stagger, reaching out to the wall for support. The hallway began to blur, and she gasped for air. It was as if someone were holding her underwater. Scamp wrapped his arms around her waist to keep her from falling.

And then, very slowly, her senses returned.

She saw her mother kneeling beside René, gently wiping up the pinkish, milky liquid emerging from his gaping wound. She smelled the sickening stink of putrefied flesh. She heard Catherine telling René that he was a good man, that he would always have Suzanne's love, and that the pain would stop soon. And then Suzanne tasted her own tears, as she stood helplessly above her beloved husband.

Catherine looked up and quickly put a clean cloth over the patient's wound. "Suzanne, come talk to René. He loves you so much, you know."

Suzanne slowly began to totter forward and then felt something inside her break.

Tarot: THE SIX OF PENTACLES

Revelation: A call to offer generosity.

⁓

Jeannette's children were now back at their house, and Claire continued caring for them while the young mother napped.

Hortense, unsettled by Scamp's messages, was vigorously washing windows in the parlor. She noticed a carriage pulling up in front of Catherine's home. Setting aside her bucket and rag, with her hands on her hips, Hortense watched as two ladies got out. One woman, older, was helping the other, very pregnant one lumber toward the front door.

The maid didn't know what to expect, but she had a feeling she was going to encounter yet another shock.

First that soldier came for Madame Catherine, she thought; *then Suzanne brought that prostitute over. . . .* (Hortense did not approve, no matter how valiant Suzanne declared Millie to be.) *Plus my cousin Andre and his wife, looking for refuge, and Scamp, with his dreadful news. All this tragedy at once. This must be what war is about.*

Reluctantly, Hortense answered the knock.

She recognized the pregnant woman as a Creole client of Catherine's, although she did not know her name. The woman appeared to be in pain and leaned very heavily on her older companion, also a Creole.

"*Bonjour*, mesdames. How may I help you?" asked Hortense, mystified by this scene.

"Are you Hortense?" the older woman asked in a haughty tone.

"*Oui. . . .*"

Again on an arrogant note, the woman continued, "This is Madame Marguerite de Trahan, and I am her mother."

Hortense's eyes widened at the sound of the familiar surname. However, she politely responded, "*Oui?*"

"Well, she's in great pain, so you obviously need to—"

Marguerite gave out a moan and then spoke. "Maman, please."

Giving Hortense a weak smile, Marguerite said, "Madame Hortense, I am a friend of Madame Caresse's; we worked together preparing medical supplies for the troops. She told me I could come here when I went into labor. She said you would help me. May we come in, *s'il vous plaît?*"

Incroyable! Hortense thought, but she replied, "*Oui*, of course," and opened the door wider to let the ladies in. "Madame Caresse is not here right now. Follow me, *s'il vous plaît.*"

Hortense led the two white women to Suzanne's former room, and while Sheila tried to make Marguerite somewhat comfortable on the bed, Hortense went to get the midwife bag.

While gathering lotions and cloths, she thought, *I vaguely recall Madame Catherine mentioning this possibility. But oh,* mon Dieu—*not tonight!*

Sheila was complaining loudly. "Marguerite, I don't like this arrangement at all. In fact, this is outrageous! First the lack of qualified medical doctors, and now my own daughter being reduced to mingling with these people? And being cared for only by a slave, no less!"

"Mother, please."

"And this tiny room—totally inadequate! Why, the absurdity of our being in this neighborhood at all! If Jacques knew about this . . ."

So, thought Hortense, *it's just as I surmised. Marguerite is the wife of Jacques. Well, she is obviously in great discomfort, but if I'd had a choice, I would have slammed the door on that overbearing mother of hers.*

Then Hortense heard Marguerite cry out.

Oh dear! I wonder if I will be delivering the baby myself, and with that despicable mother carping away. C'est la vie—but I do hope that Madame Catherine will be coming home from the hospital soon.

Tarot: THE FIVE OF PENTACLES

*Revelation: Signaling a period of loss
and impoverishment.*

~

S camp was hopping from one foot to the other. "Uh-oh!" he said. "Uh-oh! Uh-oh! Uh-oh!"

Normally, Catherine would have admonished him to hush. But she was stunned.

Suzanne was dumbfounded, too, and stared at the puddle gathering around her shoes and trickling across the slightly sloping pine floor. She grabbed the back of a nearby chair for support.

At that moment, Sister Angelique walked into the hallway briskly, passing Suzanne with a nod of her head. The nun was carrying a stack of cloths and bandages. "Ah, good news, Catherine," she said quietly, with a smile. "Millie has brought us some fresh supplies!" She bent down to place the stack on another chair.

"Uh-oh!" Scamp repeated once more.

While bent over, Sister Angelique noted the puddle and quickly straightened to look at Catherine, and then at her wide-eyed daughter, still clutching the chair. "Oh, my!" exclaimed the nun. "Suzanne, I see your water has broken!"

Meanwhile, Catherine had moved to her daughter's side to support her.

"Scamp, we'll need a mop and pail," directed Sister Angelique.

"I know where they are, Sister."

After removing the linens, the two older women lowered Suzanne gently onto the chair beside René's pallet. Her face was ashen, her eyes now glazed.

"Ohhhh," she murmured, looking down at her abdomen. She massaged it and looked up at her mother. "Maman? What should I do?"

"The baby's arriving a little early, but, given the circumstances, it's not unexpected. And look—I believe René is awake now!"

"Oh, *mon amour*. René!" Suzanne quickly got out of the chair, knelt down, and leaned over her husband, delicately holding his face in her hands. "Oh, my beloved," she whispered. "I am here for you."

René opened his eyes and attempted a smile.

"Suzanne . . . my dearest." His breathing was labored, but he struggled to continue talking to her. "You have made me . . . so very happy. Now, you must be brave. With our baby. . . ."

"René, my love, please . . ." She reached for his hands.

"Remember me, my darling, but not with tears; remember our sweet times together. . . . *Je t'aime*."

Still looking at her with tenderness, he breathed his last, exhausted sigh.

"*Non*, René! Please don't leave me! Don't leave us!"

As Catherine tenderly wrapped her arms around her sobbing daughter, Sister Angelique gently closed René's eyes and drew the blanket up over his face.

Tarot: THE HERMIT

*Revelation: A time to be mindful of limitations
and acquire the wisdom of patience.*

⁓

As Suzanne keened on top of her husband's covered body, Catherine motioned to Sister Angelique to follow her into one of the classrooms.

"Is Millie still here?" she asked the nun. "She could take my daughter and me back to my home."

"Yes, I think she is resting in the supply room. I gave her a cup of tea to help revive her. Poor dear. She's really doing a terrific service. I'll get her now."

While the Ursuline sister walked swiftly down the hallway in search of Millie, Catherine turned to console Suzanne.

Suzanne looked up at her mother and cried, "Maman! How can I go on? There are so few wounded—why René? And why couldn't you save him?"

Catherine knelt down by her daughter and put her arm around her.

"Suzanne, René had a very severe wound and had lain on the battlefield for an hour or more before Miguel found him. We should thank God that he lived long enough to see you. It is clear that it was to say *au revoir* to you and his child that he willed himself to live as long as he did. You must remember that he sacrificed his life to protect us and your child. Now it is your turn to be as courageous as René."

Suzanne's sobbing lessened.

Catherine cupped her daughter's chin in her hands and looked into her eyes. "Sister Angelique is getting Millie to take us back home. Are you having contractions now?"

Suzanne shook her head no, but then she turned and put her head down on her husband's blanketed chest, clasped his shoulders, and began sobbing again.

Sister Angelique approached them in the hallway with Millie, who looked quite stunned. The nun gave her a quick hug.

"I found her sharing her tea and cookies with one of the Baratarian patients," announced Sister Angelique, in an effort to be buoyant.

Suzanne looked up, her eyes rimmed red from her grieving. "Oh, Millie," she said, "René's gone!"

Some inner strength appeared to galvanize Millie then, and her whole being seemingly changed, from incredible exhaustion and shock to an astounding vitality. She ran over next to Catherine and took Suzanne's face in her hands. "Suzanne, my dear friend, I'm so terribly sorry. But"—and Millie's tone sounded more stern—"your baby is on his way to join us. This is no place for him to be born. So your mother and I are going to get you to her house, where we can take care of you. You know that's what René would want. And I'm here to help you—always, my good friend. Are you ready?"

Without waiting for an answer, Millie began scooping up Suzanne, and Catherine quickly moved to assist her.

Catherine turned to Scamp, who was uncharacteristically subdued.

"Scamp, I want you to stay here and help Sister Angelique.

I think this baby is going to be born within the next few hours. Then Hortense will take care of Suzanne and the baby, and you and I can check on General Jackson. We have a hectic time ahead of us."

She shook her head and looked at the nun. "If you can take care of . . ." She looked back at the covered corpse.

"Yes, of course, Catherine. God be with you!"

Tarot: THE FOUR OF PENTACLES

*Revelation: A mean condition; too attached
to a worldly position.*

⁓

Hortense heard Catherine's voice at the door and ran to open it.

"Thank heavens you're here," she said to Catherine. "I have everything ready!"

"*Très bien*, Hortense!" Catherine responded, and then stopped. "But wait—how did you know about the baby coming?" she asked.

Hortense looked beyond Catherine and saw Millie helping Suzanne to the house. "*Mon Dieu!* Suzanne!"

At the same time, Catherine heard a scream coming from the rear of her home.

"Madame de Trahan?" asked Catherine.

"In Suzanne's room. She's all right. Just started. But what about Suzanne?" asked Hortense.

"Her water broke, but she's not far along, either." Turning back to the two younger women, Catherine said, "Millie, can you stay a while longer with Suzanne, until we get everything organized?"

"Of course," said Millie. "I'll stay as long as you need me."

"Good!" Catherine turned back to her servant. "Hortense, if you will help Millie take Suzanne to my room, I'll see how

Madame de Trahan is faring. Join me after you get Suzanne settled."

Still gripping her medical bag, the midwife hastened into Suzanne's childhood room. She saw her Creole friend sitting up in the bed, but not in obvious discomfort.

"Ah, Catherine, I'm so glad to see you!"

"How are you doing, Marguerite?" Catherine asked, as she washed her hands in the basin Hortense had left.

"She's cried out several times and is clearly in a great deal of pain," declared another voice in the room.

Catherine looked over her shoulder and saw an older woman standing by the window.

"She should be at home in her own bed, with a real doctor. Instead, here we are, in this inferior neighborhood with you people. These conditions—this situation—is very unsatisfactory." Sheila folded her arms tightly across her chest, her fists clenched, as if to shut out the surroundings.

"And you are . . . ?"

"Maman! I'm sorry, Catherine. Please forgive my mother's ungracious behavior. She has forgotten how a guest should act."

"Ungracious! Well, Daughter, you forget yourself! Let me tell you—"

Marguerite let out another scream. Catherine wondered if it was due to her labor pains or to her mother's bad manners.

Catherine got down on her knees to examine Marguerite's cervix. She was not fully dilated. Catherine took Marguerite's wrist to gauge her heartbeat, then said, "You're going to be fine, Marguerite; just remember to pant like a dog when you have a contraction. They'll be coming more quickly now."

"Well?" demanded Sheila, putting her hands on her hips. "What do you propose to do?" She walked to the foot of the bed and glowered down at Catherine.

Catherine stood up and regarded Sheila with a slight smile. "I am going to deliver your grandchild, Madame. However, I quite agree with you."

Sheila looked at her with surprise.

"My home may be modest, and this room is very small. But it is my house. My maid, Hortense, and I will need every space available to set up our supplies for Marguerite's comfort. And although I did not invite you, you are my guest. I expect you, as a courteous Creole lady, to act as a guest should."

Catherine removed some of her ointments and instruments from her medical bag and, placing them on the bed, deliberately nudged Sheila aside.

"And so, now that you know that your daughter is comfortable, I would strongly suggest that you stay in a place more suitable to your station until after the birth," she continued, still laying out her tools, cloths, and lotions. "Our friend Millie will take you there. But you must leave immediately, as curfew will soon be upon us."

Marguerite's mother, for the first time in her life, was speechless.

Catherine nodded to Hortense, who was standing in the doorway. She turned then and faced Sheila. "Now, if you will come with me . . ."

"But . . . but," sputtered Sheila.

"Go, Maman. I may be in labor for quite a while," said Marguerite.

Putting her right arm around Sheila's shoulder and her left hand under the woman's left elbow, Catherine commandeered the flabbergasted woman out of the room and hustled her to the entry door.

"Now, don't worry about your daughter, madame," Catherine said in a soothing tone. "Hortense and I will see that Marguerite is comfortable and that the birth goes smoothly. I will send word to you as soon as she is ready to receive visitors."

Millie was already outside, waiting in her wagon.

Hortense handed Sheila her cloak. *"Au revoir,* madame," she said, with a big smile.

"Harrumph!" said Sheila, as she flounced past Hortense.

Shutting the door, Hortense rolled her eyes at Catherine. "That woman has some nerve," she said.

"I agree," said Catherine. "But I'm sure she's worried about her daughter. As am I. How's Suzanne?"

"She's settled. Crying a lot, but Millie calmed her down a bit. I'm so sorry about René. *Le pauvre.* But, knowing Suzanne, she'll get through this. She's always been resilient."

Tarot: THE LOVERS

Revelation: A choice in love and responsibility.

⟶

Both births occurred late that night. Both mothers cried out in pain. Not unusual during childbirth.

But Catherine wondered about Marguerite's distress; much of it seemed to be caused by a fear of someone or something she alone sensed. Besides her screams during obvious contractions, she also shrieked, "You're wrong! No, leave me!" "Stop telling me that!" "Go away!"

Suzanne's anguish only compounded her trauma. Her mutterings, between labor pains, were simpler to understand: "Oh, René . . ."

Both birthing mothers were exhausted. Catherine and Hortense wiped off their sweat, prompted their panting, and ignored the swearing. They gave them sips of water and soothed them with words of comfort and encouragement. After washing their own hands, the midwife and assistant went back and forth from one "delivery room" to the other. They massaged the patients' vaginal openings, made the surgical cuts to their perineums, and instructed them when to breathe and when to push. They were drained, too.

Catherine received Marguerite's baby boy first. An hour later, Suzanne's son was born.

Both infants were wet, bald, with long heads, and dark red

in color, and had bluish-tinted hands and feet. After cutting the umbilical cord, Catherine handed each baby to Hortense, who cleansed him, clearing away the mucus from his nose, mouth, ears, and anus. The newborn was then swaddled and placed into his own basket.

Both mothers promptly sank into a deep sleep after delivery. The caretakers restored their birthing rooms to everyday conditions; cleaned the umbilical scissors, forceps, needles, and thread; and put away the unused portions of ointment.

Hortense lit several candles in the parlor and brought the babies in, and Catherine settled herself on the sofa to watch over them. Hortense went back to her cabinet and was soon snoring softly.

Both babies seemed to be sleeping peacefully. Catherine closed her eyes and tried to rest, but, although her body was weary, her mind was churning with a peculiar foreboding.

After an hour of fidgeting, she got up to check on the babies. Holding one of the candles, she tiptoed over to the baskets, knelt down, and examined the first. Perfect. His coloring was good, his breathing steady.

Then she observed the other little fellow. Something didn't seem quite normal. He appeared to be having difficulty breathing.

Putting her candlestick down, Catherine carefully picked the baby up for a better look. Even though she supported the back of his head, it still flopped forward like a rag doll. And she could see, even in the flickering glow of the candlelight, that his coloring was wrong; his face had turned yellow.

Alarmed, she immediately felt his forehead. He had a fever. As she held him in the crook of her arm, he arched his neck backward and opened his eyes. The whites, too, were yellow. He gave a high-pitched cry, and, as she clasped him to her breast, tears came to her eyes as well. She knew he would not survive much longer.

Every baby she had delivered was precious; losing one was always heartbreaking. The loss of this child would be no different. Especially in this instance, difficult grief and despair were soon to follow. And Catherine knew tonight's consequences would be colossal. Appealing to St. Jude, known for aiding in desperate causes, she began to gently rock the baby in her arms. Softly, she told him about his father and mother and how much they loved him.

Carrying the baby out to the water barrel by the kitchen, Catherine dipped her handkerchief into the water and, squeezing drops onto the baby's forehead, pronounced, "I baptize thee *in nomine Patris, et Filii, et Spiritus Sancti.*" Then she called to Chamuel, one of the two angels who comforted Jesus in the garden of Gethsemane. Knowing the inevitable, Catherine asked that the angel lead the child quickly into heaven and return to help her deal with the family's bereavement. She was still petitioning the saints and *loas*, cuddling the baby, when he took his last, little breath.

Catherine put the infant's body back into his basket and covered it with a cloth. Hortense awakened, wordlessly acknowledged the situation, and sadly embraced her employer. She would call upon Père Antoine the following morning.

Catherine went back into the parlor and gazed at the other infant. He sleepily opened his eyes and blinked back at her. She picked him up, kissed him tenderly, and said, "Hello, my darling. Today is your first full day in a new world. You must be strong; you must survive." The baby blinked again as she gently laid him back in his basket.

A few hours later, Catherine sat at the dining room table, head down in her arms. She felt like one of the candles—melted down to the nub. Hortense was quietly pouring her a morning cup of coffee, when a baby's cry came from the parlor.

Catherine raised her head, her eyes bloodshot, her face haggard. She pushed her hand through her hair, took a deep breath, and looked fixedly at her maid.

"Hortense, will you please get the baby for Marguerite to nurse?" she said.

Hortense cocked her head in shock and dropped the coffeepot.

Tarot: THE CHARIOT

Revelation: Conflict and struggle will be
faced with strength and a conquest.

⁓

December 25: a very foggy morning. "Happy Christmas, mates, and God bless America!" Peter called out to his fellow Baratarians on the *Carolina*, as they continued blasting the British.

December 26: a very misty morning. "It's St. Stephen's Day, mates!" Peter called out to his fellow crewmen. "Where I'm from, the feast day of St. Stephen the martyr is celebrated with food, drink, music, and dancing, in contrast with your more solemn, religious Christmas Day. But today we're celebrating St. Stephen with fireworks, bombarding the Redcoats!"

December 27: a very frosty morning. The rising sun revealed that the *Carolina*'s routine was about to change.

Over the prior three days, the Redcoats had lifted, rowed, dragged, and carried dismantled cannons through forest and swamp from their ships on Lake Borgne to the banks of the Mississippi River. There, overnight, the cannons were remounted and aimed at the *Carolina*. While the cannons were being emplaced, the cannon balls were heated in the plantation's blacksmith's forge until they were red hot.

The first English salvo splintered the *Carolina*'s bulwarks and shredded its rigging. Before the *Carolina*'s crew could load and return fire, the red-hot cannonballs of the second English salvo ruptured the *Carolina*'s hull and started fires near the magazine containing the store of gunpowder.

Captain Henley immediately gave the order to abandon ship. Peter scrambled over the side into a boat, grabbed an oar, and, along with other escaping crewmembers, rowed to the opposite shore.

Moments later, the *Carolina* erupted with a roar; burning wood and iron cannon barrels sailed through the air. Peter heard the British gunners cheer.

Although Peter was furious about the loss of the *Carolina*, he was grateful to be alive. Not all of his mates were so lucky.

The *Louisiana* was safe, too; her crew of Baratarians, in row-boats and pirogues, against the wind and current, had pulled her upstream, around a bend in the river.

December 28: a very sunny morning. The *Carolina* destroyed and the *Louisiana* now withdrawn from sight, the English commander General Packenham decided to push the American rabble out of the way and take the city. Behind a barrage of artillery and rockets, ranks of English troops began advancing, eighty abreast, one column in the field along the river, the other adjacent to the swamp.

General Jackson watched their advance from the second floor of the Macarty plantation house. The English army made an impressive and intimidating sight. They covered the fields like red ants swarming from a kicked anthill.

Then Jackson turned his attention to the rampart where his men were hurrying to their assigned positions. He watched a group of Baratarians turn off River Road and run to Battery 3 to man the two twenty-four-pounder naval cannons Jean Lafitte had supplied. The general smiled to himself; Dominique Yu, Lafitte's half brother, knew what to do.

Dominique quickly gauged the distance to the advancing English and ordered the cannons loaded with chain shot. Although normally used to destroy the sails and rigging of ships, the two balls, attached by a chain, would also shred the ranks of Redcoats.

The British were now about six hundred yards away from the rampart.

Aiming slightly high so that the chain shot would not just bury itself in the muddy ground, Dominique ordered the cannons to fire. The other American batteries, including the cannon of the *Louisiana* anchored along the opposite bank of the Mississippi, followed suit, and large gaps appeared in the red-coated ranks.

The experienced Baratarians immediately swabbed the insides of the cannon muzzles to extinguish any sparks, before reloading again with bags of gunpowder and the chain shot.

More gaps.

Yet the English continued to push forward, and Peter, who was positioned close to Dominique Yu, could see the effects of the Americans' salvos with red mist and parts of human torsos rising above the oncoming ranks.

As the English advanced to within musket range, the American infantry moved up to the rampart and began firing. At that point, Dominique switched the cannons' projectiles from chain to grapeshot.

Although the smoke rising from the muskets and cannons made visibility difficult, Peter noticed the English lines becoming even more fragmented; some Redcoats were trying to take cover in the contours of the fields and behind the mounting bodies of their dead and wounded.

Meanwhile, Andre was squatting down behind the infantry, clutching his shovel in his right hand and his gris-gris in his left.

Along with the other wide-eyed and inexperienced recruits in his group, he was terrified. Andre could hear the English drums and bugles, he could see their colorful uniforms, and he could smell the pungent smoke from their rockets. He also heard Tobias trying to soothe the frightened group. "Compose yourselves, men. They'll stop when they realize our cannons will get them."

But the English did not stop.

Andre and all the new recruits, along with the seasoned American soldiers, as well as Peter and the Baratarians, were astonished by their discipline.

The American artillery continued firing at intervals to keep the British pinned down.

Finally, as more and more of their comrades fell, the British troops broke ranks and took cover in the wet ditches of the sugarcane fields. The survivors waited until nightfall, seven hours later, to begin their humiliating retreat to their camp.

By that time, Andre no longer was frightened and Peter's bitterness had abated. After the hours of crossfire between ship and rampart, the explosions of the rockets and cannons, the blazing of the guns, and the shrieks of the wounded, the two men were drained of any feelings at all.

Tarot: THE SUN

*Revelation: Achievement; intent to move forward
and plan for the future.*

~

December 30, 1814
Residence of the American Peace Commissioners,
Ghent, Belgium

"Thank God Britain's Parliament has finally ratified the peace treaty," said John Quincy Adams. "It's been a long five months. We can return home now and submit it to Congress for approval."

"I'm writing to President Madison to advise him that the English government has approved the December twenty-fourth draft of the treaty," said American Peace Commissioner Albert Gallatin. "And just in case this letter reaches him first, I'm including the key provisions. It will end the war and remove English garrisons from US territory."

Henry Clay added, "And the English have agreed to reimburse owners for property, including slaves confiscated from southern ports."

"I doubt you'll ever see a halfpenny," responded Adams.

"You could say that our agreeing to restore the Indian lands to the boundaries of 1811 is just as insincere," commented Clay. "The Indians are not subjects of the English king; we will deal with them directly."

"There has been give-and-take on both sides," said Gallatin. "We have guaranteed England's complete sovereignty over all of Canada east of the Rocky Mountains, and they have pledged to stop interfering with American shipping and impressing our sailors."

Clay responded, "Perhaps. But I think the reason Britain gave in is that Napoleon has returned from exile on the island of Elba. The English are worried about a resurgent French empire."

"Well, Henry, you can't blame them for wanting their troops back," said Adams.

"It's over; we proved ourselves as a nation to be reckoned with. And our men can go home," said Gallatin. "The sooner, the better!"

Tarot: THE TWO OF PENTACLES

Revelation: Spirit of harmony in the midst of change.

⁓

December 31, 1814

Andrew Jackson was again using his telescope, peering out of the Macarty mansion's second-floor window.

"I can't see anything in all this fog," he complained to his aides. "What in tarnation are those British doing? Digging and hammering all day and night . . ."

"General, our scouts report that they are building redoubts. Ah! It's stopped now, sir," said a breathless Major Reid, who had just rushed into the headquarters and raced up the stairs. "They are located across the field, about six hundred yards to our front."

"We must pinpoint the location of each so that our cannons can be sighted and ready to open fire as soon as their targets are visible," said Jean Lafitte.

"I'll order Captain Jugeant to make up scouting parties of a couple Choctaws and a Baratarian cannoneer each; they should be able to gauge the distance and locations."

"Good idea, Major Reid; please proceed immediately. We don't want any surprises."

Tarot: THE TEN OF CUPS

Revelation: True friendship.

~~~

It was the first morning of the year 1815, and, although the gloomy fog still cloaked the field, the American camp was in a jubilant mood. Recognizing the local custom of New Year's Day visiting and feasting, but not in a position to allow the local volunteers to return to their homes, General Jackson had invited the entire civilian population of New Orleans to bring their feasts and attend a review of the American army. The troops had spent New Year's Eve repairing and washing their clothes, cleaning muskets, and polishing boots. By midmorning, Camp Jackson had taken on the appearance of a county fair. Older men, women, and children gathered along the top of the river levee for the best view.

With the exception of those who had to remain on duty at the rampart, almost four thousand troops were filing into place, assembling to march in the dress parade. Even the slaves, although lacking uniforms or weapons, stood proudly in formation, some holding their shovels, spades, and pickaxes. Musicians entertained and flags fluttered as cheerful officers trotted up and down the ranks. They were all waiting for the general to appear; he was still getting ready at the Macarty mansion.

Jacques brushed some of the dried swamp mud off his

uniform jacket as he hastened to join his regiment. He glimpsed Tobias, who was already at the head of his formation.

"Tobias!"

The tall, handsome slave grinned broadly at his master. *"Bonne année!"* The men exchanged buoyant salutes.

Still grinning, Jacques found the ebullient Tennesseans in the open cane fields, nodding and calling out, "Happy New Year!" to one another. Some of the men waved gaily to the women and children who had arrived in carriages from the city. Jacques searched the crowd for Marguerite and her mother, without success.

This fog is terrible, he thought. *I can barely see the levee by the river. They could be here, but it's too difficult to pick out their faces. I hope the sun breaks through this haze soon.*

Several yards away from the Tennesseans, Millie pulled up in her cart and lifted out a picnic hamper. Even through the mist, she quickly spotted Peter's companions at Battery 3, each freebooter colorfully dressed to please only himself. She could also make out the thickset half brother of Jean Lafitte, Dominique Yu, commanding the battery.

As Millie walked toward the Baratarians, she heard someone call out her name.

"Millie! Is that you?"

"Miguel! Hello! How are you?"

"Good, thank you. I almost didn't recognize you in that dress; I've grown accustomed to seeing you with pants on." Miguel glanced down at the picnic basket. "Seeing someone special here, perhaps?"

Millie blushed. "I hope so. His name is Pete; he's one of the Baratarians."

"Well, you sure look pretty," said Miguel.

"Merci! Suzanne lent me this dress and cloak, since she can

only wear black now. She also helped me do my hair and fix the picnic food."

"Um, 'since she can only wear black now'? Millie, I'm afraid to ask." Miguel hesitated. "René?"

"Oh, my! You don't know! Miguel, so much has happened since we last met. René is with the saints. His wound was too deep, and infection had set in."

"God rest his soul! He was so young." Miguel shook his head. "But I am not surprised. René was covered with blood and very weak when I found him. Suzanne must have been devastated."

"Yes, and there's more. Catherine sent Scamp to fetch Suzanne once we got René to the hospital, so she was with him when he passed. But then her water broke and she went into labor. Later that night, she gave birth to a boy."

"One departs, one is born."

"Oh, Miguel. Things just got worse. The baby died, too. I thought both deaths would destroy her. She just stayed inside her home, with all the shutters closed, and refused to speak to anyone. Baskets of food were left at her door, but they remained untouched."

"And what about Catherine?"

"Suzanne still won't see her. Suzanne blames her mother; she thinks Catherine did not do enough to save either her husband or her baby."

Miguel's eyes widened. "I'm sure that Catherine did everything in her power to save both René and the baby. She once told me that one out of every three babies dies within a few months of birth. Suzanne should know that better than anyone, considering her *maman*'s profession. She also knows that a battle is not a parade—most men who receive bad wounds do not survive." He shook his head sadly. "How could Suzanne even consider blaming her *maman*? Catherine is the best healer in

New Orleans—maybe in all Louisiana!"

Miguel thought a moment and then asked, "Well then, how did you . . ."

"I went every day and knocked on Suzanne's door to see her. Finally, after three days, she did let me in, and I just sat and talked to her. About anything—the battlefield, the hospital, Pete—and I told her that René would not want her to be miserable. That was not the person he fell in love with. I couldn't tell if she was listening; she just had a dazed appearance—not right."

Miguel nodded, understanding Millie's choice of words.

"Finally, she allowed me to feed her some soup. We had some heart-to-heart conversations, and she started getting better. She regained some of her spirit, which I always admired. Plus"—and Millie smiled—"she opened the shutters."

"You're a good friend, Millie. You may have saved her life."

"I was worried about her, Miguel; her grief was so apparent. I decided to ask her to help me look nice for today's parade, to take her mind off her suffering. It was her idea to make this shrimp rémoulade salad and pecan pie for a picnic. Giving her something else to think about seemed to soothe her."

"But she still won't see Catherine. I just can't imagine . . ."

"Suzanne is heartbroken, and, as I said, at first I was really afraid she was becoming unhinged. Now, though, she's angry. I think she feels the need to blame someone or something."

Miguel nodded again. "I understand. Unfortunately, her *maman* is the target. Catherine must be wretched."

"I'm sure she is. I hope time will help. They have both lost very special people."

Miguel noticed someone trying to get Millie's attention. "Say, Millie! I see one of the Baratarians over there, waving at you. He's got a huge smile on his face! Could that be your fellow?"

Millie whirled around to see whom Miguel was pointing at. She called out, "Pete! I'll be right there!"

Turning back to Miguel, she said happily, "*Oui*, that's my pirate!"

Miguel gave her a warm hug. "Pete's a lucky man, Millie. Enjoy your picnic and the parade. And thank you for your caring friendship to Suzanne. Catherine and I are most grateful."

Millie looked at Miguel with certainty. "Suzanne is like a sister to me, Miguel; I would do anything for her."

She picked up her hamper, waved at him, and ran off to meet her pirate.

All the while, the bands had been taking turns playing merry tunes. Women and children had been clapping in time to the music. Troops had been making themselves as presentable as possible, readying for the parade. And as Millie was reaching out to grab her beaming boyfriend's hand, the mist finally lifted. The sunlight was dazzling. Peter and Millie smiled at each other. Perfect. Fireworks seemed to go off.

But no. These weren't fireworks.

They were muzzle blasts, thirty of them, from the big British cannons. Each weighed six thousand pounds, and each had been lugged, heaved, and dragged through the swamps and marshes and cane fields by the English sailors. They were now just six hundred yards away, and manned by the same Hearts of Oak who had destroyed the French and Spanish fleets at Trafalgar.

Tarot: JUSTICE

*Revelation: A balanced combination of
the right components*

—⁓

Peter's instincts took over immediately. He grabbed the very startled Millie, slung her over his shoulder, and ran to the rampart. Carefully putting her down behind it, he yelled, "Hug the wall and cover your ears, Millie; those damn British are ruining our day!"

Millie had to smile. Spoken like a true American.

Miguel was in shock. Smoke and chaos were everywhere. He caught sight of Peter picking up Millie and running toward the protective barricade. Following the privateer's lead, Miguel also dashed to his post behind the rampart, leaping over a few men trying to hide from the cannon shells roaring overhead.

At the first blast, Jacques was still looking for Marguerite. He threw himself on the ground, covering his head with his arms.

"To your stations on the rampart, men!"

The voice sounded familiar. Jacques glanced up and saw General Coffee cantering back and forth along his regiment, yelling instructions to the anxious troops. Jolted into action, Jacques jumped up and joined the Choctaws and the Tennesseans rushing off to the cypress swamps.

Andre was paralyzed with fear. He saw most of the troops rushing toward the wall. The women and children who had come to watch the parade, like horses, stampeded in different directions, some to the levee, others up the road leading to the city. Two little girls, however, did not bolt. They stood holding each other's hands, sobbing. A woman was running toward them, a babe in her arms and another one in tow.

Andre could not move. What happened next, though, seared itself in his memory forever. He saw the black man he knew as Tobias dash by and scoop up the two little girls. Suddenly, the tall slave disappeared in a yellow-orange flash. At the same time, Andre felt engulfed by a searing wind and threw his hands up to his face for protection. A second later, he was able to open his eyes again and was stunned to see Tobias, still clutching the girls, ejected from a cloud of debris.

The black man and the little girls landed in a heap at the shocked woman's feet. Although mud-splattered and covered in blood, the children straightened up and scurried, apparently uninjured, to their mother's side.

The man, however, did not move or make a sound. Andre staggered over to Tobias, who was lying on his stomach. The exposed muscle and gore on his back led Andre to assume he was dead. Then he heard a muffled groan.

Kneeling down at the injured man's side, Andre said, "Tobias, I'll get help. Stay still now."

"T-t-t-t."

"Shh, now. Help is on the way."

Andre waved his arms toward a couple of fellows from his unit. "Over here," he called. "This man needs assistance!"

A pushcart was brought over, but as the two men gently lifted Tobias onto it, they shook their heads.

Nonetheless, Andre tried to comfort the injured slave with a lie: "You'll be all right, Tobias."

"T-t-tell Jacques. Jacques de Trahan."

"Do you belong to him? Monsieur Jacques de Trahan?"

Tobias tried to smile. *"Oui."* And he passed out.

Once the smoke cleared at the rampart, Miguel saw Jackson inspecting the artillery batteries. The general's uniform was coated with white plaster dust from the Macarty house. At the first sound of the cannons, he and his staff had rushed from the mansion. Although no one was injured, the building was severely damaged. As it was the largest target to sight on and likely Jackson's headquarters, the English had made it their initial target. This proved disastrous to the English, as the scouting teams of Choctaws and Baratarians had mapped the position and distance to the English batteries.

"Confidence, men! We'll not panic, and we will teach them again that we are better soldiers than they." Jackson spat to emphasize his remarks.

Because the enemy positions were predetermined, each of Jackson's batteries had its cannons aimed at a specific English target and its powder charges measured. As a result, the first rounds fired from the American artillery did severe damage to the English batteries. When the firing from the enemy cannons slackened, Miguel joined in as the Americans cheered and the general waved his hat to them in return.

Millie crouched down behind the fortification, holding her hands over her ears. She had never been this close to a battle and watched with admiration as the Baratarians loaded, aimed, and fired their cannons in what resembled an intricate dance. Even when a defensive cotton bale was knocked out of place and caught on fire, Peter and his crew did not lose their focus. Others immediately jumped over the rampart and knocked the smoldering bale into the canal, where it smoked itself out. Meanwhile, the Baratarians continued loading, firing, and reloading, discharging twice every minute.

By two o'clock, the English cannon fire had slackened, and then it stopped altogether. It was a welcome respite for the American cannoneers.

Looking toward the guns on his left, Peter saw Dominique Yu's arm bound up.

"Dominique!" he called. "Are you all right?"

"Only a scratch," the pirate rejoined. "But I can see through my spyglass that the battery we targeted is a complete wreck. The barrels of sugar the English used to protect their cannons have been blown to bits, leaving the artillerymen exposed. They cannot work the cannons if they are hiding on the ground. But you'd better get over to that girlfriend of yours; she's still got her eyes closed and her ears covered!"

Peter left his post and went over to tap Millie's shoulder. As he helped her up, he said, "Are you all right, Millie? That must have been a terrifying experience. I was afraid maybe you would faint."

Millie joggled her head, as if to shake out any cannon noises still echoing inside her.

"I'm fine, Pete. It was pretty scary, but then I noticed that most of the shells flew way over our heads. They just made a lot of noise."

Peter nodded. "The Macarty plantation house seemed to be the main English target; the place is in shambles." He looked at her anxiously. "You're sure you're all right, then?"

"I am, Pete," Millie assured him. "And besides," she added, gazing up at him with a coquettish look, "I felt safe here with you."

"Millie, I don't know what I'd do if anything happened to

you!" He felt himself redden but then paused and cocked his ear. "Do you hear that?"

"Oh! It's the fiddlers!" she said. "And French horns, too. They're playing music!"

"Yes! The bands are playing again. I'll bet the Brits can hear them also," said Peter, smiling. "We got them good; we held our own."

Millie threw her arms around her pirate and said, "I'm so proud of you, Pete. You're a hero!" And the intensity of her kiss proved that she meant it.

She pulled away reluctantly and looked around at the upheaval. People were milling about all over the "parade grounds." The few wounded were being moved to the field hospital, officers were rallying their units, women were looking for their men, and some children were still crying.

"Well, I've got to get to work," said Millie.

"What do you mean?" Peter asked. "What about our picnic?"

"Gosh, I'm sorry, Pete. I suspect the food is long gone, along with the hamper. But I hope Bella is all right; I hitched her up by the field hospital. Now, I must get back there; I may be needed. Would you like to help me?"

"Yes, but I can't; I'm required to stay by my post. The English may be planning an infantry attack. I hear musket fire even now, coming from the end of the rampart by the swamp."

He bent down to enfold her with another powerful kiss, and the passion of his touch was just as intense as a gigantic muzzle blast.

Tarot: WHEEL OF FORTUNE

Revelation: An unexpected turn of luck;
a change of assets.

⁓

Millie walked quickly back to the field hospital and ducked inside to see whether she was needed to transport any wounded. A doctor was examining a soldier, shaking his head sadly. He addressed another man, standing nearby. "I'm sorry, Mr. Shepherd, but your friend Private Judah Touro is very badly injured. You yourself can see that a large mass of flesh has been torn off his thigh. I suspect a twelve-pound shot hit him."

"I won't give up on him, Doctor. I'm going to get him back to the city, where he can be cared for."

"Good luck. I don't think he'll make it, though."

"Oh my goodness; is that Mr. Touro?" exclaimed Millie, looking down at the prostrate figure. "Why, I've bought soaps and candles from his general store. I am so sorry to see him hurt."

Turning now to Rezin Shepherd, she said, "I can take Mr. Touro to the Ursuline convent; my wagon's just outside."

"Thank you, miss. However, I will take him to my house in the city. We live in the same neighborhood, and I am certain that the local women there will care for Judah. I, too, have a cart, along with this brandy to give him on the way." He thought a minute, then added, "Ironic, isn't it? Judah was not strong enough to fight in the army, so he volunteered to carry ammunition to one of the batteries. And now this . . ."

He bent down to pick up his wounded neighbor. "I won't let you go, my friend," he said to the semiconscious man. "I won't let you go."

Tarot: THE NINE OF CUPS

_Revelation: Victory; a satisfied validation
of commitment._

~

General Jackson met with his officers to tally their losses and deliberate their next moves.

"The cotton bales are worthless as breastworks, sir," declared Captain Humphrey. "They were knocked over, and some even caught on fire. I suspect they might make good platforms for the cannons. There, the ground is muddy, and the cannons dig into the ground when discharged. We can move the cannons to the side, excavate the soil, lay down the cotton bales, use the soil to fill the gaps in the rampart, and replace the cannons."

Jackson replied, "Let's try it on Battery 1 first, to make sure it works. If the English attack while we're making the change, the _Louisiana_ can cover that section of the line."

"Well, if that doesn't succeed, perhaps the soldiers can use the cotton bales for bedding or to stuff under their uniforms," Colonel Butler said.

"One way or the other, the cotton bales will be practical. I suspect the British were surprised to discover that their sugar barrels are useless," said Reid.

"Right," agreed Humphrey. "Our cannons blew them apart. The hot sugar must have coated their guns, crews, and ammunition with a sticky mess."

"Do we have a casualty report?" asked Jackson.

Butler replied, "Eleven killed and twenty-three wounded. Some of those were civilians who were here to visit relatives. Unfortunate turn for their holiday."

"Anything else?"

"We're getting more deserters. They're telling us that the British are low on food. They're eating horseflesh, oranges from the groves, and even that burnt sugar blown out of the hogsheads!" reported Colonel Butler.

"It is said that their hospital is overflowing with sick and wounded. They are short on ammunition, but they're expecting reinforcements. Morale is down—not surprising, since they've been turned back three times; they probably thought they'd take the city without much of a fight. Not a bad record for our patchquilt army," commented General Morgan.

"Have we heard from General Adair and his Kentuckians?"

"Nothing, sir. But they can't be far."

"We haven't heard anything from the Capitol, either. I wrote to Secretary of War Monroe that we have bloodied the English nose but they haven't given up. I also asked for more supplies, but none yet."

Jackson's staff shook their heads in exasperation.

"Colonel Kemper, I'd like you to make a reconnaissance through the woods and swamp to the east and south. Find the place where the English are landing their supplies and these reinforcements they're expecting. I must know immediately if they, in frustration, try to slip around us by another route to the city. Take a couple dozen men who can live in the woods, and enough pemmican to feed them for two weeks. You'll have to keep the landing site under observation without revealing your own presence."

"I understand and will send a man back every few days to report, sir!" said Reuben Kemper.

"General Coffee, I want a reconnaissance in force down the Gentilly Road toward the Chef Menteur Pass into Lake Pontchartrain. About two hundred of your horse soldiers should be enough to put up a delaying fight if they run into the English. I'll ask General Humbert to go along as assistant commander. He's familiar with the area."

The men all nodded in agreement.

"But tonight, gentlemen, I want to make sure the troops know that I'm proud of them. They are each to have a quarter pint of whiskey to celebrate today's victory."

Jackson paused and looked at each of his aides with resolve. "Happy New Year to you all, and God bless the United States of America!"

Tarot: THE ACE OF SWORDS

Revelation: Change and struggle; out of conflict,
a new viewpoint will be revealed.

~~~

January 2, 1815

On the second day of the new year, Catherine set off for the convent. Walking briskly through her quiet neighborhood, she pondered the recent events and changes that had occurred—not only outwardly throughout the city, but deep within her as well.

Earlier that morning, an exhilarated Sheila had arrived in a carriage to take Marguerite and the baby to Claudia's house. Every day after the birth, the Creole mother had called upon her daughter and the baby in the quadroon neighborhood. The visits were brief but gracious. Besides bringing gifts from friends, Sheila always presented Catherine with a box of biscuits or candy.

Nevertheless, Catherine had been especially surprised that morning when, upon leaving, Sheila had reached out to embrace her and thank her for helping their family. Hortense had been even more flabbergasted when she, too, received a hug.

Catherine smiled as she thought about Sheila. She understood the mores and prejudices that the white mother's Creole class had inculcated in her. New Orleans' rigid social conventions limited professional expectations and dictated lifestyle behaviors; one's prestige and privileges were instilled at birth.

Creole culture depended upon these unwritten laws and traditions. Those same community conventions had been implanted in Catherine by her own mother, and faithfully observed by her relatives, friends, and neighbors, while the Church asked no questions.

Catherine had never before examined these notions and practices, and when the Yankees had moved in, she had simply regarded their different customs as very odd, sometimes silly, or simply uncouth.

But circumstances of these past few weeks were now making her confront and reshape her perspectives on New Orleans laws and traditions, as well as her culture's positions on loyalty and love.

She was uneasy with these thoughts, this questioning of the familiar and, she admitted, the comfortable. But now, for the first time in her life, she felt vulnerable.

It wasn't only because the British were invading her homeland. The fact that hitherto considered bizarre behaviors and serendipitous occurrences, such as her friendship with Marguerite, Suzanne's marriage to René, or the esteem and appreciation now given to Millie—regardless of her background—were no longer controlled by traditions left her mind conflicted. Catherine felt as if these changes should dismay her. Yet . . .

This was unmapped territory. Her mind worried itself back and forth as she continued her contemplation of the present insecurities she was facing.

When had these abnormalities begun? With Suzanne's wedding announcement? *However, René and Suzanne were so much in love; why shouldn't they have been married?* The day General Jackson had arrived in New Orleans? *Because of his dysentery, he needed me, and I needed . . . What do I need?* Partnering with Marguerite in organizing the Ursuline "hospital"? *But we enjoy each other's company, so why shouldn't we be friends?* Or the most painful aberrance: relinquishing the baby? *For whose benefit?* Le bébé's? Oui, *I kept my promise to René, but I betrayed my daughter. Can I ever—will I ever—forgive myself?*

The future? She no longer had any confidence in knowing the direction it would take.

And still another thought nagged at her: Had she really chosen the direction of her life? Wasn't it prescribed by society? Who made these rules, why, and to what end?

And now? Doubts and confusion.

She looked forward to tending to the wounded; the busy work would suppress her brooding. She hurried into the Ursuline convent, carrying her medical bag.

She had not been to the hospital since the babies were born. Her spirits lifted somewhat, as she noted the quiet yet competent atmosphere within.

As she rounded a corner, she bumped into Sister Angelique.

"Hello, Catherine! How are you? And how is Suzanne?"

"*Bonjour*, Sister. I'm fine but tired. Suzanne is . . . I don't know. She has practically locked herself away inside her home and won't see me. Whatever I know about her is by way of Millie."

"Well, she's been through quite a lot for a young girl. So many emotions—grief, melancholia, and anger, not to mention exhaustion—are squeezing her. She's mourning the loss of her husband, her son, and her plans for the future. Give her time, Catherine."

"I hope you're correct, Sister. All of this suffering, the pain, the deaths we have witnessed . . . and yet to me her estrangement is even worse than death. It's been dreadful, so unexpected, and it caught me so unprepared. I have never before felt such anguish." Catherine's shoulders sagged as she admitted her despondency to this woman.

The nun studied her through narrowed eyes. "You seem to be going through quite an emotional battle of your own, Catherine."

Catherine looked up in surprise. How could the Ursuline sister know about the churning thoughts within her?

"Please take care; you won't be any good to anybody if you become ill yourself," the nun continued.

Catherine braced herself. "You're right, Sister Angelique. This has been a strain on us all, emotionally and mentally. But we must remain strong."

Changing the subject, she asked, "By the way, has Scamp been assisting you?"

"That boy has been such an asset, Catherine. He rides with Millie back and forth to Camp Jackson and checks up on the general, then returns here to help clean up. I do believe the lad has matured a great deal these past couple of weeks!"

"I agree. And he's been quite conscientious in updating me on General Jackson's, um, condition."

Sister Angelique laughed. "Actually, he's absolutely delighted to inform everyone about our good general's intestinal affairs. And Millie reports that he also nags the general about drinking his teas and eating properly."

Catherine chuckled. "Well, I'm glad everything is working out. And the nursing staff is still functioning?"

"Yes, Suzanne's organizational skills are commendable and we have plenty of supplies and medicines. We were lucky not to have too many injuries in the New Year's Day battle."

She paused. "There is one case, however, that I'm hoping you might be able to help with."

"Of course."

"A colored man is dying; he was severely wounded at the parade grounds. His master has been with him since he was brought in yesterday, and insisted that he be put in a room. The Creole refuses to eat or sleep and just keeps mumbling and crying. He was already rather muddy when he came in and now is completely disheveled, but he won't let anyone come close to him. We have had to move the other patients out of the room. I fear for this man's sanity. If he continues in this manner, we may have two deaths on our hands."

"I'll see what I can do."

"Thank you. He's in that chamber across from us."

Catherine entered the room and saw the profile of the Creole kneeling by the lone bed. He was holding the dying man's palm in one hand while tenderly stroking his forehead with his other.

"I am with you," Catherine heard him say quietly to the dying man, but his words were punctuated with a heaving sob.

"Monsieur?" she said in a hushed voice.

The man turned toward her and gazed at her questioningly, with tears in his eyes. Tears in his very green eyes.

Taken aback, Catherine said, "Jacques?"

He did not seem to recognize her. She rushed over to his side and knelt down beside him. "Jacques! *C'est moi*, Catherine!"

"Catherine," he said, now sobbing openly. "He's leaving me. Tobias is leaving me. I don't know how I can go on without him!"

Catherine put her arm around the quivering man.

"I am here to help you, Jacques. Please let me do that for you and Tobias."

Jacques nodded.

Leaning over the patient, Catherine pulled back the coverlet and quickly appraised his condition. From his labored breathing, she knew that he was not going to live much longer. Actually, given what acute injuries he had sustained, she was surprised he was still alive. He just wasn't ready to die and was tenaciously determined to stay a little longer. She suspected she knew why.

She gently covered the patient's torso again and turned to the grieving Creole. "Jacques, I know this is hard for you, but you need to let him go."

Jacques stared at her through his tears and then broke down again, his shoulders heaving. "But I can't, Catherine. I can't let him go. Don't you see? I'm in agony!"

"And so is he, Jacques. He is distressed because he is worried about how you'll get by after he's gone. You're prolonging his pain."

The awfulness of that last detail appeared to shock Jacques into lucidity.

Catherine continued, "Tell him how significant he is to you, and that you'll miss him terribly but that you'll be all right. And then, when it's your time to go, he'll be waiting for you and you'll be together again."

Jacques looked at her, shaking his head. "I'm not sure I can . . ."

"You need to do this, Jacques; you need to do this for Tobias."

Jacques hesitated, then put his mouth down to Tobias's ear and whispered his final farewell to his slave.

Within seconds, Tobias's discomfort seemed to cease; his face looked serene. He took his last few breaths and passed.

Jacques began weeping silently.

"He's at peace now," Catherine said, closing the dead man's eyes and again putting her arm around Jacques. "How very fortunate he was to have you, his good friend, with him when he died."

Jacques looked at her, smeared the tears away with his sleeve, and managed a small smile. Then he shook his head. He gazed back down at the dead man and reached out to gently caress his cheek. "Ah, Catherine," he said, "Tobias was more than just my friend; he was my love."

Tarot: THE PAGE OF SWORDS

Revelation: Irritability; indicates vigilance and scrutiny.

~

January 4, 1815

"Finally, Major General Thomas, you and your two thousand very tired volunteers from Kentucky have arrived in New Orleans. But you say that only five hundred have guns?"

"Yes, sir, and not only no muskets but almost no clothes, never mind blankets or tents."

"It's January fourth. The weather is cold and rainy. They're not reinforcements; they're handicaps!" Jackson was livid as he paced haltingly in his tent.

"Since we were sent at the request of the secretary of war, the governor of Kentucky believed that the federal government would provide weapons, equipment, and supplies. In fact, we passed a steamer carrying such. It's reported to be moored at Natchez."

"What? Corporal Madden, have General Coffee send one hundred of his men on his best horses up there, find this ignorant captain, and arrest him on my authority. Tell Coffee to put his ablest officer in charge of commandeering the ship and bring it here immediately!"

Jackson shook his head and took a deep breath. "Well, we're glad you're here," he said. "We need all the help we can get."

"Sir, the women of our city were embarrassed for the men,"

said Captain Beale. "They saw them shivering as they marched through the city. Some of those men were even clutching their pants and shirts together with their hands to keep from being immodest."

"From what I hear, the city's females are most grateful for that thoughtfulness," said Corporal Madden, with a restrained chuckle.

Captain Beale continued, "Our ladies have volunteered to sew clothing for the men. They're gathering materials now."

"Well, it's gratifying to know that all of the citizens of Louisiana are supporting us in this war," said Jackson. "I just wish Washington would do the same." Jackson was still seething, but then he softened.

"Major Thomas, I want you to take your suitable Kentucky militiamen who are armed to the rear of the line at the Rodriguez Canal. The others can go to backup positions closer to the city. That way, they should be able to rest and hopefully will soon get the clothing they need."

"Yes, sir," said Thomas.

"I'm going to make the rounds again of our lines, encourage the men, and then head to the Macarty mansion. The Brits' artillery made a mess of the house, but I can still climb to the top and look out through my telescope at their camp. Meanwhile, I want all troops to continue fortifying our positions and stay on the alert. Is that flag in the center of the line still in one piece?"

"Yes, sir," responded Major Hinds.

"Good. I want it to continue flying so that both armies can see it. Let me know immediately when Colonel Reuben Kemper and his scouts return. They may have information about possible English reinforcements and their supplies. Meanwhile, we'll just have to wait and watch."

Tarot: THE QUEEN OF CUPS

*Revelation: Wives having the gifts of vision,
imagination, and dreams of love.*

⁓

Several Creole women were gathered around Claudia's dining room table, measuring out long sheets of cotton and then threading their needles. Five slaves were kneeling on the floor, placing patterns onto fabric and cutting the pieces, to be fitted into shirts, trousers, and coats.

"Ladies, I have a plan. I think we'll be able to make our items faster if we individually do the same piece every time," said Sheila.

"What do you mean, Sheila?" asked Annabelle.

"We'll each have a pile of the same shirt sections. For example, Annabelle, you will always sew the front to the back of each shirt at the shoulders. Then you'll pass your finished part to Elizabeth, who will put in the right sleeve. Then she'll give it to Claudia, who will sew in the left sleeve."

"I see," said Clara. "Then I'll sew up one side of each shirt, and you can finish the other side."

"Exactly. I think it will save time, which is just as precious as these clothes are for the troops from Kentucky," said Sheila.

"Such a good idea, Sheila," said Annabelle.

"Let's get going, then," said Sheila.

The servants brought the cut-up shirt and trouser sections

separately to the Creole women, who began to assemble the clothing, passing the progressing pieces along.

"Ah!" said Henriette, as she completed the last stitch and snipped the knot's tail. She held up the first finished shirt. "Well done, ladies!"

"I don't believe I will ever have sewn so much or so quickly in my life!" exclaimed Elizabeth, looking at the stack of woolen sleeves a servant set before her.

"True," said Sheila. "And these shirts aren't exactly high fashion!"

The ladies laughed.

"But," continued Sheila, "they'll be just fine for those poor men from Kentucky now wearing rags. Plus, I heard that Monsieur Louis Louaillier was quite persuasive in winning approval from the Louisiana legislature to appropriate six thousand dollars for further equipping these troops."

"And many of our citizens agreed to donate another six thousand dollars to support the army," added Henriette.

"Contributions, not only from our city, but also from surrounding counties. All in all, Père Antoine told me that over sixteen thousand dollars has been raised to help these needy men," said Claudia.

Two hours later, along with having acquired the latest news and gossip, the women also had a large stack of completed shirts and trousers. They heard a female voice from the street call out, "Whoa, Bella!"

Sheila got up to look out the window. "I see Millie's arrived with another load of cottons and woolens," she said, smiling.

"I'll help you bring them in," said Henriette.

"It's a good time for us all to take a little break. Perhaps a drink, ladies?" said Claudia.

While the servants withdrew to the back kitchen to prepare

the beverages, Sheila and Henriette went outside to assist in unloading some of the supplies. Millie jumped down from her wagon with an armful of coverlets.

"Thank you for your help," she said, as she handed the pile to Sheila. "I have some wool fabric here, too, and more is on the way." She reached into her cart and grabbed another stack of woolen material that she handed to Henriette.

"Whew! Heavy stuff," said Henriette. "And it's so humid today, especially riding in your wagon. Why don't you come in for some lemonade, Millie?" asked Henriette.

"No, thank you, madame. I have one more delivery to make this afternoon, and then I will be visiting a friend who is in mourning."

"Would that friend be Madame Suzanne Bonet?" asked Sheila softly.

Millie nodded, adding, "I appreciate your offer, though."

"Wait just a moment, then," said Henriette. "I'll get some biscuits and fruit for you to take to your friend's home."

While Henriette hurried into the house, Sheila said, "Poor dear. I know how hard it is to lose a child and a husband. And so close together! Please give her my sincere condolences, and do let me know if there is anything I can do."

"I will, madame. Thank you."

Henriette returned with a small basket full of persimmons, oranges, and baked goods. "Here, Millie. The biscuits just came out of the oven."

Taking the container, Millie lowered her head to sniff the contents. "Mmm! They smell wonderful!"

"Next time, perhaps, you can join us for some refreshments. Take care, now!" said Sheila, as Millie climbed into her wagon.

"I'll be back tomorrow," said Millie, smiling. Lightly tapping her mule with the reins, she said, "Let's go, Bella!"

Making their way into the house, Henriette said, "That young girl is priceless, Sheila. Not only is she pleasant, but she's also reliable and talented. I certainly wouldn't know how to drive a wagon! And I can see why she wears those trousers—so much easier to do her job."

"True," said Sheila. She set the blankets down on the dining room's sideboard. "I remember when she volunteered to help that day at the church. I noticed several eyebrows were raised when she spoke out. But I have to give her credit. And I agree with you: she certainly is unique!"

"Are you talking about Millie?" asked Elizabeth. "I saw her at the New Year's Day parade, all dressed up."

"In a dress?" asked Claudia.

"Yes, and she looked lovely! I do believe she was meeting one of our troops."

"Why, I saw her, too," said Clara. "And I agree—I suspect she was planning to get together with someone. I saw her carrying a picnic basket."

"Well, now," said Claudia, "who do you think our Millie has in mind?"

"I know!" said Annabelle, with a smile.

"Do tell," the women exclaimed.

"I saw Millie reach out to embrace . . ." Annabelle paused.

"Come on, Annabelle! Tell us!" said Elizabeth.

"A Baratarian!"

The women gasped.

"Really! A pirate!"

"Yes, and a handsome one!"

"And . . . ?"

"Well, that's all I saw. The shooting started, and, as you all know, the whole parade ground turned into chaos."

The women nodded, some with disappointment at not

knowing any more about Millie's beau, others remembering the horror of that day.

Just then, they heard a baby's cry. At a gesture from Sheila, one of Claudia's servants put down her scissors and went to the second floor.

"Oho, Grand-mère! What's the latest on *le petit prince?*" asked Adelaide, who, along with Henriette, was rapidly stitching the inseams of pants.

"He is just beautiful," Sheila replied. "Eats and sleeps well. And sometimes, after he's nursed, he's a bit fussy, but after I burp him, he smiles at me."

"Because he has passed the *gaz,*" said Elizabeth, laughing.

"And Marguerite?" asked Annabelle. "How is she responding to motherhood?"

"I have seldom seen her so happy," said Sheila. "Of course, she's still worried about Jacques's safety and is very much looking forward to presenting him with his son."

"May that happen soon," said Claudia. "And may it be a joyful time for us all."

The women nodded, and a quiet descended over them as they continued sewing, absorbed in their hopes and fears for family and friends.

Tarot: THE KING OF WANDS

*Revelation: A new leadership idea that will
promote powerful change in the immediate setting.*

$\sim$

January 6, 1815

"General, we have guests," announced Captain Pierre Jugeat, as
he forced the sailors inside Jackson's tent.

The English seamen had been captured in a small supply
boat seen sailing to Bayou Bienvenue.

"Welcome, gentlemen," Jackson said, grinning. Turning to
Captain Jugeat, he asked, "And to what do we owe this pleasure?"

The captain answered, "One of my scouts, Nakni, observed
their boat leaving the English fleet, headed for the supply base
on Lake Borgne. I sent a messenger to our navy commander at
Petites Coquilles, who dispatched three brigs to intercept the
boat. And *voilà*—the navy has a cargo of gunpowder and cannonballs, and we have nine impressed sailors and one arrogant
lieutenant."

"Send the lieutenant away, and we'll talk with the sailors."

The nine British seamen happily revealed everything they
knew in exchange for the promise that they could remain in the
United States.

After the sailors were taken away, Jackson conferred with
his staff.

"We now know from the English sailors that the Redcoats

are enlarging the Villeré Canal to move their barges from Bayou Bienvenue to the Mississippi. That tells me two things. First, the Redcoats still plan to take the city by advancing along the river. Second, they may use the barges to ferry troops and artillery to the south bank for a two-pronged advance."

"That's quite an undertaking," said Colonel Butler. "Widening the canal and pulling the barges two miles to the river."

Jackson looked glum. "Yes. What we need is to get a better look at this canal work."

Commodore Patterson spoke up. "General, I'll take a couple of my sailors with telescopes down the south bank to a point opposite where the Villeré Canal meets the river. We'll see what the English are up to."

"Good, Commodore; please make that a priority and report back as soon as possible."

"Yes, I understand."

"I'll have a couple of my Choctaw scouts circle east through the cypress swamps tonight, observe the enemy activity on the Villeré Canal tomorrow, and report back," volunteered Captain Jugeat.

"All right. We can never have too much information about the enemy. Let's meet again at ten tomorrow night. Please see to your troops. Good evening, gentlemen."

Tarot: STRENGTH

*Revelation: A clash—spiritual power overcomes
physical power through trust.*

~~~

January 7, 1815

Sister Angelique stood at the doorway of the convent, quietly greeting the city's women who had come to make a novena in the chapel. They were a somber assembly, some silently hugging one another, others discreetly wiping away tears, worrying about their men. They had been gathering for the past seven days, since the assault on New Year's Day. The full strength of the invading army had not yet been employed against the city.

The late-afternoon sun shone on the large golden statue of Our Lady of Prompt Succor, making it glow. There was a humble hush as the faithful and hopeful knelt before her image, praying their rosaries, petitioning the mother of Jesus for help in their time of need.

Two years before, Sister Angelique and the other Ursuline nuns had gathered before another, smaller image of Mary and her baby son. They had placed the figure in a window of the convent and prayed for the Madonna to intercede on their behalf and save their home from a horrific fire that was heading their way. It had already destroyed most of the city's buildings. Sister Angelique would never forget the words "Oh, Lady of Prompt Succor, ask your son to save us, or we are lost."

Suddenly, the wind had shifted direction. The flames had blown back into the burned area and soon died out. The nuns had all been quite certain that because of Our Lady's intercession, the convent remained unscathed.

Word of the marvel spread. Our Lady of Prompt Succor was her title; Mary of Immediate Help was the claim. Many considered this saintly woman's renown miraculous, perhaps even magical.

Now, New Orleans was desperate for another miracle. As Sister Angelique knelt down in a pew in the crowded chapel, she perceived a peculiar solidarity among these diverse women: upper-class Creoles, free women of color, immigrants, slaves, and even a few Yankee Protestants.

Like the troops, regardless of background or social position, they had joined together and done everything they could to help the effort: donating mattresses, blankets, food, and clothing; mobilizing supplies and coordinating pickups and deliveries; organizing themselves to work in shifts, as well as providing childcare; and nursing the wounded in their homes and the convent.

So far, General Jackson had foiled the English invasion. His mostly inexperienced army had held its ground and forced the English to withdraw from the field, all while suffering far fewer casualties than their enemy. However, despite their difficulties, the English had not given up. Rumor had it they were awaiting reinforcements.

The women had seen the sorry reinforcements that General Jackson had received. They knew the outlook was grim and were afraid not only for their men, but also for themselves and their families. "Beauty and booty," the British motto, terrified them.

And so they gathered to seek divine intervention through this novena. Sister Angelique closed the chapel door and led the women in prayer. "Please, Our Lady of Prompt Succor, intervene with your son, Jesus, to provide us Americans a bloodless victory."

Courage. Commitment. Love. Sacrifice.

Please! A miracle! Victory!

As the evening wore on, more candles were lit and the votive lights gleamed. When various women left, some genuflected, but many simply took a last look at the statue and breathed a final appeal, imploring her aid not just for their husbands, sons, brothers, and neighbors, but also for those volunteer courageous countrymen who were fighting valiantly for their fair city.

Sister Angelique made her personal prayer: "Our Lady of Prompt Succor, help all of us in our time of need. Please make the battle short and the deaths few, and bring victory to our side."

Her conscience pricked her a bit, so she added, "And don't be too hard on the enemy troops; just send them all back to England. Quickly. Amen."

Making the sign of the cross, the Ursuline nun went back to her nursing duties.

Other petitions, too, included individually unique appeals.

Catherine prayed, "Please, bring my Miguel back to me. I know this sounds selfish, but I am worn out, physically and emotionally. I really need Miguel. I need him—his care, his support, his strength."

She bowed her head and covered her face with her hands. Then, taking a deep breath, she continued, "Speaking of strength, please help General Jackson and his army. They are so committed to saving our city. Bless and protect them; let them return safely to their families."

"Keep our young Scamp safe and out of General Jackson's way!" murmured Hortense. "Yes, he can be a little too lively and curious, but he's a good boy; please don't let him get hurt!"

"Watch over my Andre," said Claire. "He doesn't have any weapons, except that shovel he's been digging with. I hope he's not afraid too much. Not like me!"

"I know René is with you and the baby in heaven, Blessed Mother," prayed Suzanne. "He made the ultimate sacrifice. Isn't his death enough? Yes, I'm angry. Yes, I'm wretched, too. Help me get through this struggle. Please don't let anyone else suffer like I have."

"Hi, it's me, Millie. I know you don't see me very often. But this isn't about me; it's about Pete. Please, please protect him. He and his fellow Baratarians are so brave. Now, I know he's not a churchgoer, but watch over him anyway. He's a good man. In fact, he's the best man I've ever known. And I've known quite a few."

"For my son-in-law, Jacques, may he return safely to his wife, Marguerite, and the baby. She loves him so," whispered Sheila. She glanced at her daughter, kneeling next to her, and saw that she had cradled her head in her arms. *As if she hears the cannons*, thought Sheila. *My poor dear.*

What Sheila did not see was Marguerite releasing her self from her body, floating down the aisle, and gliding out through the closed chapel door.

Tarot: THE KING OF SWORDS

*Revelation: A wise man of intellectual leadership
who strategizes the future.*

~

"*B*onsoir, gentlemen. Are you ready to report?"

"Yes, General," responded Commodore Patterson. "From the levee on the west bank of the Mississippi, opposite the Villeré Canal, over a period of several hours I was able to watch the enemy assembling artillery, ammunition, and other supplies in preparation to cross the river. I assume they are only waiting for additional boats. With more infantry support, I could move my battery closer to the crossing point and open fire while they're crossing."

"Captain Jugeat, anything to report?"

"My scouts confirmed the prisoners' information that the English are widening and deepening the Villeré Canal. Where it meets Bayou Bienvenue, they're beginning to move their barges into the enlarged canal. The English are in a hurry. They're digging in shifts around the clock."

"Thank you, gentlemen. Captain Jugeat, once again, my compliments to your Choctaws.

"Commodore Patterson, I need your battery to cover the river and the right flank of the rampart; my observations from what's left of the second floor of the Macarty house show that the majority of the English infantry are still in their position facing us. However, I will send you every soldier and cannon I can spare.

"Major Arnaud, I believe your second regiment is already with General Morgan on the west bank of the river."

"Yes, sir."

"Tomorrow, take the rest of your battalion back to the city, cross to the south bank, and, staying out of sight, march them to General Morgan's position.

"General Adair."

"Yes, sir."

"Attach all the members of your Kentucky volunteers who are fit and armed to join Major Arnaud's march to General Morgan's camp."

"I'll see to it, sir."

"It's been a week since the last assault. I expect that the British are going to attack any day now. General Adair, please accompany me while I inspect our defenses."

"With pleasure, sir!"

"I believe you'll be impressed by our fortifications. The rampart is over five feet high and twenty feet thick in some places. Our gun platforms are solid, and the canal makes a nice barrier. Considering that only the canal existed two weeks ago, our rampart is a manifestation of the population's, as well as the army's, overwhelming desire to defeat the acclaimed English army."

His staff members nodded their heads in agreement.

"When I return from making a final round of the lines with General Adair, I'll be back in the upper gallery of the Macarty house, watching the British through my telescope. Again, I believe the attack is imminent. I want you all to try to get some sleep tonight, but do so fully dressed, with your sword and pistol by your side, ready for battle."

Upon this final command from the general, Marguerite began trembling, then hurtled back to her self in the chapel.

Tarot: THE HANGED MAN

Revelation: a pause in one's life;
waiting with fear and anxiety.

~

My dearest Catherine,

Tomorrow the British will probably attack us again. Our luck has been good so far; I just hope it lasts. And even though I'm scared, I'm proud to be a part of this effort and doing my share to protect our beautiful New Orleans.

I deeply miss you and am so sorry I cannot be with you during this terrible time with Suzanne. But you need to keep your spirits up, no matter the outcome. I have always admired your pluck and am grateful to have shared the past two years with you. Truly, you have made them the best years of my life.

I hope to see you soon, but if that doesn't happen, I just need you to know how much I love you.

Always,

Miguel

Tarot: THE WHEEL OF FORTUNE

Revelation: Unexpected turn of luck; success.

⁓

January 8, 1815

Jackson had slept a couple of hours in his tent when he was awakened by a messenger from General Morgan, commander of American forces on the southern side of the river.

"Sir, the activity on the riverbank at the English camp makes General Morgan certain that the main attack will be against his position on the south side of the river."

After a long yawn, General Jackson said, "Horse manure! Return to General Morgan and remind him that the city is on *this* side of the river. The English know that if they advance on the south bank, I will hold the interior lines and can easily move this army parallel to the English and be prepared to prevent any attempt by them to recross the river. Also, an English advance west on the south bank will allow me to cut their supply line to their fleet. So far, we have held our own, but it's not because the English are stupid."

Jackson yawned again and then added, "And having said that, Monsieur Shepard, please deliver my message to General Morgan with a little more tact."

"Yes, General Jackson, I will relay your message in the manner of a Creole gentleman!"

Blinking at his pocket watch, Jackson continued, "Twenty minutes after one. I may as well stay up. We don't need to awaken the troops for another two hours. The English will probably attack at daybreak or a little before, so three o'clock a.m. will give us plenty of time to prepare. Light another lantern, Rufus; I'm going to the Macarty house to keep an eye on the English camp."

It was not so much what General Jackson saw from the second floor of the ruined Macarty house as what he heard. From the direction of the English camp came the sound of digging and hammering, but, oddly, Jackson could see no fires or even candles burning. Clearly, the English were trying to conceal their activity and apparently thought that the sleeping American troops' snoring would drown out the noise.

Jackson observed that the English had been almost correct about the snoring, and he presumed that the hammering came from sappers making plank bridges to cross the ditch and ladders for scaling the rampart. The digging and other noise could be the English repairing and rearming the artillery emplacements that the American artillery had decimated on New Year's Day.

After detecting the futile English attempt to conceal their preparations, Jackson gave the order to awaken the troops so they could cook, eat, and take their positions before sunrise. Fourteen-year-old Jordan B. Noble, a drummer of Major Daquin's Battalion of Free Men of Color, began the long roll for reveille, although most of the soldiers did not actually need to be awakened.

Leaving the Macarty house, Jackson walked the 280 yards to Battery 1 at the river end of the rampart. The battery's light cannons were manned by regular US Army artillerymen and supported to their north by Captain Thomas Beale's militia company of New Orleans riflemen. Covering the next eighty yards was the 7th US Army infantry regiment. Old Hickory praised the men of these units for the fighting spirit they had shown to this point and was confident in their ability to inflict another defeat on the enemy.

Shaking hands and slapping backs, he moved to Battery 2. The general warmly greeted the former sailors of the USS *Carolina* who manned one of the ship's cannons, now landlocked. He commended the seamen, a mix of Yankees and Baratarians, for their steadfast bravery in having shelled the English camp during the December 23 night battle and the following days.

Encouraging more men of the 7th Infantry, the general moved along the forty yards of rampart to Battery 3 and the aroma of brewing coffee. Battery 3 consisted of two heavy naval cannons under the command of Jean Lafitte's half brother, Dominique Yu, and crewed by Baratarian privateers, including Peter. Resting by his cannon, Millie's beau was packing his ears with cotton while watching Jackson's approach. The general gladly accepted a cup of hot coffee from the diminutive Dominique, jubilantly thanking him and his brother for the coffee, the cannons, gunpowder, projectiles, musket flints, and, most of all, the experienced gun crews. Jackson noticed Peter and nodded to the observant Baratarian; Peter saluted in return.

Savoring his hot coffee, Jackson smiled to himself. Perhaps because these men were more accustomed to confronting an enemy, they had enjoyed their early-morning meal of coffee, beignets, cornbread, and bacon. Jackson knew that his men from Kentucky and Tennessee had had a simple breakfast of cornbread and whiskey. The citizen soldiers from New Orleans, he supposed, preferred not having any food. Tension, anxiety, and fear already filled their stomachs. The general understood; he was familiar with those sensations.

The next two hundred yards to Battery 4 were defended by

Major Jean Baptist Plauce's Battalion of New Orleans Volunteers and Major Pierre Lacoste's Battalion of Free Men of Color. Although Major Lacoste's men were untested, Jackson told them he knew they were the equals of the brave Creoles of Major Plauce's battalion, who had held the left flank of the American army during the night battle and beaten off a determined bayonet charge by the English reinforcements, preventing the American army from being outflanked.

Battery 4 possessed the largest cannon in the American arsenal: a thirty-two-pounder naval gun served by more former USS *Carolina* crewmen. Upon Jackson's greeting, they voiced their readiness for the enemy assault.

The general next encountered Major Jean Daquin's Second Battalion of Free Men of Color, who manned the 160 yards of the rampart between Batteries 4 and 5. Andre had been assigned to help clean their weapons. He was crouching down next to Miguel as Jackson stopped to talk to the 250 men. They all listened quietly as Old Hickory said that he had not forgotten how they and the Creole volunteers had stood their ground and defeated a charge by the exalted English army. He assured them that all citizens of the United States would always remember their bravery. He counseled them to be vigilant while exuding confidence that victory could be theirs. Miguel and Andre, along with the rest of the men of color, felt more assured as the general acknowledged their service.

Batteries 5 and 6 were only a few yards apart and consisted of light field pieces manned by US Army artillerymen and veterans of Napoleon's army. They saluted their general, indicating their preparedness.

The final functioning battery, Battery 7, was 200 yards to the east and roughly 240 yards from the edge of the swamp. The general took his time making his way to the last battery while encouraging the Tennessee volunteers under General William Carroll. Although they had missed the night battle, many had served gallantly in the Indian War and had turned back the English advance on December 28. He advised that they now were the defenders of the center of the American line because of their famous accuracy and the range of their rifles.

Walking toward the lightening sky, Jackson encountered General Coffee. Coffee's Tennessee volunteers held the eastern end of the rampart, such as it existed, for its 520-yard extension through the cypress swamp.

"Well, General Coffee, as always, your men have the toughest assignment: standing in the water with their rifles, waiting for the English to appear."

"Don't worry, General, we have Captain Jugeat's fifty Choctaws scouting out in front, so we'll have plenty of warning if the English come this way."

"Well, remind your men not to worry about their feet, but to keep their powder dry!"

"Andy, if you think my men needed that information, you and me would be here alone. The others would be buried back at Emuckfaw Creek, Enotachopo Creek, or Horseshoe Bend."

Jacques, who was still mourning Tobias's death, had nonetheless returned to Coffee's side to assist as needed. Right now, though, he was wet and shivering in the bitter cold. But he smiled at Coffee's words. He knew that the woodsmen he accompanied were not inexperienced; they were seasoned in the use of firearms, had seen combat, and were far better marksmen than the enemy. Whatever action the British had planned, these Americans were guaranteed to perform valiantly.

Jackson laughed. "You are right, as always, John Coffee. The Tennessee volunteers have endured hardships worse than wet feet and fought with courage, resolution, and like professionals."

Glancing at the sky, Jackson changed the subject. "Today is the day. I can hear the Redcoats. I can feel them. I just can't see them yet."

Coffee replied, "Just a few minutes ago, that Choctaw Nakni captured two Redcoat deserters: Irishmen runaways through the swamp. Figured not much difference between an Irish bog and a Louisiana swamp; got lost real fast. Said they were part of a work party repairing English artillery redoubts. In return for a promise that we wouldn't trade 'em back to the English, they were more than happy to let us know the English will attack today, as soon as their cannons are in place."

"Well, that agrees with all the other observations and reports. Like to borrow one of your horses, John. Want the men to be able to see me when the lead starts flying."

"Well, if you promise to return it in as good a condition as you get it. On top of a horse, you'll be showing above the rampart. Lot of that lead will be flying at you."

"Brave men are braver when they can see that their leader is not hiding someplace. But if it will make you happy, get me your shortest horse."

"Just what I had in mind; unfortunately, I don't have a billy goat handy."

"Now, John, an old goat riding an old goat might confuse the men."

"Yes, but the real goat would probably have more sense than to go trotting along behind the rampart!"

As Jacques listened to the two friends bantering, he briefly forgot his troubles. He just continued smiling and thinking, *Mon Dieu! These crazy Americans!*

Mounted on a stallion and rejoining his staff, Jackson looked at his defenses through the enemy's eyes. He was confident that General Coffee's Tennessee volunteers could hold his northern flank and the cypress swamp. The weakest point in the defenses was from Battery 7, where the artillery support consisted of only one six-pounder and one eighteen-pounder cannon covering a stretch of about 250 yards to the swamp. Although General Carroll's seasoned Tennessee militia defended that section of the rampart, Jackson ordered General Adair's Kentucky volunteers who did not have firearms to form a reserve line twenty yards behind the Tennesseans.

As the sky began to brighten, the men of the various units moved to their assigned positions. A thick mist hovered above the ground, obscuring the view of the fields extending to the English camp. The elevation of the parapet gave the Americans a slight advantage, but the English did not appear. The Americans waited in silence, each man reflecting on his own thoughts and the coming battle.

Satisfied that his army was as prepared as possible, General Jackson walked his horse to a point just south of Battery 7. This gave him a view both along and across the weakest portion of the American line.

Suddenly, a rocket roared into the air and zigzagged across the sky. The Americans craned their necks to follow the rocket's path. Then it quickly fizzled and disappeared. But still there was no sign of the English attack. The Americans along the rampart waited in anticipation for several minutes, which felt like hours. Then, suddenly, the roar of thunder boomed as the English artillery opened fire. The American cannons promptly replied. The air in the one-thousand-yard-wide battlefront was quickly filled with various-size projectiles of iron, from cannon-balls to exploding shells.

General Jackson remounted his horse and moved with his staff a few yards farther back from the rampart, opening up access for the foot soldiers and providing an extra margin of safety for his officers. As both sides continued their artillery duel, Jackson thanked God that he did not have to order his men to charge into that storm of missiles.

As the mist continued to thin, the general's assessment was proven, as the multiple ranks of Redcoats became visible to the Americans along the rampart.

The initial English advance was along the river, directly in front of American Batteries 1, 2, and 3, and within range of the battery on the west riverbank.

As the English infantry advanced, their artillery support slackened to prevent them from hitting their own troops. With targets in view, the American batteries stepped up their fire as their pickets scurried back to the safety of the rampart. When the American pickets reached safety, the men of Beale's New Orleans Rifle Company and the US 7th Infantry opened fire, adding a storm of rifle and musket balls to the cannon fire. The musket and rifle fire tumbled scores of Redcoats, while the three American batteries along the rampart began firing grape-shot, turning the English soldiers into a haze of red mist. The attack along the river disintegrated as fleeing Redcoats tried to take refuge on the riverside of the levee, only to come under fire from the American battery on the south side of the river. The common English soldier believed he had only one real option. Advancing against the American rampart meant certain death. Therefore, he chose the wrath of his officers, and a possible prison term for cowardly conduct. Knowing that many of the officers were dead or wounded hastened the decision.

The English attack along the river melted away as the common soldier spontaneously, and against orders, began to take shelter in ditches or amongst the bodies of their dead or wounded comrades. Those who could withdrew to their camps.

General Jackson had been correct: the main English attack

was directed toward the section of American line with the least artillery support. The northern portion of the rampart was defended by General Carroll's Tennessee volunteers, but with only the three cannons of Batteries 6 and 7 in support.

At the end of the rampart, the English signal rocket had been followed by salvos of inaccurate rocket and artillery fire. The American artillerymen held their fire as mist still obscured the fields to their front. However, the beating of drums and trumpeting of bugles could be heard clearly.

Slowly the fog lifted and the sunlight revealed an advancing wall of scarlet. It took the American artillerymen only a few minutes to adjust their cannons for the estimated range and commence firing. The interim was filled with a cheer from the Tennessee volunteers, as they finally had a target so massive, even the poorest shot among them could not miss. The privateers who had manned the USS *Carolina* and regular army artillerymen repositioned the cannons of Batteries 4 and 5 to enfilade the lines of Redcoats. The cannons were loaded and fired with minimal adjustments for aim. Holes began to open in the first rank; as the survivors moved forward, the second rank stepped into the fire. With every cannon shot, men and parts of men were filling the air over the red wall.

General Carroll's Tennessee volunteers and those of General Adair's Kentucky volunteers who had obtained arms were arrayed in four ranks behind the rampart. When General Carroll gauged the Redcoats to be two hundred yards away, he shouted the order to fire. The first rank of riflemen fired, stepped to their left, and moved to the rear to reload, as the second rank then stepped forward and fired. This maneuver continued for rank after rank, pouring continuous fire on the English.

The oncoming human wall appeared to be painting the field red as it advanced. Soon the air in front of the rampart was so choked with gunpowder smoke that the Redcoats were no longer visible. The Americans began to just tip their rifle barrels over the front edge of the rampart, hoping to hit any Redcoats who had reached the ditch.

And still the Redcoats continued their rush, leaping over their dead countrymen.

And still the Americans continued the slaughter.

Those Brits who did reach the ditch, however, were horrified to find that whoever had been assigned the responsibility had failed to bring the bundles of canes for bridging the canal and the ladders for scaling the barricade. A fatal blunder. Pandemonium.

A few Redcoats waded across the canal. With their bayonets, they tried to cut steps into the rampart. The Americans shot them down.

Some tried standing on one another's shoulders, but they, too, were greeted with gunfire.

Others, noting the confusion and futility, turned back to escape to the rear. They ran into a regiment dragging the missing fascines and ladders toward the rampart. These troops, seeing their bolting comrades, dropped their scaling equipment and joined them in flight.

British commanders rode forward on their mounts, urging their demoralized troops relentlessly forward. The Kentucky marksmen quickly eliminated the officers.

Just like their comrades who had attacked the American line along the river, even elite English soldiers could take no more. With many of their officers, including Commanding General Edward Pakenham and Second-in-Command General Gibbs dead, the common soldiers retreated to their camp. Those who had advanced closest to the American lines dropped to the ground to shelter in ditches and behind the bodies of their dead and dying comrades, rather than risk a rifle ball in the back. As the English drums and bugles fell silent, the American gunfire began to slacken.

Finally, General Jackson gave the order to cease firing. Glancing at his watch, the general noted that only one half hour had passed since the English artillery had opened fire.

A sound similar to that of a large herd of cows replaced the roar of cannon, rifle, and musket fire. As the smoke in front of the rampart dissipated, the Americans beheld the source of the noise: fields that appeared to be a boiling red ocean, red from the English uniforms, the illusion of surf the result of the wounded and dying rolling in agony and attempting to rise.

As the stunned Americans stared, hundreds of English soldiers, either unharmed or slightly wounded, rose from the midst of their prone comrades, most picking their way back to the English lines, others stumbling toward the American rampart with their arms raised in the air.

Even as these survivors moved off, the Americans knew that it would be possible to walk across the battlefield without stepping on the ground. The all-encompassing screams, cries, and pleas of the dying caused many of the Americans to move back from the rampart and cover their ears. Others proceeded beyond the rampart to provide what aid they could.

General Jackson, who had witnessed the massacre of Creek Indians at the Battle of Horseshoe Bend, was stunned by the slaughter, the result of the English generals' battle plan, which apparently had presumed that the Americans would run away at the first sight of the English army. But the general had no pity for the enemy. Dismounting, he walked east along the rampart, congratulating the Tennessee and Kentucky volunteers, praising their valor and marksmanship, while his staff collected casualty numbers. Jackson paid the highest praise to those who had manned the artillery. Turning west, he extended the same compliments and congratulations to each unit along the rampart while instructing the officers to send salvage parties among the English dead to collect their muskets and ammunition.

A white flag of parley was waved, and a formal, twenty-four-hour cease-fire was called. Jordan Noble, who had kept up a continuous drumroll throughout the battle, sounded his final beats.

Tarot: THE TEN OF PENTACLES

Revelation: A creative idea for a sense of security.

~⁗

A ndre smelled gunsmoke mixed with the stink of blood. He gathered the courage to raise his head above the rampart and look out over the battlefield. Instead of its usual yellow-gray stubble, it was furrowed with hundreds of scarlet clods. Then he rubbed his eyes in dismay. Many of those clods were moving!

"Do you see that?" he asked Miguel. "Some of those Red-coats aren't dead; they're alive!"

"Uh-huh," agreed Miguel. "They were hiding behind the piles of their own dead."

"And now they're heading to our lines with their hands up. They were just pretending to be dead!"

"Yes, but by so doing, they avoided their own demise. They knew that if they continued coming this way toward the rampart during the battle, the American backwoodsmen would pick them off easy. Their rifle barrels have grooves inside that make the bullet spin and go straight."

"Maybe," answered Andre. "But most of our troops have smooth-barrel muskets. Those weapons aren't nearly as accurate as the rifles."

"That's true, Andre," said Miguel, as he patted his beaten-up fowling gun. "This old thing has a smooth inside barrel that doesn't control the bullets. But the British know that once it's shot, the ball tends to go above where the gun is pointed, so if a soldier lies down, he's less likely to be hit."

"Hmph. So they knew they'd be slaughtered if they kept marching in this direction, and instead they just fell down in the heaps of their dead comrades and waited it out."

"Right. Now they're coming in as prisoners. Looks like about five hundred of them. Playing possum saved their lives."

Tarot: THE KING OF CUPS

Revelation: Meeting a feature of oneself.

~

The men gathered in Jackson's tent were giddy.

"Congratulations on this great victory, sir. You will definitely be a national hero!"

"Well, thank you, Colonel Butler. We must also give credit to our troops. But, most of all, I thank God for helping us in our time of need. Speaking of which . . ." Jackson looked around the room, and his eyes landed on Scamp, crouching in a corner.

"How old are you, son?" he asked.

"I'm almost eleven, sir," responded the boy.

"When I was about your age, I served the country as a messenger. How would you like to be promoted and serve as my courier?"

"Yes, sir!" Scamp scrambled up, straightened himself to his full height of four and a half feet, and, with a huge grin, saluted Jackson.

"All right, then. There's a young woman out there picking up the wounded and taking them in her wagon to the convent hospital. I've heard about her—I believe her name is Miss Millie. See if you can get a ride with her and let the townspeople know that the battle is over and we won. I'm fairly certain that many of them are in the chapel, praying for us. It's an important assignment, Soldier."

"Yes, sir. Don't worry, sir. Consider it done, sir!" And Scamp ran out of the tent, yelling, "Miss Millie! Miss Millieeeee!" at the top of his lungs.

Jackson turned to his aides with a smile and said, "He's young, spirited, and plucky, just like our country! Now, back to business."

$\mathscr{Tarot:}$ THE SUN

Revelation: Liberation, achievement, gains.

The women and children had gathered together for early Mass in the chapel of Our Lady of Prompt Succor. Once again, the hands of each participant were clasped together in prayer, hoping for a miracle. The minutes passed slowly. Chalmette plantation was on everyone's mind. The cannons had been heard booming earlier. And then nothing.

As the priest prayed the Agnus Dei, the congregation repeated the solemn request. "Lamb of God, you who taketh away the sins of the world, have mercy on us." Seldom had this prayer meant so much. Heads were bowed, breasts were lightly thumped, tears were still spilling.

The participants lined up to receive Holy Communion. As each woman knelt at the railing to receive the host from the priest, she again begged God to help save those dear to her.

After the last communicant had returned to her pew, the chapel was quiet, each person meditating.

Suddenly, the door flung open, slamming against the wall, and Scamp burst into the chapel.

"Victory is ours! We won the battle!" he cried out. "We beat 'em!" He raised his arms up to the ceiling. "We did it! Hooray for General Jackson and our army!"

Everyone turned to the boy in surprise.

"Scamp?" asked Catherine.

"*Oui*, Madame Catherine!" said Scamp, with a huge smile. "It's true! General Jackson promoted me to be his courier and sent me to tell you all that the city is safe and the battle is over! Wahoooo!" He took off his cap and waved it in circles above his head.

"Glory be to God," added the priest.

"Amen!" agreed the congregation.

"Thank you, Our Lady of Prompt Succor," whispered Sister Angelique.

The cathedral's bells began pealing, the churchgoers hugged, and all of New Orleans exhaled a sigh of relief.

Tarot: THE EMPEROR

*Revelation: Control and leadership in creating
a governing structure.*

⁓

Jackson had praised the troops on their brilliant victory, had notified the New Orleans citizens that they were safe, and had sent a message to Secretary of War Monroe that although the battle was won, the enemy was still on American territory. He now needed to address the near future.

"Many of our men are on the battlefield, gathering British weapons, in case the English renew their assault," said General Adair.

"Good," said Jackson. "They're probably collecting souvenirs, too. While we have this truce, however, I want them to take the dead Redcoats to the Bienvenue plantation for burial. That way, the British won't get too close to our line. I don't trust them."

"Perhaps we should pursue the Redcoats ourselves and attack them further, sir," Major Hinds urged.

"No. I don't want our men to leave the protection of the rampart. We have trounced the British, and New Orleans is now safe. Most of their officers are dead or wounded. The rest will soon lead the way to their ships and will not sully our soil any further."

Jackson noticed that Hinds looked doubtful.

"However, Major Hinds, I want you to organize a scouting party. Watch the Redcoats very closely to make certain that they are evacuating. And, just to make sure, after the truce is ended, we will continue shelling them during the day and harass them at their picket lines at night."

Major Hinds smiled.

Tarot: THE EMPRESS

Revelation: Cycles of change; endings must occur.

~

M iguel and Andre loaded yet another bloody body onto a British scaling ladder.

"These corpses sure are awkward and difficult to stack," said Miguel.

"Not to mention all the stink and the blood," agreed Andre. "But that fellow over there with the basket has an even worse job. He's picking up all the severed arms and legs scattered about."

"Here's a body with two arms and two legs, but the fella lost his head. Guess the shot made it explode."

"Yup. Just bone, brain, and blood left on that one. I don't know what's worse: the sight of these mangled bodies or the stench of their rotting corpses."

The two men transported their load to an enormous mass grave and laid the bodies on the ground nearby. One Redcoat, upon seeing a corpse they'd brought, began weeping.

"I guess he recognizes one of the men," said Miguel.

"He's not the only one of this British burial party crying," observed Andre. "It must be difficult to see a dead friend and have to pitch his body, almost like trash, into a hole."

"Well, not everybody is being tossed into this giant plot. Did you hear what the Brits are doing with two of their dead generals?" asked Miguel.

"Do they get a special grave around here?"

"No, their bodies are actually being gutted and then sent back to England, preserved inside casks of rum."

"What a waste of good alcohol!" snorted Andre.

Tarot: THE STAR

Revelation: A need for hope and courage;
no collapse is final.

~

The occupants of New Orleans were finally informed about the signing of the Treaty of Ghent, which had ended the war two weeks before the Battle of New Orleans. Two weeks after the battle, the British were completely gone from Louisiana, as well as the entire country.

A victory parade, led by the New Orleans battalions, was held in Place d'Armes, and the hero Jackson was crowned with a laurel wreath. The general congratulated the male citizenry for their roles in protecting their homes, praised his countrymen who had come to defend the city, recognized the Belles of New Orleans' impressive efforts, and thanked the good nuns for their nursing. And, to give credit where credit was due, he promised to honor Our Lady of Prompt Succor every year with a Mass of thanksgiving.

Other festivities within the city, big and small, were joyous and full of music and dancing. The largest celebratory ball, given in Old Hickory's honor, was held the evening of January 23. Everyone was invited, and, although Suzanne was in mourning, she did convey to Catherine that she was considering attending the festivities with Millie and Pete, if only just to watch.

The mother and daughter were now on speaking terms. Very civil. Very polite. Very crushing to Catherine.

Miguel kept saying, "She needs time; don't rush things!"

Upon arriving at the ball, Catherine began scanning the crowd, hoping to find her daughter. Perhaps this dance would be a breakthrough for them.

"Do you see her, Miguel?" she asked her husband.

"Not yet, but look, Catherine. The general has arrived, along with his wife!"

Amid applause, Andrew Jackson proudly escorted his spouse into the ballroom.

"I always wondered what Rachel Jackson was like. She's just his opposite!"

"True," answered Miguel. "She's short and obviously not thin, and the way she's chattering away and waving to people seems quite vivacious in nature. She fits in well with us Creoles!"

A fiddler began a lively tune, and, as the crowd formed a large circle around them, the Jacksons began to dance.

"Just look at them hopping up and down, Miguel!" exclaimed Catherine. "I've heard some of the Kentuckians singing the lyrics to this song; it's called 'Possum up de Gum Tree.'"

"Madame Caresse?"

It was a familiar voice. Catherine turned around and was delighted to see Andrew Jackson's doctor.

"Doctor Morell!" she exclaimed. "Miguel, this is the general's physician. A month ago, he was captured by the British. I am so glad to see you again, and you're looking well."

"Thank you. The British released all of their prisoners, including the navy purser and me, on January twelfth. Considering the circumstances, I am quite healthy. Even better, I am happy to know that you have cleared up General Jackson's dysentery. He is dancing tonight, thanks to you!"

"*Oui*, and he has even put on a little weight. I suspect you are responsible for that. Enjoy the evening, Doctor, and welcome back!"

Catherine and Miguel continued to make their rounds, mingling with all the diverse citizens—free men and women of color, Creoles, Yankees, and Baratarians—who had banded together to save their city. They greeted exuberant friends and neighbors, buoyant soldiers and jaunty seamen, slaves and their merry masters. Even Sister Angelique and the Ursuline nuns were there, animated with smiles and hugs.

Yet, despite the laughter and joy around her, Catherine grew increasingly uneasy. She still didn't see Suzanne at the celebration. Or Millie and Peter.

She immediately knew why when she returned home and found the folded letter on her dining room table.

Tarot: THE PAGE OF WANDS

Revelation: A message of tidings;
an alteration in life.

~

My dearest Maman,

I hope you had a good time at the celebration. You deserve it. All of our people do. The men and women of New Orleans showed the rest of the country, as well as the world, that we are unified in patriotism and bravery.

I am happy that Miguel has returned unharmed. You two share such an exceptional warmth that many couples seem to lack. And your success with General Jackson's illness is so commendable. You are a true heroine in your own right. Your gift of healing will continue to relieve suffering. The people depend upon you for so much.

So, the city is safe now and prosperity will return. The future is bright.

But not for me. Not in New Orleans.

Of course I cannot, will not, enter another plaçage; plus, I do not have your gifts. Thus, the prospects of supporting myself are absent. Although I know, dear Maman, that you would disagree, I would be a burden to you.

I am sorry. I do not want to hurt you. But I had to leave.

I am with Millie and Pete. The steamboat is taking us up north to the town of St. Louis, and there we will start anew, *with different identities. We will look up René's old friend Monsieur Lisa. He is an important person in St. Louis and can recommend trustworthy people to get us started. Pete is planning on using his skills in carpentry, Millie will open a boardinghouse, and I will be the business manager for both.*

Please do not look for me or try to communicate in any way. That could be dangerous for all of us.

Please do not worry. René gave me money before he left for the battle. "Just in case," he said.

I am lucky, Maman, to have loved René, even for so short a time. He connected me to a new world, one of different ideas and exciting possibilities. I trust that our sweet baby is in a far better place, as Père Antoine would say. I know that René is with him, as he is with me, always.

Give my best wishes to Miguel and Hortense, and tell Scamp to study hard so he can follow in your healing footsteps. You will always be in my thoughts and prayers, Maman, and I hope you understand and forgive me.

Your loving daughter,
Suzanne

You were wrong, René. Suzanne is strong. Strong enough to leave me.

Tarot: THE WORLD

Revelation: Completion of a goal, reward,
and assured success.

⁓

May 1815

Several months after the battle, the city of New Orleans was thriving, the river bustling, the theater and opera flourishing. As in a gumbo, the flavors of the different cultures sometimes clashed, but then adjustments were made, assimilations occurred, and adaptations were taken, and the outcomes were generally palatable.

It was a particularly lovely spring day, sunny and warm. Catherine was shopping on Royal Street. She had just purchased some new linens and was now shopping in Judah Touro's fine-merchandise store, when she saw a familiar figure pushing what looked like a small cart nearby.

"Madame de Trahan?" she called out. "Is that you?"

The woman stopped, turned around, and then smiled. "Hello, Madame Caresse! How wonderful to see you!"

The woman of color and the Creole embraced. "You look well, Marguerite," said Catherine. Then, eyeing the vehicle, she added, "What an ingenious contraption! It's like a cradle on wheels! Wherever did you get it?"

"They sell something similar in England, but Jacques had this one specially made for me here in the city! It's just perfect, not only for our outings, but indoors, too. I always want the baby to be near me."

"*Oui*, it is a wonderful design. Very clever, and practical indeed! And the *bébé* likes it?"

"Loves it! He's asleep now; this is his naptime. But it's such a delightful day that I thought some fresh air would do him good. Here . . ." She moved the small attached parasol aside. "Now you can see my little sweetheart!"

Catherine bent over and peered into the small carriage. "Ah! Your *petit garçon*, Marguerite. He's grown so!"

"He has, Catherine." Marguerite carefully lifted the sleeping infant out of the pram. "He's just a love," she continued, beaming. The mother gently adjusted the baby's blue bonnet further back on his head. "So good-natured, sleeps through the night, has been gaining weight steadily, and the doctor says he's robust and healthy. Would you like to hold him?"

"*Oui!*" Catherine set down her items and held out her arms to receive him.

"*Bonjour, mon coeur!*" she said to him softly. As she gently rocked him back and forth in her arms, she looked carefully at his features. Small copper curls peeked out from under the brim of his baby cap. Suzanne's curls. His face was heart-shaped— again, like Suzanne's. *Just as I thought*, mon petit!

As Marguerite had said, he was a good weight and size. She bent her head to kiss his forehead softly and inhaled his warm sweet baby smell. *Innocence.*

As the baby shifted his weight sleepily in her arms, he clasped her finger in his tiny fist. *Strength*, she thought. *You will need it!*

Then Catherine perceived something else: a tingling vibration, a sparkling energy, and it was emanating from the child. Still lost in her thoughts, she nodded her head. Oui. *And I suspected as much*, mon petit fils! *You've also got the power, hmm? I will try to guide you in whatever ways I can, so that you use your gift wisely.*

Realizing that Marguerite was staring at her, Catherine exclaimed, "Oh! I'm sorry, Marguerite! It's just been so long since I've held a baby. He is so precious! And how handsome he is. Obviously, he has his mother's good looks!"

Marguerite laughed and said, "Thank you, Catherine. You are one of the few people to see any resemblance to my side of the family. Everyone else says he looks mostly like Jacques."

The baby stirred and gazed up, almost knowingly, at his grandmother. Catherine continued to rock him tenderly as she looked into his emerald eyes. "Yes, I'm not surprised. Those gorgeous green eyes are a very distinctive family trait!"

She looked back at her Creole friend. "I'm glad to see you both thriving, Marguerite."

"And what about you, Catherine? You look wonderful! And pardon me for noticing, but isn't that a Hollie Point christening cap you're about to purchase? It's beautiful! Is it for Suzanne?"

"No, it is not for Suzanne, Marguerite."

Catherine did not volunteer any more information; she just continued rocking the baby in her arms, with a smile on her face. A very demure smile.

Marguerite looked at her questioningly. Then her eyes grew wide. "Oh, *mon Dieu*!" she exclaimed. "*You're* with child!"

"*Oui!*"

"Congratulations, my friend! When?"

"Not for five more months. Plenty of time to prepare. But I gave away all of Suzanne's baby things, so we must begin anew."

"And Miguel? How is he with this news?"

"Oh!" Catherine replied. "He's thrilled. And attentive, and nervous, and tells everyone he sees that he's having a baby. Plus, he's gaining weight right along with me!"

"I'd like to see him go into labor," Marguerite said, laughing.

"I suspect he would if he could. He's already converted Suzanne's former room into a nursery and reorganizes the baby clothes and blankets on a weekly basis. Each day he suggests different names for the baby. Today he's being very patriotic; he proposed Andrew for a boy and Jacqueline for a girl. I suspect he'll adapt to fatherhood quite well and the child will be completely spoiled."

"*Merveilleux!* The baby has already snuggled into his heart!" said Marguerite.

"And what about Jacques? How does he feel about his beautiful boy?" Catherine asked, as she gave Marguerite's baby a kiss on his forehead and reluctantly handed him back to his mother.

"Oh, my goodness. He couldn't be happier! He's already planning his future, from fencing lessons to his education in Paris," said Marguerite. "I suspect Jacques will make this child the most indulged youngster in all of Louisiana!"

Looking down at the baby in her arms and still beaming, she added, "Your papa absolutely adores you, doesn't he, Tobias?"

Again, Catherine smiled.

Tobias did, too.

Thus, the circle is complete.

Further Revelations

~

Treaty of Ghent: will be ratified by the US Congress in February 1815, officially ending the War of 1812.

Andrew Jackson: will run for president of the United States in 1827.

Albert Gallatin: will be quite apprehensive about a Jackson presidency, saying that the general was "altogether unfit for the office."

John Quincy Adams: will become the sixth president of the United States in 1828, although Andrew Jackson, his opponent, will win more electoral votes. Adams will lose to Jackson four years later.

Henry Clay: will run for president against Andrew Jackson in 1832. He will lose; Jackson will serve two terms.

General John Adair: will become governor of Kentucky and later serve in both the US House of Representatives and the Senate.

Commander Jean Baptiste Plauché: will become lieutenant governor of Louisiana.

General John Coffee: will be appointed by President Jackson to accomplish the Indian Removal Act of 1830. The five civilized tribes forced to surrender their ancestral lands and relocate to the Oklahoma territory will include the Choctaws, as well as the Cherokees, Creeks, Seminoles, and Chickasaws.

General William Carroll: will serve as Tennessee's governor from 1821 to 1827 and from 1829 to 1835.

Major Arsène Latour: will write *Historical Memoirs of the War in West Florida and Louisiana in 1814–15.*

Edward Livingston: will become a US senator and minister to France.

The Baratarian Privateers: will receive official pardons on February 6, 1815, from President Madison. Most will choose to give up plundering forever.

Dominique Yu: the half brother of Jean Lafitte will settle in New Orleans and become a politician.

Jean Lafitte: will be forced to leave Louisiana in 1817; he will establish another "privateering" domain in Galveston, Texas.

Our Lady of Prompt Succor: will become the patroness of the city of New Orleans and the state of Louisiana.

Père Antoine: will remain the popular and revered pastor of St. Louis Cathedral until his death in 1829.

The Ursuline Convent: will, two hundred years later, still be located on the same site in New Orleans' French Quarter. It will be the oldest surviving French-colonial structure in the lower Mississippi Valley and will welcome tourists, instead of the sick and wounded.

James Madison: will die in 1836 at Montpelier, the last of the US Founding Fathers to pass into eternity.

Dolley Madison: will die in poverty in 1849, at the age of eighty-one.

Edward Coles: President Madison's personal secretary and first cousin to Dolley Madison will become the second governor of the state of Illinois.

Commodore Oliver Hazard Perry: will have thousands of male children and more than thirty counties and municipalities named in his honor.

General Jacques Villeré: will become Louisiana's second governor.

Lieutenant Thomas ap Catesby Jones: will rise to the rank of commodore in command of the US Navy's Pacific squadron. At the end of the Mexican-American War, he will accept the surrender of Mexican towns along the California coast and will be the model for Herman Melville's character Commodore J in his novel *Moby-Dick*.

Colonel Reuben Kemper: will settle down to become a planter in Mississippi; a county will be named in his honor.

James Derham: will become the first licensed African American physician in the United States.

Dr. James Tilton: will, at the age of seventy, develop a malignant tumor in his knee. While having his leg amputated, he will give advice to the operating surgeon and assistants.

Judah Touro: will become a millionaire and will found the New Orleans Almshouse, the Touro Infirmary, and the Touro Synagogue.

Rezin Davis Shepherd: will inherit half of Judah Touro's fortune and will use the money to restore a New Orleans street, renaming it Touro Street.

Jordan B. Noble: will become a popular New Orleans musician.

Manuel Lisa: will continue trading through his Missouri Fur Company and will become a leading citizen of St. Louis and a trusted representative for Indian tribes living along the Missouri River.

Choctaw Indians: will face hunger and death on the first Trail of Tears in 1831; sixteen years later, hearing of a people suffering a similar catastrophe, they will send $170 (approximately $3,000 in today's currency) to Ireland to help peasants and tinkers starving in the potato famine.

"The Defence of Fort M'Henry": Congress will make this poem the US national anthem in 1931. It will become known as "The Star-Spangled Banner."

Francis Scott Key: will have a distant cousin, F. Scott (Key) Fitzgerald, born three generations later, who will become known for his writing of the Jazz Age.

Congo Square: will be a venue for music festivals and community parades.

New Orleans: will hold its first Mardi Gras in February 1826.

The Spotted Dog Pub, Penshurst, England: will continue in operation successfully into the twenty-first century (open daily— watch out for the press gang!).

So be it!

Acknowledgments

Many thanks to my own personal "saints and loas":

- Laura Ingalls Wilder, my distant relative, who also wrote her first novel as a senior citizen.
- My book discussion group, AAUW friends, local librarians, and writing clubs for their ongoing advice and support over the years.
- The authors of the published books regarding this period, including *The Battle of New Orleans* by Robert V. Remini, *Jackson's Way* by John Buchanan, *The War of 1812* by John K. Mahon, and *Gumbo Ya-Ya* by Saxon Dreyer and Robert Tallant.
- My She Writes Press "overseers" Brooke Warner, Lauren Wise, and Annie Tucker, plus fellow SWP authors for their contributions and camaraderie.
- My sons, Seán and Rauri, and sister, Anne Ingalls, for their ideas, encouragement, and humor.
- Jim, my husband and partner, whose knowledge, creativity, and enthusiasm helped shape this book.

Let the Good Times Roll!

About the Author

Sue Ingalls Finan is a graduate of University of Illinois Urbana-Champaign and Loyola University Chicago. She has taught creative writing and American history in Chicago, IL, Pittsburgh, PA, and Sonoma County, CA, and her stories have appeared in textbooks, anthologies, magazines, and newspapers. Now living in Sonoma County with her husband Jim, she writes for her local newspaper and volunteers at hospitals and libraries with Duffy, her Irish wolfhound therapy dog.

SELECTED TITLES FROM SHE WRITES PRESS

She Writes Press is an independent publishing company founded to serve women writers everywhere. Visit us at **www.shewritespress.com**.

Eliza Waite by Ashley Sweeney. $16.95, 978-1-63152-058-7. When Eliza Waite chooses to leave a stagnant life in rural Washington State and join the masses traveling north to Alaska in 1898 during the tumultuous Klondike Gold Rush, she encounters challenges and successes in both business and love.

To the Stars Through Difficulties by Romalyn Tilghman. $16.95, 978-1631522338. A contemporary story of three women very different women who join forces in a small Kansas town to create a library and arts center—changing their world, and finding their own voices, powers, and self-esteem, in the process.

Light Radiance Splendor by Leah Chyten. $16.95, 978-1-63152-178-2. Set in Eastern Europe in the first half of the twentieth century and culminating in contemporary Israel and Palestine, *Light Radiance Splendor* shows how three generations of the Hebrew Goddess Shekinah's devoted mission keepers grapple with betrayal, love, and forgiveness.

South of Everything by Audrey Taylor Gonzalez. $16.95, 978-1-63152-949-8. A powerful parable about the changing South after World War II, told through the eyes of young white woman whose friendship with her parents' black servant, Old Thomas, initiates her into a world of magic and spiritual richness.

The Wiregrass by Pam Webber. $16.95, 978-1-63152-943-6. A story about a summer of discontent, change, and dangerous mysteries in a small Southern Wiregrass town.

Dark Lady by Charlene Ball. $16.95, 978-1-63152-228-4. Emilia Bassano Lanyer—poor, beautiful, and intelligent, born to a family of Court musicians and secret Jews, lover to Shakespeare and mistress to an older nobleman—survives to become a published poet in an era when most women's lives are rigidly circumscribed.